*It was the storybook era of
silent films . . .
and her matchless beauty was all
the rage—and whisper—of Hollywood . . .*

Chosen in an international search for the perfect *Irish Rose,* Abbie Dare, raven-haired and inno-cent, is soon whisked from her family's humble English home to the banner-headline and back-stage-gossip whirl of stardom.

Opulent mansions, glistening limousines, and gala grand openings fill her life, but her heart still searches for the man who will not treat her beauty as a bauble, her dreams as fantasies, and most importantly, her love as his stepping stone to greatness . . . and other women's hearts . . .

HOLLYWOOD'S IRISH ROSE

The tender story of a woman's true love
and the heartbreaking fantasies of an era.

Hollywood's Irish Rose

Nora Bernard

AVON
PUBLISHERS OF BARD, CAMELOT AND DISCUS BOOKS

HOLLYWOOD'S IRISH ROSE is an original publication of Avon Books. This work has never before appeared in book form.

AVON BOOKS
A division of
The Hearst Corporation
959 Eighth Avenue
New York, New York 10019

Copyright © 1979 by Nora Bernard
Published by arrangement with the author.
Library of Congress Catalog Card Number: 78-67801
ISBN: 0-380-41061-3

First Avon Printing, January, 1979

AVON TRADEMARK REG. U.S. PAT. OFF. AND IN
OTHER COUNTRIES, MARCA REGISTRADA, HECHO EN
U.S.A.

Printed in the U.S.A.

Hollywood's Irish Rose

Chapter 1

IN the gilded lobby of the Lamont Hotel, guests were lounging in white satin chairs, some reading papers or books, a few writing letters or waiting for luncheon companions, many simply watching each other. The most conspicuous person there, a gorgeous young thing in lavender silk, had removed her matching silk pumps and was stretched out on a love seat, her foot dangling over the side and swinging against the powder blue plush carpet.

On the far side of the lobby, Abbie Dare, the lovely receptionist, watched three prospective guests with amusement. The tall man and the elegant, middle-aged couple had that certain look of consternation and bewilderment. At length, the three caught sight of her and approached the desk.

"Dr. and Mrs. Ivan Mikhailovsky," the tall man said, respectfully. The bearded man and his imperious wife stood proudly erect, as if at attention. She had been right, Abbie thought. They were foreigners. Russians. The tall man was probably their interpreter.

Abbie dutifully handed him the keys to their rooms.

"Room 518," she told him, and smiled. "And you're next door in 520."

His eyes acknowledged her charm. He lingered for a few seconds as if he wanted to say something but

1

Abbie looked away, and the three turned and walked toward the elevator, trailed by bellhops with their trunks.

Abbie searched through one of the desk drawers, looking for a pencil. Flora, the receptionist who worked nights, had stuffed all the drawers full of *Screen Stars*; an American magazine that she read whenever she was bored on the job. Abbie was never bored. She loved watching the elegant hordes of people who frequented the opulent hotel, the shining figures of the moneyed. The young husbands and wives looked like pairs of beautiful twins, with the same flawless complexions, straight, white teeth and lithe, athletic bodies. Their parents were always regally graceful, immensely handsome people with thick, grey hair, fine skin, and youthful figures. The women seemed not older, but only more delicate than their daughters. Even the ugly among the rich were blessed with radiant health. Their irregular features simply made them more exotic than the rest. The rich, it seemed, could purchase perfection for themselves.

Abbie enjoyed watching the women more than looking at fashion magazines. The models in the fashion dailies only simulated the look of wealth, and the imitation could never compare with the original. Each of the real lady's dresses was created especially for her, and she wore each as if born in it. The fabrics and colors were as splendid and varied as a flower garden.

Abbie never felt envious. How could one be jealous of gods and goddesses? Being privileged to observe such loveliness was thrill enough.

It was nearly six in the evening, but as usual Abbie was in no hurry to go home. Leaving work was almost like being exiled from an enchanted palace. Outside the hotel, her Mum waited for her at home with a din-

ner of stew. Bill waited for her, too. He was her intended and was ready to marry her whenever she
wanted. He was twenty-five, seven years older than she
and eager to start a family. He had been waiting for
Abbie since she was thirteen. Abbie's beauty had been
striking even then and there was promise of her becoming more exquisite as she matured. It was thought
that her maternal great-grandmother had been Irish,
and Abbie seemed to bear the story out. She had jet black
hair, smooth ivory skin, and intense blue eyes. Her
features were strong and clear: a long, chiseled nose,
high cheekbones, and a well-defined chin. But her lips
were pink and as tender as a child's. Abbie was small,
just over five feet, and her figure was dainty, but her
gait was firm and erect. Bill had loved her from the
first day he saw her. It was not only her loveliness, or
the charm of her low, soft voice. It was that proud,
steady walk—it seemed to him impressive in a girl so
young.

Abbie was flattered by Bill's attention. He was tall,
handsome, and hardworking. He was even-tempered
and a moderate drinker. In the neighborhood, the older
girls often whispered his name, and sighed and giggled.
It was not unusual to see one of them walking beside
him, trying for a flirtation. But he was oblivious to all
of them. Abbie had won him without any effort.

Abbie loved Bill, but the excitement of their first
summer together had expired. Then, Bill had seemed
to her the finest of men. Large and strong, powerful,
but gentle. His passion for her thrilled her. She loved
feeling his heart beating, his beautiful, manly chest, his
shoulders, the texture of his skin, his silky, blond hair.
Every day that August, they embraced and kissed, held
each other, lay down together in the woods in back of
his parents' house. Sometimes, she imagined the two

of them naked together, but she never dared voice such thoughts. They were shameful, the kind only a bad girl would have. How shocked and even angry Bill would have been if he could read her mind. He was so proud of her virginity.

"I've never known a girl as pure as you are," he'd tell her, and she'd feel guilty about her secret desires.

But now, she loved Bill as she had loved her father.

"It's 'ow it is," Flora told her. "It's that way for everyone. Familiarity, you know. Look around."

Flora had been married for a year, herself, and her words conveyed her own experience. It was true. People settled for being comfortable with each other. Perhaps even Mum and Dad had burned for each other at one time, but babies and holiday camps soon replaced passion.

"Hey love, bet you're glad to see me."

It was Flora. Large, good-natured Flora.

"How's the day been?" she asked.

"Not much," said Abbie. "Pretty quiet."

"Well, I hope it stays that way," Flora said. She opened the drawer and pulled out a copy of *Screen Stars*, with a picture of Rudolph Valentino on the cover.

"Ain't he gorgeous?" Flora purred. "I'd leave home for him."

"I like Wally Reid better," Abbie told her.

"I hear he's a dope addict," Flora whispered.

"Oh, that's nonsense!"

"That's what I hear."

"I don't believe it."

"Have you seen *The Sheik* yet?" Flora asked.

"No, not yet."

"You gotta make Bill take you to see it. Then tell me Rudolph Valentino ain't gorgeous!"

4

"I didn't say he wasn't, I said I like Wally Reid better." Abbie winked playfully. "See you tomorrow, Flora."

At the side entrance, designated for hotel employees, Bill was waiting for her.

"God, Abbie! Late again," he groaned.

She had forgotten he would be there. It was Wednesday night, and he always ate at her house Wednesdays and Fridays.

"Sorry," she said, embarrassed.

"I've been out here for fifteen minutes," he said.

"Bill, I said I was sorry. I'll remember next time."

Abbie felt irked with him. She even felt mildly resentful that he ate so many dinners at her house. She couldn't recall the last time his mother had put herself out.

"How's work?" he asked, forgetting his annoyance.

"All right. You?"

"Got a stairwell to build for some bloke on Cardiff Street." Bill was a carpenter.

"Nice house?"

"All right. Ordinary."

They circled the old Anglican church that stood on the corner of her block. Spring had even made Newbury Street attractive. The flower boxes were crowded with poppies and tulips, and some of the houses were freshly painted. Though it was getting dark, the noise of playing children filled the street.

Abbie opened the door to her house.

"I'm here, Mum," she called.

Her mother came out from the kitchen. She was not yet forty, but her figure was thick and most of her hair was grey. Ten years ago, she had still been beautiful, but work and worry had since taken her looks.

They were having corned beef and cabbage for dinner. Abbie could smell it all over the house.

"Sit down, Bill," Mrs. Dare said.

"I'll help you serve, Mum," Abbie told her mother.

Abbie's mother had made great efforts to give the small house a cheery look, but all the prints on the walls and all the Oriental trifles and vases crowding the tables just made it look cluttered and haphazard. Mrs. Dare thought such knick knacks exotic. Abbie knew they were gaudy, but whenever she tried to advise her mother on interior decoration, the older woman protested that she was "putting on airs." Abbie had tried to persuade her to at least sell the old wrought-iron tables that were being used as flower stands, but Mrs. Dare insisted that she needed everything.

Mrs. Dare had been forced to take a job when her husband died. Like most working-class people, they had never managed to save any money. They had spent his salary as he had earned it. Heaven knew they barely got by as it was. Mr. Dare had been an unskilled laborer, and what with the rent, food, and Abbie, there was just enough money left for his cigarettes and ale, the privileges of every working man.

After his death, it was Mrs. Dare's brother, Leonard, who had come to her rescue. She hadn't spoken to him for years since he had married a shop owner's daughter and had risen into the middle class. But after her husband died, Eleanor humbled herself and asked Leonard for help. She had no choice. The dole was her only alternative. She had married at sixteen, and the only work known to her were the duties of a housewife. Leonard had worked zealously for his father-in-law and had inherited the tobacco shop as his reward. He brusquely offered Eleanor the job of cashier. Each night, thereafter, she blessed her brother Leonard and his family. She never missed a day of work and often stayed overtime without expecting to be paid extra.

Still, she did not earn enough to support herself and Abbie as well. She had hated to ask Abbie to look for a job. Because people were young for such a brief time, she thought, they should be allowed to enjoy themselves before the hard work of raising a family and "contriving" began. Her own parents had been able to indulge her, giving her spending money for sweets and trifles the year before she married.

Abbie, at least, enjoyed her job. When she first started she would come home and spend the evening telling her mother about the grandeur of the hotel and its dazzling guests. Her glowing face mirrored the splendor of the lobby, the ballroom, and the people. She had been allowed inside one of the suites and described it vividly—the chandelier; the rose-colored wall-to-wall carpeting; the white, French provincial furniture; the frothy, canopied bed. Mrs. Dare had never known upper-class people; for her they hardly seemed to exist. Only Abbie's stories confirmed that they were real.

"Abbie, why don't you go join Bill at the table? I'll serve dinner," Mrs. Dare said.

Abbie seated herself next to Bill. She decided that, for a change, he could start the conversation and keep it going. Usually, he hardly said a word, and whenever she commented on his silence, he smiled and said, "I'm one of those quiet chaps."

She usually felt obliged to talk, but today she was simply not in the mood.

Bill looked at her and smiled quizzically. "You're quiet, Abbie."

She returned his smile. "Nothing to say, dear."

Her mother entered with the pot of corned beef and cabbage and ladled it onto their plates.

"You sit down, too, Mum," Abbie said.

"In a sec, dear."

Mrs. Dare returned to the kitchen, then joined Abbie and Bill.

"You're coming to Rosalie's wedding, aren't you, Bill?" Mrs. Dare asked.

"I am," Bill replied.

Rosalie was one of Abbie's cousins. She was marrying a welder that Saturday.

"I took a peek at her gown," Mrs. Dare said. "White taffeta with orange blossoms."

"Guess it set her Dad back a bit," Bill said.

"No," Mrs. Dare told him. "She sewed it herself."

"Clever girl," Bill commented.

"So much nicer than storebought," Mrs. Dare said. "I keep telling Abbie she should make hers too, and I'd help." A day seldom passed when Mrs. Dare did not mention Abbie's impending marriage.

"I don't sew very well," Abbie said.

"We'd find a nice, simple pattern," Mrs. Dare told her.

Abbie shrugged.

They gossiped about the neighborhood. Harold Wiggins was bedeviled by drink and was destroying his home.

"Whiskey can be a terrible thing," Mrs. Dare said, "but teetotalers are no fun at all."

"A man's got to know his limits," Bill remarked.

Mrs. Roper was pregnant with her sixth child in seven years; the Browns were going to Kent to see relatives; and the Stocktons and Bartons were still feuding.

"What's it over, anyhow?" Abbie asked.

"Oh, you know, the fights that Mr. and Mrs. Stockton get into? Well, the Bartons had their fill one night and called the police."

Mrs. Dare shook her head over the situation. Why couldn't people behave decently? The good Lord knew she did her best to be proper. People couldn't point when they passed *her* house.

After Abbie cleared the table, Bill suggested they take a walk.

It was a soft night. A warm wind was blowing, and Abbie could smell the sea-tang of the Thames. Light shone from the small houses lining the street, and people sat on their front stoops, talking in the dark.

"Let's walk over to Graham Street," Abbie suggested.

Graham Street was several blocks away in the middle-class area where her Uncle Leonard lived.

"You've been so quiet tonight, Abbie," Bill said. "Is everything all right?"

"Yes," she said, smiling. "I'm one of those quiet girls."

Chapter 2

SATURDAY was a rare and splendid day, clear and brisk and sweet smelling, more like early autumn than late spring.

"Happy is the bride the sun shines on," Mrs. Dare said while she and Abbie were dressing.

Mrs. Dare had been a little hurt that Rosalie hadn't asked Abbie to be one of her bridesmaids, but Abbie had pooh-poohed it. They hadn't been close for years. Mrs. Dare suspected that Rosalie was afraid Abbie might steal all the attention. Even in the simple, yellow cotton frock she was wearing, Abbie would be lovelier than the bride.

"Does this look all right, Mum?" Abbie asked.

"Fine, dear," her mother told her.

Abbie thought the shapeless, droopy print her mother wore was far too matronly, but whenever she tried to encourage Mrs. Dare to buy nicer clothes, she would say, "I never was a fashion plate! I couldn't afford it!"

Abbie put on her cloche.

"Ready Mum?" she asked.

"Coming."

Mrs. Dare fastened a pin in her hat and the two of them stepped outside. They linked arms and walked toward St. Agnes'. It seemed the whole neighborhood was already there in their finery. The girls Abbie's age wore "stylish" chemises, cheap, mass-produced copies of the dresses worn by the young ladies at the Hotel Lamont. The young fellows looked uncomfortable in their dress suits. Their fathers looked as if they'd been stuffed into theirs. The older women were dressed like Abbie's mother, in hanging prints, with seams that had been stitched and restitched for the past dozen years or so. Home-made bows had been attached to their pumps, and many of them had decorated their hats with ribbons and artificial flowers.

The people congregated on the steps of the church and talked about their families, their jobs, the wedding, the weather.

"Hey Abbie!" It was Helen Winters, a girl who lived in the neighborhood. She was engaged to Tom Colton, one of the bridegroom's brothers.

"Can't believe that me and Rosalie will be practically cousins or something," Helen said. "Maybe it makes me related to you, too."

"I don't think so," Abbie said and laughed.

"How's Bill?" Helen asked.

"Well—there he is, right behind you!"

Bill swept forward and kissed Abbie on the mouth. "How are you, Helen?" he asked.

"All right, Bill. Yourself?"

"Can't complain."

Abbie noticed that people were starting to file into the church.

"Got to find Tom," Helen said and walked on ahead of them.

Abbie and Bill joined Mrs. Dare in a center pew and the organ started playing "Oh Promise Me." The three bridesmaids, dressed in blue taffeta and wearing flouncy picture hats, walked down the aisle, their heads held high and stiff, as if they were imitating models. The best man followed, then the bride's mother. Finally, Rosalie came down the aisle on her father's arm. She was a pretty, red-haired girl, with freckles and green eyes. She blushed and smiled at the guests as she passed. She was joined by Davey, her bridegroom, at the front of the church.

"Dearly Beloved, we are gathered here, today. . . ."

People were stirring, and Abbie looked around. Her own mother was starting to snivel. Middle-aged couples were holding hands. Young girls watched, hypnotized.

"To love, cherish, honor and obey. . . ."

"For better or worse. . . ."

"In sickness and in health. . . ."

"Till death do you part. . . ."

"I do. . . ."

"I do. . . ."

Rosalie's new husband gave her a rousing kiss, and the congregation cheered.

Rosalie's mother had rented the Masonic Hall for the reception. The members had practically given her the space for nothing, asking only the minimal fee to satisfy club regulations. Some of the men had put a makeshift band together—a piano, an accordion, a saxophone, and a ukulele. Rosalie and her bridesmaids had decorated the hall with papier-mâché roses and colored streamers.

"I've never seen a prettier room," Rosalie's mother gushed.

There were roast chicken dinners, a three-tiered cake "exclusively prepared" by a bakery in town, and a keg of beer donated by the Masons.

On Newbury Street, a wedding was a very important occasion, not only for the families of the couple, but for everyone invited. A wedding meant food, music, dancing, laughter, and good company. It meant pleasure, and in a hardworking existence, pleasure meant a great deal. The festivities usually lasted all day and on into the night.

"You're next, Abbie!" laughed Rosalie. She was flushed, a little drunk, and dancing a fierce jig with one of her brand new brothers-in-law.

Abbie smiled and waved.

"The bouquet!" a cry went up.

"Rosalie! Throw the bouquet!"

Girls started giggling, self-consciously. Rosalie ran to the front of the hall.

"Line up, girls!" she hollered.

All the single women in the room formed a group in the center. All except Abbie. Bill nudged her.

"C'mon Abbie," he said.

"Oh, I don't want to. It's a bother."

"Don't go puttin' on airs," he said.

"I'm not," she insisted.

"Go on, Abbie," her mother joined in.

Abbie got up reluctantly and joined the rest of the girls. Some of them were nervously holding their breath. They liked to pretend it was all nonsense, but they were just as superstitious as their mothers.

The accordion player sounded a suspenseful chord.

Rosalie closed her eyes, swung her arm around a few times and threw the bouquet.

There was a great deal of squealing, and then Helen Winters emerged triumphant, the flowers clutched in both hands. She ran to Rosalie and they hugged each other. Abbie looked on, wistfully.

Chapter 3

ABBIE had planned to tell Flora all about the wedding on Monday evening, but her news was overshadowed by some excitement at the hotel. One of the managers had called the entire staff together and announced that two film stars, Jack Pickford (Mary's brother) and his wife, Marilyn Miller, would be registering at the hotel that week. They were touring the continent and had chosen the Lamont for their stay while in London. They were to be treated like royalty, which in a sense they were. Their movie studio was sending photographers and journalists to cover their arrival in London.

The chambermaids chattered eagerly. It could well be the most thrilling event of their lives; a glamorous tale to dazzle their neighbors and families.

Abbie was not as thrilled as the others. All the guests at the Lamont were very important people, and she wondered why the Pickfords should be thought especially splendid. Abbie was not mad about film stars. She enjoyed the cinema, and paid close attention to the stories, but she had no favorite actors or actresses. She could just imagine how excited Flora would be when she found out about the Pickfords.

Indeed, Flora rushed in that evening, flustered and rosy, clutching the latest issue of *Screen Stars*.

"Abbie, I've got to talk to you!" she cried.

"You've heard about the Pickfords," Abbie said.

"No, no, not that—well, that too! Just fancy—you know, she's supposed to be one of the most beautiful women in the world?"

"That's what they say."

"Can't wait to have a look at her—but listen!" Flora started leafing through her magazine, furiously.

"Flora, catch your breath," Abbie said. "You look as if you might faint."

"Here!" Flora said, her finger on one of the pages. "Read this!"

She folded the magazine and handed it to Abbie. The page featured a drawing of a beautiful girl with a heart-shaped face. Underneath the picture, in bold letters was the question: COULD YOU BE ABIE'S IRISH ROSE?

Abbie read the smaller print.

Century Pictures has already selected lovely new actress, Carlotta Lynn, as the leading lady of our forthcoming production of the Broadway hit, "Abie's Irish Rose." Still, the search is on for a beauty who best typifies an "Irish Rose." If you are that lucky she, you may find yourself on fame and fortune's doorstep! The winner of our contest will be awarded $1,000 in cash and have a wardrobe designed especially for her by Gloria Stone, the lady who dresses the stars.

Our lucky rose will also be granted a chance at stardom! She will be given a screen test by Century Studios and regardless of the results, guaranteed a small part in the picture, "Abie's Irish Rose." If Century is impressed enough, our winner may just find herself in pictures!!

To enter, send a recent photograph of yourself, with your name, age, height, and weight, to: Abie's Irish Rose, Century Pictures, Box 524, Hollywood, California. Finalists will be chosen and brought to Hollywood, where they will be Century's guests at the luxurious La Paloma Hotel, all expenses paid! Our winner will be selected by a panel of judges that include America's sweetheart couple, Rod LaRoche and Vilma Banky. The deadline is July thirtieth of this year, so hurry!

"What of it?" Abbie returned the magazine to Flora.

"What of it!" Flora said, shocked. "It's a great opportunity, that's all!"

Abbie wasn't sure what to say. She knew how film crazy Flora was, but she was definitely not destined for a screen career.

"Are you thinking of entering?" Abbie asked, cautiously.

Flora burst out laughing. "Of course! Two-ton Tessie, here! Whatever would they say to that!"

"Well, why did you show it to me?"

"Because it's a chance for you, Abbie!"

Abbie was as stunned as she could be. She was Abbie Dare, a working girl who lived on Newbury Street. Stardom was not for the likes of her.

"Why, that's too ridiculous, Flora!"

"Why?" Flora argued. "Look at you! You're beautiful! Your coloring, your figure—you could win it, Abbie!"

Abbie blushed. "I'm flattered, Flora. But there's nothing special about me."

"Oh, you're a fool, Abbie. If I had your looks I'd mail my picture out in a jif!"

"Flora, it's sweet of you to think of me, but I just couldn't!"

"Why not?" Flora demanded.

"It's just a ridiculous publicity stunt."

"You could still win money, and the clothes, and the part in the film—"

"No, Flora," Abbie said, firmly. "That's all there is to it. It's too silly to think about."

"Oh, all right," Flora said, downcast. She shoved the magazine in one of the drawers.

"I only wish I stood half a chance," Flora said, bitterly. "You could win and you won't even try!"

"Flora, you're dreaming! I don't want to hear another word."

She gently kissed Flora.

"Still you're a love for thinking of me. I have to go home now," Abbie said. "See you tomorrow."

"So long."

On her way home, Abbie felt unsettled. In a vague, indescribable way, Flora had upset her world. Abbie had never considered herself beautiful. Beauty was for women far above her—film stars and princesses and the ladies at the hotel. Bill told her she was beautiful, but all men told girls that. It was true the chaps paid a lot of attention to her, but as Mum said, most fellows looked at anything in skirts.

She and her mother had a rather subdued dinner that evening. Mum's lumbago was kicking up, and so she spent most of the meal complaining to Abbie about all her ailments and how hard it had been to be on her feet all day.

"How about you, love?" her mother asked. "Anything exciting happen at work?"

"Jack Pickford and Marilyn Miller are going to stay at the hotel next week."

"Well, that's quite a nugget!"

"Yes," Abbie said.

"You don't sound too thrilled," her mother remarked.

"Something else happened today," Abbie said, slowly. "Oh . . . it's funny, really. Flora tried to talk me into entering a beauty contest. A beauty contest leading to a screen test in Hollywood."

"Why, I never heard of such foolishness!"

Abbie was taken aback. "You mean, you don't think I'm pretty enough?"

"Pretty, pretty, pretty!" her mother said, impatiently. "That's all you young girls think about! Well, let me tell you something, Abbie. Pretty doesn't raise a child or feed a husband!"

Abbie was silent.

"You forget this silliness," Mrs. Dare went on, "and attend to the business of your life. Actresses! Ha! When I was a girl, we called those sort of women by a different name. I'm not going to say what!"

"I'll be in my room, Mum," Abbie said, and got up abruptly.

Mrs. Dare sighed and started clearing the table. She carried the dishes into the kitchen and scraped them. Maybe she had been too hard on Abbie, but she had never been given to complimenting her daughter. Abbie had a sweet, modest nature, and Mrs. Dare didn't want to spoil her by giving her a swelled head. Mrs. Dare knew from experience that beautiful women tended to expect too much from life and were often more disappointed than plainer-looking women. And, as much as Mrs. Dare hated to admit it, she was also a little envious of her daughter. Those marvelous eyes, that translucent skin!

In her small room, Abbie stared at herself in the mirror on her dresser, as if looking at a stranger. Was the girl beautiful? Abbie turned her head and surveyed her profile. It was like seeing herself for the first time. Why had she paid so little attention to her looks? If she was beautiful, why wasn't she happier, why wasn't the world at her feet?

Perhaps it could be. No, she mustn't think that. She had never thought about such things until taking her job at the hotel. It was as if she had lived in a cave all her life, shut off from the sky and the sea, and then all of a sudden, she'd been exposed to sunlight. The Lamont made her own life seem grey and trivial, and she longed to live in the sun.

She stretched out on her bed, her mind buzzing with thoughts of Flora and Bill and Mum. Presently, she fell asleep.

The next day, Flora mentioned the contest again in a roundabout way. Somehow, she got started talking about jobs she'd had; cooking for a crotchety old bag, having great fun in a candy factory.

"How do you think I got to the state I'm in," she laughed, patting her stomach. "But the best job I ever had was with this photographer. I was his assistant."

"Really? Did he show you how to work the gadgets?"

"Oh, yes. We got to be great chums. He told me anytime I wanted my picture taken, he'd do it for a tuppence."

"Very sweet of him."

"He takes wonderful pictures, too," Flora said. "The best. Why, I could just imagine the shots he'd get of you. Real beauties!"

"Oh, stop it, Flora. My mind's made up. Not another word."

"You're a stubborn fool, Abbie!"

"Don't be too hard on me, now. I am going to see

20

The Sheik tonight with Bill, just because you told me to," Abbie said.

"Well, you're not hopeless."

"See you tomorrow, love," Abbie told Flora. "Have a good night."

Bill met Abbie outside; they had dinner at a local pub, then headed for the cinema. Bill wasn't fond of films. He just couldn't get worked up over something that wasn't real. But women had so much emotion inside, bless them. They needed something to cry over and let some of that emotion out.

Abbie was enchanted with *The Sheik*, and Rudolph Valentino *was* gorgeous. She talked excitedly about the movie as Bill walked her home.

"It was so full of action," Abbie said, "and adventure! Didn't you like it, Bill? I thought it was an awfully good story."

"It was all right."

"Is that all you can say?"

"Sorry, love," he said. "I just don't see much to it."

Abbie fell silent. Bill had no imagination at all.

Bill watched her quietly. He loved her, but he didn't know what she expected of him. He wanted to give her his name, and provide a home for her. Wasn't that enough for any woman? Wasn't that proof of his love and devotion?

"I love you, Abbie," he said.

She drew closer to him, but her eyes were sad.

She was strange, he thought. More restless than the other girls. He wondered if she ever dated any of the rich sports at the hotel. He knew they probably made eyes at her, she was such a pretty kid. He also knew they'd only take advantage of a working girl. But Abbie had a good head on her shoulders, she couldn't be taken in so easily.

"Abbie, is there anyone else?" he asked, just so she would reassure him.

"Why Bill, what are you talking of?"

"I mean those rich gents where you work. I know how fancy they talk and the grand places they could take you."

"Oh Bill, they don't interest me," she said, lying a bit.

"They could turn a lot of girls' heads."

"Not mine," Abbie said.

"Just hope I don't bore you too much when we're married," Bill said.

"Oh Bill," Abbie sighed. She kissed him so he wouldn't say any more.

Chapter 4

THE day of the Pickfords' arrival the entire hotel staff and the newspaper reporters were fluttering about like nervous birds. The chambermaids' uniforms were more starched than usual. The hotel manager wore a boutonniere and studs. He walked back and forth, shouting orders, dabbing his forehead with a handkerchief. Only the guests remained cool and amused over the affair. For her part, Abbie could hardly wait for the day to end. The hotel seemed to be compromising its dignity for the sake of the Pickfords. She had never seen Mr. Hardy, the manager and a man she respected, behave like such a fool.

Huge bouquets of roses, lilacs, and gardenias lined the lobby. Reporters hovered near the doors like expectant fathers.

"They're here!" one cried, spotting their limousine.

A silence fell over everyone, and when the Pickfords entered the lobby, all the flashbulbs went off. Abbie tried to see Marilyn Miller, but she was surrounded by reporters and Abbie only caught glimpses of her beautiful blond hair and bright green frock. She and her husband were posing for photographers. More flashbulbs popped. Abbie blinked her eyes.

Mr. Hardy came over to her and took her arm. "Get

the key to their room and give it to them," he whispered.

Abbie hung back from the rest of the hotel employees, who were gathered around the Pickfords in adoration, and waited for them to turn their attention to her. She watched them talking graciously to reporters and found herself studying Marilyn Miller. She was absolutely exquisite, a woman whose natural beauty had been heightened and glorified by master beauticians and designers. Her expertly applied makeup made her loveliness even more vivid, her carefully tended blond hair shone, her striking dress emphasized the elegant lines of her long-waisted figure.

"Mr. and Mrs. Pickford, the key to your room," Mr. Hardy announced grandly and nudged Abbie forward.

Abbie shyly handed Marilyn Miller the key. Miss Miller gave her a dazzling smile.

Abbie returned to her desk. She watched the Pickfords as Mr. Hardy guided them toward the elevators, other puny mortals trailing behind them.

Marilyn Miller was gorgeous, even breathtaking. Yet she seemed unreal, more an ideal in the mind of an artist than flesh and blood. She was a fantasy more suited to the screen than reality. Without the clothes, the jewels, the makeup, she would simply be a very lovely woman—a woman no more beautiful than Abbie herself.

Abbie suddenly felt a new power, and lifted her head proudly. She saw Flora come through the door and waved.

"I know I just missed them," Flora said. "Maybe I'll get a look at them later on. What's she like?"

"She's stunning," Abbie said.

Flora smiled.

"Flora, I've got something to tell you," Abbie said, firmly.

"What, love?"

"About the contest—I've changed my mind. I've decided to enter."

"Abbie! What made you change your mind?"

"I don't know . . . you've only one life. Why not take a chance!"

"Now you're talking!" Flora said.

Chapter 5

FLORA had made an appointment for Abbie with her photographer friend, Jack Desmond, on Saturday afternoon. Abbie told her mother that she and Flora were going to Lacey's Bridal Shoppe to price wedding gowns. Abbie thought it best not to mention the contest to Bill, either. She knew he wouldn't approve.

She took the bus to Flora's flat, two rooms in a busy section of London.

Flora's home was painstakingly proper, dull, dark colored and innocuous, the sort of rooms one had seen countless times before and would forget immediately upon leaving.

"I expected your place would be a lot different," Abbie remarked.

"It's my husband," Flora sighed. "He's such a stiff. Says bright colors make him dizzy."

Flora had already set jars of cold cream and assorted makeup on her bureau. "Sit down, love, and let me work on you," she said.

Flora's sister ran a beauty salon and had taught her every trick there was. Abbie only used lip rouge usually, but Flora insisted on smoothing color on her cheeks and adding mascara to emphasize her eyes.

"Your eyebrows could be tweezed, I guess," Flora

said, "but I won't touch them, unless you want me to."

"Leave them be," Abbie said.

Flora arranged Abbie's thick, shining hair in soft appealing waves that framed her face. "OK, love. I don't think I can improve on what's already done."

"We're ready?" Abbie asked, her voice suddenly high.

"Ready as we'll ever be," Flora answered.

The girls took a bus to Princes Road, where the photographer kept his shop. It was an undistinguished-looking store with a placard in the window reading simply, "J. Desmond, Photographer."

"He doesn't have to display his work in the front window," Flora insisted. "When you're good, you don't have to prove things to anyone."

Flora rang the buzzer, and Desmond greeted them. He was an older man with glasses and a mustache, hardly taller than Abbie. She had pictured him as being young, masculine and romantic-looking, perhaps because Flora kept referring to him as an "artist."

"Come in, come in, ladies," he said. He smiled at Abbie and looked at her carefully.

He led them into his studio. It was small and dark and smelled like the inside of an old coat. The walls were covered with autographed portraits he'd done of evidently famous people. Some of them were theater stars that Abbie vaguely recognized. She was impressed by the quality of Desmond's work. Especially through his use of lighting, he had succeeded in making each subject dynamically interesting in some way.

"Can I offer you tea?" he asked Abbie and Flora.

"Oh no, thank you," Abbie said.

"Well, I'll have some," Flora told him. "I never pass up food or drink."

Desmond brewed some tea for her, and while Flora drank a cup, he had Abbie sit in a chair in the center of the room. He looked at her intently like a sculptor appraising a block of marble, then stood behind his camera.

"Hold your head high . . . tilt your chin just a bit . . . face forward . . . now, a profile shot . . . turn your head to the side. . . ."

When she didn't follow his instructions precisely, he went over and turned her head as if she was a manikin.

He took perhaps ten shots in all.

"Will they be all right, do you think?" Abbie asked, anxiously. She had never sat for a professional photographer before.

"My dear, I'm sure it's quite impossible for you to take a bad picture. I should get at least five shots that are nothing less than superb."

Abbie beamed.

"They should be ready by Tuesday," he told her. "Come by and you can decide on the picture you want. I'll blow all of them up."

"Oh, thank you!" Abbie said.

Mr. Desmond nodded and smiled.

Abbie returned by herself Tuesday evening after work. She had told her mother that she was having dinner with Flora and her husband. It was a raw, rainy night and Mr. Desmond thoughtfully greeted her with tea and biscuits.

"How are the pictures?" Abbie asked, eagerly.

Mr. Desmond smiled and went into his office to get them. He brought back a large envelope.

"First, I'm going to show you the best of the lot," he said. "This is the one you must send."

He took it out of the envelope and handed it to her. Abbie stared at it in wonder. In the portrait, she looked like a dark-haired angel. Desmond had captured Abbie's essential appeal; a soft, haunting quality.

"I've made a duplicate of it, so I can blow it up and hang it with the others," he told her. "That's all the payment I want."

"I just can't thank you enough," Abbie said.

"You can promise me that you'll autograph the portrait some day," he said.

Abbie blushed.

The two of them looked at the other pictures while they finished their tea. They were all lovely, but the one Desmond had selected was indisputably the best.

Abbie slipped the pictures inside her coat to protect them from the rain. She was so excited, she felt drunk. She thanked Desmond again and ran to the corner to catch the bus.

When she got home, her mother tried to take her coat as soon as she stepped inside the door.

"You must be soaked to the skin," Mrs. Dare clucked.

"Here, Mum. Please put this away," Abbie said, handing Mrs. Dare her umbrella.

While Mrs. Dare put the umbrella in the hall closet, Abbie slipped into her bedroom. She put the pictures in one of her bureau drawers.

"Abbie?" her mother said and entered her room.

"Just shaking out my coat," Abbie said.

"Well, why here?" her mother scolded. "For goodness' sake, Abbie, at least do that in the front hall! Honestly!"

Mrs. Dare shook her head in annoyance. The older girls got, the sillier they were.

"Sorry, Mum," Abbie said, lightly.

"Have a nice meal at Flora's?" her mother asked.

"All right," Abbie said. She knew she was expected

to tell Mum about her evening out, but she felt too excited. She wanted to be alone in her room. She wanted to look through the photographs once more. Desmond's artistry had made her face unforgettable, and she couldn't wait to show the pictures to Flora.

"What did she serve?" Mrs. Dare asked.

"Oh . . . lamb stew," Abbie said, feeling exasperated. She was almost tempted to tell her mother the truth and show her the pictures. They were proof that she could win the contest, that it was all within her reach, not foolishness or nonsense. . . .

"Mum," Abbie said.

"Yes, dear?"

No. Abbie realized it would be a bad idea to tell her mother now. She would have to have solid news for Mum before sharing her secret.

"Nothing. Just that I'm not feeling all that well," Abbie said.

"Oh no!" her mother said, alarmed. "What's wrong?"

"I just don't think the dinner agreed with me," Abbie said. "I'm going to go to bed."

"Yes, love, you do that. How about some milk first to settle your stomach?"

"Oh no, Mum. I really don't think I could drink it."

"Poor dear," her mother said. "You go straight to bed."

"Yes, Mum. Good night."

Abbie kissed her mother and closed the door of her room. After she undressed, she looked at the pictures again. She had never before experienced the luxury, the fun of admiring herself. She put the photographs back in the drawer as if they were hidden diamonds.

"Please make it happen," she whispered, and dimmed the lights.

Chapter 6

THE next day she showed the pictures to Flora.
"They're gorgeous," Flora said, awestruck.

Her praise reassured Abbie that she had a chance of winning, and she decided to tell Century Pictures to get in touch with her at the hotel. She was determined to keep her plans secret from Mum.

"What happens when you're chosen?" Flora asked. "You'll have to tell her then, won't you?"

"Oh, Flora, I'll cross that river when I come to it," Abbie said, not sure which she was more afraid of: losing or winning.

A day or so after mailing out her picture and vital statistics, Abbie was able to clear her mind of the contest. Her initial excitement had dwindled. Tens of thousands of pretty girls would be entering, girls very much like herself, smalltown beauties eager to see how far their looks would take them.

Nevertheless, there was a change in Abbie. She was straighter, bolder, and steadier; more sure of herself. She no longer jumped when Mr. Hardy asked her to do something. She was not the subservient little girl she had been, always eager to please, scrambling here and there as people bade her. She had become less impressed by the ladies at the hotel. The deciding force that separated them from her was money, she had de-

33

cided. Money nurtured their refinement and taste. Before, Abbie had believed they had been born with graces inherited from their aristocratic forbears. She had learned differently and now could look each one directly in the eye.

"Regardless of what you might think," the look in her eye informed them, "we are equals, and don't you dare walk over me."

Indeed, one of the guests complained to Mr. Hardy that that sweet girl, Abbie, was becoming arrogant. The lady, Mrs. Peter Prescott, a regular guest at the Lamont, had expected Abbie to handle some irksome dinner arrangements entailing many phone calls and letters, that she, herself, couldn't be bothered with. Abbie had once done a similar favor for her in the past, but now Abbie refused.

"That isn't my job," Abbie had told her, firmly.

When Mr. Hardy reprimanded her, Abbie's eyes blazed.

"I'm not her secretary!" she said angrily.

Mr. Hardy was impressed. This was not a young woman who was easily cowed. She had always been a competent worker, and after all, she was justified, so he told the lady as tactfully as he could, "I'm afraid the hotel does not provide such services, Mrs. Prescott. You must find your own means of handling your affairs."

"Well, I never—" she said in a huff, but she didn't move to another hotel and a week later, she apologized to Abbie for imposing on her.

Abbie had also become less docile where Bill was concerned. If he suggested they visit his relatives and she wasn't in the mood, she said so. Before, she had always trudged along on family outings and even watched his brother's children when she was asked.

Bill wasn't sure how he felt about this new side of Abbie's character. At first, he had been pleased that she felt secure enough to be honest with him. But lately her wishes often interfered with his own. He had never realized how much she hated visiting his brother and sister-in-law.

"I feel like I'm just tagging along," she told him. "All the three of you do is discuss family business that has nothing to do with me."

"But Abbie, you're going to be part of my family," Bill said. "It all concerns you, too."

"I just don't enjoy visiting them. That's all there is to it."

Bill felt anxious enough to ask his brother, George, about Abbie's behavior. Did all women change this way? Was she just having a fit of nerves before taking the plunge into marriage?

"A working man's got to be master in his home," George said dubiously. "It's all right for those rich blokes to take some grief from the wife. They're kings in the world outside. But all we've got is our home, and if the Mrs. makes things tough for you there, what's left?"

Of course, George made perfect sense, but Bill chose to ignore his advice. It was inconceivable for him to think of sharing his life with anyone but Abbie. She would settle down after they were married.

Abbie planned her wedding because Bill and Mum prodded her, but she felt the shopping and the tentative lists of guests were all a pretense to satisfy her friends and family. Bill wanted to wed as soon as possible and thought mid-July would be perfect. Abbie knew that the finalists of the beauty contest wouldn't be chosen until early August, so she pushed the wedding date to October.

She had already prepared herself for the possibility of losing. If that happened, it would mean she had gotten her hopes too high and had been mistakenly encouraged. She would be deeply upset, but not devastated. She would marry Bill and become Mrs. William Reid. But somehow, marrying Bill seemed less likely than winning the contest.

By July, Abbie and her mother had put a deposit down on a dress they'd found in Lacey's Bridal Shoppe. It had puffed sleeves, a high collar, and an empire waist. They also purchased a simple lace veil. Abbie only wished she would hear from the movie studio soon. Mum was pressuring her to select her bridesmaids and their dresses.

"Oh please, please," Abbie often caught herself praying.

She had vacation time coming and she and Mum were planning to spend a week at a holiday camp near the beach. The trip was for Mum's sake. Mrs. Dare loved the foolish festivities, relays, and contests of the popular resorts. For her part, Abbie had outgrown such vacations. She was glad, however, that the trip would mean a respite from all the shopping and planning.

A week before she and her mother were to leave for their holiday, Abbie got a phone call at the hotel.

"Hello, is this Miss Abbie Dare?" a male voice inquired.

"Yes," Abbie said. The connection was bad and she could hardly hear him.

"Miss Dare, this is Century Pictures calling."

Abbie's heart leaped. "Yes?" she said.

"Miss Dare, it is my pleasure to inform you that out of thousands of entries from America and the United Kingdom, you have been selected as a finalist in our search for Abie's Irish Rose."

"Oh, good Lord!" Abbie cried.

Both she and the man on the phone started laughing.

"We will arrange for your trip over to the States and your stay at the La Paloma, if you're still interested."

"Of course, of course, I am!"

"In that case, your steamer tickets will be mailed to you within the coming week. Should they be sent to the address included with your picture?"

"No," Abbie said. "I want them mailed to my home address. Twenty-three Newbury Street, London, England."

"Very well," the man said. "You'll be sailing for the States on August 15." That was just two weeks off.

"Is there any way I can get in touch with you if I have to?" she asked.

He gave her a number she could call collect at Century Studios and told her to ask for Michael Lewis.

"Do you have any questions, Miss Dare?" he asked.

"Oh, I can't think of any."

"Well, I'll see you in a month," Mr. Lewis laughed. "Best of luck."

"Goodbye," she said.

Abbie did not think of anything for perhaps two minutes, then the news penetrated. She had been chosen as a finalist! She would be leaving for California in two weeks! A golden chance had been placed in her hands like a gift. It seemed as if her hopes had been powerful enough to make them choose her.

She wanted to tell someone. The news was too thrilling to handle alone. But Flora wasn't due at work for another two hours, and Abbie would have to collect her thoughts before speaking about the contest to Bill and Mum. Despite her exceptionally high spirits, she was able to attend to her work that afternoon, as poised and efficient as ever.

That evening, when Abbie saw Flora walk through the door, she started waving frantically. "Flora, Flora!"

"They called?" Flora said, her eyes wide.

"Yes!" Abbie told her. "I've been chosen as one of the finalists!"

"Oh Abbie!" Flora threw her arms around her friend. "Oh, don't forget me, Abbie! Don't forget when you're a film star, it was me who got you started!"

"Oh, Flora, stop it! How could I ever forget you? The best friend I've ever had?"

"Tell me everything!" Flora begged. "Everything they told you!"

"They're mailing me the steamer tickets."

"An ocean cruise to the States," Flora said, rapt. "Just fancy!"

"I'm frightened, Flora!" Abbie said, suddenly.

"Why?"

"About telling Mum and Bill. I went against their wishes."

"Oh, Abbie. You're a grown woman now," Flora said. "If you're old enough to get married, you're old enough to make decisions about your life."

It was a good argument. Abbie would keep it in mind when she had to speak to Mum that evening.

"I guess I should go now," Abbie said. The sooner she confronted Mum, the better.

"Good luck, love!" Flora said, warmly.

"Thanks, dear," Abbie said and kissed her.

On the walk home, Abbie's feelings twisted in two directions. She was thrilled over her good fortune, but worried about her mother and Bill. She had deceived them both with regard to the wedding. How could she have been so underhanded? She almost wanted to cry.

Should she tell Mum before dinner and ruin their meal? Or, would it be wiser to tell Mum later that evening? In that case, Mum would probably not be able to sleep. If Mum was in a good mood, Abbie's news would destroy it. If she was feeling sour, Abbie would make things worse. Abbie shook her head, despairingly.

"Hello, love," her mother greeted her when she walked in the door. "How was the day?"

"All right," Abbie said, quietly.

"Just all right?" her mother asked. "Nothing new?"

Every word Mrs. Dare spoke took on a double meaning for Abbie. Perhaps Mum was suspecting things— "Nothing new?" Abbie decided to tell her mother that very minute. She could barely control herself. How would she be able to eat a morsel of dinner under these circumstances?

"Mum," she began, heavily. "There's something I have to tell you."

"What is it, Abbie?" Mrs. Dare whispered, alarmed. "Oh Abbie, you're not—you're not pregnant?"

"No, no," Abbie said.

Mrs. Dare looked relieved. "Well, what then?"

"You know the beauty contest I told you about?" Abbie said, slowly. "Well, I entered it, even though you didn't want me to. And I've been chosen as a finalist."

Mrs. Dare stared, her mouth wide open.

"I'm sorry, Mum," Abbie continued. "I just had to do it. I won't be able to go with you on our holiday. You see, the ship for New York leaves in two weeks and—"

"And you won't be on it!" Mrs. Dare thundered.

"Mum!" Abbie cried, her eyes huge.

"You are going to call that studio and tell them you've changed your mind!"

"Oh no, I'm not!" Abbie yelled back at her mother, startled by the anger she felt. "No! This is a fantastic opportunity for me, and I won't give it up! Not for you or anyone!"

Mrs. Dare was taken aback.

"If I'm old enough to marry Bill Reid, I'm old enough to decide what is best for me!" Abbie said.

Mrs. Dare wrung her hands. "Oh, Abbie! Don't you know I want the best for you? It just doesn't seem a decent life for a young girl. Hollywood sounds like such a wild place!"

There were two common ideas about Hollywood— one that it was a city as decadent as Sodom, the other that it was a paradise of gods on earth. Mrs. Dare held the first idea.

Abbie put her arms around her mother. "Oh please, Mum!" she pleaded. "Please let me try. I'd never forgive you or myself if I threw such luck away. If a person's going to misbehave, they'll do it on Newbury Street as well as Hollywood! Don't you trust me, Mum?"

Mrs. Dare sighed. The girl made undeniable sense. "All right, Abbie. You're not a child anymore. It's your choice. But I insist that you at least let me come with you. I don't want my girl in that place by herself!"

"I'm sure I'll be properly chaperoned," Abbie said. "But I'll call the studio to make sure."

"What about Bill?" Mrs. Dare asked. "Have you thought what you're going to tell him?"

Abbie sighed, wearily. "Not yet, Mum. But he'll have to understand. He'll just have to."

"We'd better eat dinner," Mrs. Dare said. "It's getting cold."

The next evening Abbie told Bill about the contest while they were dining out at Wakeley's pub. In all the time she'd known him, she had never seen him so angry.

"You led me on like a fool!" he yelled.

Abbie shrank in her chair. People at other tables were looking at them.

"Please, Bill, lower your voice," she whispered. "Maybe we should leave."

"We're not going anywhere," he said, more quietly. "Why didn't you tell me about this before? Why did you keep on with your cock-and-bull plans for the wedding?"

"Because I knew you wouldn't want me to enter the contest."

"You never planned to marry me at all, did you?"

"Yes, yes, I did, Bill!" Abbie was almost crying.

"Then why did you enter that bloody contest?"

"For the money, Bill. That's all, and the clothes," she said.

"Things I couldn't give you, eh?" Bill said, bitterly.

Abbie didn't know what to tell him. She had wounded his pride, and to Bill, that was unforgivable.

"Well, there's no purpose in me waiting around for you after that contest," he said. "You probably won't be back, anyway."

"What do you mean, Bill?"

"It's over between us, Abbie. That's what I mean."

Abbie looked at him, stunned. She could not imagine him out of her life. It would be almost like losing Mum. She started sobbing. "Oh please, Bill, no!"

"That fancy stuff means more to you than I do," he said. "It's plain to me I can't give you what you want."

"That's not true!" Abbie said, desperately.

"Then tell those people at that cursed movie studio you're not going to Hollywood."

Abbie stared at him. His blue eyes were steely and appeared almost cruel to her. He was testing her, and she hated him for it.

"No, Bill," she said, composing herself. "I can't do that."

"Then don't expect me to sit here waiting for you."

"No, Bill. I can see that I can't."

"It's over then," he said, harshly.

"I guess it is. Goodbye, Bill," Abbie said. She stood up and walked out of Wakeley's, walked all the way home without daring to look back.

When she got to her house, she went to her room and collapsed on the bed, feeling too drained to cry. She and Bill were finished.

"Abbie?" It was her mother.

"Please, Mum," Abbie said, softly. "Leave me be."

Her mother didn't say a word and closed the door. All at once, Abbie started to cry. She wept until her head hurt, and then tried to sleep.

Chapter 7

"**I** don't believe you really loved him, anyway," Flora stated flatly, when Abbie told her what had happened.

"Oh yes, I did, Flora. I truly did," Abbie insisted.

"All right, maybe you loved him, but you weren't *in* love with him, Abbie. I could tell, the way you talked about him."

"I wish I didn't miss him so much, Flora," Abbie said.

"That's only natural, love. He's someone who's been close to you for a long time," Flora said. "I know when I got married, I missed my family so much, at times I'd cry thinking about them."

"This is much different, Flora."

"Oh, Abbie. All girls go through it. I know when my first beau and I broke up, I thought I'd die. Now, I know it was the best possible thing that could have happened. He was a rotter, that one."

"Oh Flora, Bill wasn't anything like that!"

"No, love. But he wasn't for you, and you weren't for him. You'll fall in love again, and it will be so much better than the first time. It always is. Ask anyone." Flora always made life seem so simple. Like sewing or cooking or anything else, it could be mastered eventually. It was just a matter of experience and practice.

Abbie sighed deeply. "I hope so," she said.

Abbie regretted most of all the terms the relationship had ended on. It was impossible for her and Bill to be friends or have warm feelings toward each other; he would never forgive her. Whenever the telephone rang, she silently hoped it might be him, calling to find out how she was. When the day's mail arrived, she looked it over, anxiously. She was waiting for the steamer tickets from Century, but also hoped for a letter from Bill. But Abbie was never to hear from Bill again. It was as if their time together had evaporated, without leaving a trace. At times, she was tempted to write or call him, herself, but she knew it would serve no purpose. Hearing from her might only torment him, and she felt she had hurt him enough.

Abbie's last week at home was frantic. Mrs. Dare had resigned herself to Abbie's decision, and now invested the same time and energy in Abbie's trip to California that she would have spent on the wedding. Abbie tried to stop her, but her mother insisted on using her vacation money to buy some new clothes for her daughter.

"Oh, come on, Abbie. I wouldn't enjoy the seashore alone. Please?" she begged. Finally, Abbie could only sigh and nod her head.

Mrs. Dare indulged Abbie in the first shopping binge of her life the Saturday after the steamer tickets arrived. They went to Parker's department store, a middle-class establishment. Abbie told her mother the prices would be out of their range, but the older woman ignored her protests.

"You don't think I'm going to let you compete in

44

that contest dressed like a shopgirl, do you?" Mrs. Dare said.

"But, Mum, most of the contestants will be shopgirls!" Abbie told her.

"Well, mark my words, they won't look like they are."

And so they made the rounds at Parker's. Mum thought most of the dresses were ridiculously expensive. "It's the price tag that makes them middle class," she huffed.

After appraising every item in Abbie's size, they settled on a pink chiffon dress and a navy blue two-piece outfit, both drastically reduced. The pink chiffon had a small tear in the waist, and the navy blue's size had been marked improperly. They were marvelous bargains, but Abbie and her mother ignored that fact and insisted the two dresses were much prettier than the others.

After they were through at Parker's, they went to the milliner's, and Abbie bought a pair of gloves, a beige beret, and a very smart hat that resembled a man's fedora. She and her mother stopped for tea and cake at a small cafe, then Abbie bought a pair of black, patent-leather pumps at Grimley's shoestore.

When she and her mother finally got home, they were exhausted. They weren't accustomed to such extensive shopping, and the soles of their feet were burning.

"I don't know how those upper-class ladies do so much of it," Mrs. Dare groaned. "Some luxury! It's like work."

The next morning, Abbie went to Jenkins' Notions to pick up a copy of the *News*, as she always did on Sundays. Through the large picture window, she saw a group of her neighbors gathered in the store, huddled over their papers and talking. As she entered the store, one of them lifted his head.

"It's her, it's Abbie!"

"Abbie, congratulations, love!"

"What?" she said, confused.

"The contest, love," Mr. Jenkins said.

"Oh, did my mother tell you?" she asked.

Mr. Jenkins shoved a newspaper in front of her. "Look, you're famous!"

Her own face looked up at her—it was one of the photographs Desmond had taken.

LOCAL GIRL IS FINALIST IN MOVIE CONTEST

Abbie Dare, 18, of 23 Newbury Street has been selected as a finalist in Century Pictures' search for "Abie's Irish Rose." Miss Dare, a lovely brunette, works as a receptionist at the Lamont Hotel in London. The winner of the contest will receive $1,000.00 in cash, a new wardrobe, and a part in the film, "Abie's Irish Rose." Listed among the judges who will select the winner are Rod La Roche and Vilma Banky. Miss Dare leaves for Hollywood, California on August 15 and will be staying at the La Paloma hotel. The contest will take place on September 6.

Abbie's face was hot with annoyance. Mum must be responsible for this silly announcement. Why had she done it? It looked as if she was flaunting Abbie's good luck, gloating over her only daughter's attributes. "See how pretty my girl is! They're going to make her a star!"

Abbie winced, thinking that the neighbors now had a new bit of gossip to lick their lips over. She could almost hear nosy Mrs. Bain saying, "Hollywood! And what do you suppose will happen to her there? She'll turn bad just like the rest of them!"

"Best of luck, love," Mr. Jenkins said, warmly. He went behind his counter and brought her a gift-wrapped package. "This is for you, Abbie," he said. "Compliments of the house."

Abbie felt embarrassed, as she always did when someone gave her a gift. "Thank you," she said.

She carefully took the wrapper off to show Mr. Jenkins that she planned to keep it. It was a bottle of the elegant, heady new scent, "Shalimar," currently the most popular fragrance among the European elite. Abbie was awed by Mr. Jenkins' generosity.

"Oh, thank you, thank you!" she cried, and hugged him.

"I'm happy you like it," he told her.

All the other neighbors offered their sincere congratulations, and Abbie felt awful for having suspected the worst of them. She was also ashamed of herself for feeling so angry at her mother. The news item had probably been a token of Mum's honest pride in her.

Abbie left the store feeling encouraged and cheerful. She wondered if Bill had read the article. Surely, someone would point it out to him, or he would hear people discussing it. It seemed they could not be out of each others' lives completely until she left for the States.

Three days before she was scheduled to leave, Flora came to work with an uncharacteristic look of worry on her face.

"What's the trouble, Flora?" Abbie asked.

"It's just that I've lost one of my earrings. You know,

47

the opal ones my husband bought me for my birthday?"

"Oh no, Flora! Have you tried retracing your steps?"

"I've looked all over creation for it," Flora sighed. "I've practically torn my flat apart searching for it."

"Do you think you could have lost it here? When did you discover it was missing?"

"Last night when I was taking them off. You're right, Abbie. I could have lost it here."

The girls looked behind the reception desk and scanned the lobby floor.

"Do you remember where else you went?" Abbie asked. "Were you in any of the elevators?"

"I remember Mr. Hardy sent me into the ballroom to look for a couple of guests. Their child had taken ill and the baby's nanny said it was urgent."

"Well, let's look in there."

"All right," Flora said.

The girls entered the massive ballroom. It was completely dark.

"I'll turn on the lights," Flora said.

"Surprise!" shouted the entire staff.

Mr. Hardy, bellhops, chambermaids, busboys, waitresses, beauty salon operators, and a few guests who were especially fond of Abbie, were all gathered around a huge angel's food cake, baked for the occasion by the hotel's head chef. With frosting and food dye, he had rendered a likeness of Abbie's profile inside a five-pointed star. Next to that, in cherry-colored icing was the command, "Shine, Abbie!"

Everyone started singing "For She's a Jolly Good Fellow." Flora and Mr. Hardy led Abbie to her seat of honor at the head of the table while the chef wheeled his creation over to her. Mr. Hardy opened a bottle of champagne from the hotel's stock, and one of the busboys poured. Flora started cutting the cake and plates were passed to her.

"Speech, Abbie!" People tapped their glasses with forks.

"I don't know what to say," Abbie told them, breathlessly. "I never expected this." She turned to Flora. "Flora certainly fooled me. She's the one who ought to be the actress."

Everyone laughed. Abbie kissed Flora and Mr. Hardy. Brian Loring, a young guest who was friendly with Abbie, asked her to dance. The band played "Poor Butterfly" and the lights were dimmed to give the room a romantic aura.

"Years from now, I'll probably be talking about this," Brian told her.

"Excuse me?"

"When you're a star, I'll be telling people about the night I danced with you."

Abbie smiled shyly.

Chapter 8

*A*LTHOUGH Abbie and her mother arrived at the dock early, the studio chaperone and the two other British contestants were already there.

The studio chaperone, a pleasant looking middle-aged woman named Georgia Ford, introduced Abbie to the two other girls. Carolyn Holt was a delicate blonde and Evie Sebastion a pouting brunette. A few awkward attempts at conversation were made, but the girls were in no mood to chat. Abbie had spent a sleepless night anticipating the voyage and was exhausted. Carolyn seemed to be extremely nervous. Only Evie babbled on with endless questions about New York and California.

Before the four of them boarded the boat, Abbie hugged her mother.

"I'll write you as soon as I get on the boat, Mum!" she promised.

"Behave yourself. Be a good girl," said Mrs. Dare, close to tears. She turned to Mrs. Ford. "Take care of her."

"I will," Mrs. Ford assured her, patting Abbie's shoulder.

"I love you so much, Mum," Abbie whispered.

Tears spilled down Mrs. Dare's cheeks. She took an

embroidered handkerchief from her purse and dabbed at her eyes.

"Goodbye, love," she said softly.

The studio had provided the girls with third-class accommodations, so it was hardly the luxurious ocean voyage that Flora had envisioned. First class was reserved for established stars. Mrs. Ford and the three girls shared one cramped, stuffy cabin.

At the beginning of the trip, Mrs. Ford firmly told the girls that they could forget about shipboard romances. "I've come a long way to collect you three," she said, "and I don't plan to lose you to one of the cads on board. Any fooling around will disqualify you, no questions asked."

Little Evie pouted even more than usual when she heard that declaration, but romance was out of the question for Abbie and Carolyn. Both girls suffered from seasickness during the entire trip. It was like being on a perpetual roller coaster and Abbie was so ill she could barely lift her head. She stayed in her bunk and slept constantly to stave off nausea, though Mrs. Ford begged her to get up and eat something.

"Abbie, it's for your own good. You'll look like a beanpole by the time we reach New York," she said, but Abbie only motioned her away. Meanwhile, Evie became involved with a young student and met him secretly in the small hours every morning, when a war could not have wakened Mrs. Ford. However, one morning at seven, a ship's officer knocked on the cabin door, holding a tearful Evie by the hand. She and her young man had been discovered hiding in one of the lifeboats. The officer didn't have to say what they were doing there, his expression was eloquent enough.

"I'll take care of this, thank you," Mrs. Ford said, mortified. She closed the door behind him, and Abbie had the distinct impression that she would have thrown Evie overboard if the law had permitted.

"Evie Sebastion, you are hereby disqualified!" she shrieked. "When we reach New York, you will be sent back to England, immediately!"

Poor Evie burst into tears, but Mrs. Ford was unmoved. Evie had ruined her chances of winning the beauty contest, but things were not entirely hopeless, for when she told the student what had happened, he offered to marry her when they arrived in New York.

"We'll see," said Mrs. Ford.

When they finally reached New York, Abbie wanted to kiss the ground. She had lost ten pounds and was worried most of all about her appearance, especially since the studio had sent photographers to New York harbor to take publicity shots.

"I'll look awful," Abbie complained to Mrs. Ford. "So skinny!"

"Don't worry, dear," Mrs. Ford said, soothingly. "The camera adds ten pounds so you'll look just fine."

Actually, Abbie's thinness was fashionably attractive and made her look more sophisticated.

Abbie and Carolyn asked Mrs. Ford if they could spend just one night in a hotel instead of boarding the train for California that same day. Mrs. Ford was sympathetic, but it was impossible. Arrangements couldn't be tampered with. The girls groaned. Century Pictures didn't seem to care about their comfort any more than if they had been cattle. Abbie felt indignant, but thought it best not to say anything to Mrs. Ford. The woman could mention to the studio heads that she had been "difficult," and that would probably hurt her chances.

Evie's parents in Bristol had to be called and the new developments explained to them. Mrs. Ford tried to be as calm and businesslike as possible. At length, she handed the receiver to Evie.

"You talk to them," she said in a nasty tone. "I can hardly understand them."

"I'm getting married, Dad," Evie announced happily.

"Do what you want!" her father stormed, and hung up. Evidently, Evie had always been a problem child. She and her intended waved goodbye merrily to the girls, but ignored Mrs. Ford.

"Idiots," Mrs. Ford muttered.

The next job was to call Century in California and inform them of Evie's departure.

"She wasn't really pretty, anyway. It's nothing to cry about, that's for sure," Mrs. Ford smugly told the studio. "She probably photographed a lot better than she really looked."

"How about the other two?"

"They're pearls," Mrs. Ford said, smiling at the girls as if they were her daughters. "Sweet as can be, too."

They boarded an Erie Lackawanna train for California that afternoon. Abbie and Carolyn whiled away the hours playing cards, talking, reading magazines, and doing each others' hair. Carolyn spotted some swell-looking guys in the dining car, but neither of the girls was willing to take a chance and talk to them. Mrs. Ford watched them closely. When the train finally pulled into the Hollywood station, the girls were exhausted beyond words. They had spent the afternoon primping for the studio photographers, though, and their fresh looks belied their weariness.

"Let's see those smiles," Mrs. Ford whispered to them as they stepped off the train.

The girls responded immediately with fixed grins. A crowd jostled them, and photographers greeted them with cries of "Turn this way, baby!" and exploding flashbulbs. Abbie, numb, just wanted to crawl into bed.

A welcoming committee of five men from the studio held up a huge placard that read: HAIL BRITANNIA! WELCOME ABBIE DARE AND CAROLYN HALT!

"It's Holt!" Carolyn shrieked upon seeing the sign. "It's Holt, you bloody fools!" The ghastly sea voyage followed by the endless boredom on the train had been too much for her to bear.

"Holt," Carolyn sobbed. "Holt! Holt! Holt!"

Mrs. Ford and two members of the welcoming committee swiftly hustled her into the waiting limousine. Abbie got in too, and they quickly drove off.

Chapter 9

THE "lavish" La Paloma Hotel was a rather shabby establishment for second- and third-class tourists, with faded and worn pink stucco walls and a gaudy mural of flamenco dancers in the lobby flanked by a few dying potted palms.

Abbie shared a room with a vivacious blonde from Atlanta named Bonnie Lee Francis, who had recently been named "Miss Georgia Peach." The title had simply been one among many that Bonnie Lee had collected. In her twenty-one years, starting at the age of six months when her mother had mailed her picture to the Rose Petal Baby Soap Company, she had competed in nineteen beauty contests. Bonnie Lee took first prize in that company's search for the "Rose Petal Baby," and after that Mrs. Francis made a career of entering her little girl in every competition imaginable. Bonnie had been dubbed "Miss Atlanta Belle," "Miss State Fair," "Miss Eagle Rescue Squad," and even "Miss Georgia Dairy Association."

"Contests are nothin', honey," she assured Abbie in her soft, Southern drawl. "They're no more excitin' than a swim on a hot day and no scarier than learnin' to drive."

Though her acquaintance with Hollywood had been brief, Abbie was already intrigued. London had been a bleak charcoal drawing in blacks and greys, but Hollywood was one long, lazy, stretch of color—sunshine, palm trees, beaches, automobiles, and neon signs. It was a booming American city with a tropical climate.

In London, everyone had looked middle-aged and work-worn, but in this city, people all seemed to be young and idle. The beautiful boys and girls that came to Hollywood as to a shrine, though, were usually desperate people struggling for a chance to be in pictures. Looking into the eyes of a lovely waitress or a handsome young bellhop only made Abbie's desire to win the Century contest even stronger. It made her hug the luck she'd been granted, luck that eluded the other hopefuls in the city. The door had been opened for her, if ever so slightly. What wouldn't that beautiful manicurist or good-looking counterboy do for that?

The evening before the competition, the girls were instructed to wear their prettiest dresses and to bring along bathing suits.

"Why, I didn't even pack a bathing suit!" Abbie told Mrs. Ford, shocked. "The advertisement didn't mention anything about that!"

Both Mrs. Ford and Bonnie looked at Abbie as if she was crazy.

"My goodness, Abbie," Mrs. Ford said. "The studios just took it for granted that all the girls knew there was going to be a bathing suit competition."

"Well, I didn't!"

"I suppose our English cousins are quite a different breed after all," Mrs. Ford sighed.

"I don't know how I feel about this," Abbie said, indignantly.

"Oh, please," Mrs. Ford groaned. "Don't be difficult.

I'll pick up a bathing suit for you tomorrow before you go."

After she left their room, Abbie turned to Bonnie Lee.

"I didn't plan on being some stupid bathing beauty," she said, petulantly.

"Well, I don't see a thing wrong with it," Bonnie Lee said, fluttering her eyelashes. "Look what it did for Gloria Swanson."

The day of the contest, Abbie wore her pink, chiffon dress. At a party on Newbury Street, she would easily have been the belle of the ball, but surrounded by so many other beautiful girls on the way to the studios, she felt a bit lost. She tried to decide objectively which girl was the prettiest, but the task was too much for her.

Century Studios looked like a group of enormous warehouses. Abbie had once heard movie studios referred to as "glamor factories," and the name seemed fitting. The buildings looked as ugly as boils on the gorgeous California landscape. As soon as they arrived, the girls were led to a huge conference room which had been rearranged for the contest. The large, oblong table had been removed, and the judges were seated along opposite walls. The gentlemen smoked cigars indifferently and talked to each other. They looked thoroughly bored with the work awaiting them, hardly lifting their eyes when the girls were brought in. The ever-present photographers stood against the wall opposite the contestants.

Mrs. Ford instructed the girls to line up in alphabetical order, and, one by one, to announce their names and walk around the room in full view of the judges.

"Just be natural," she urged. "And smile."

Abbie could feel her insides shivering as she stood waiting her turn. All of Bonnie Lee's advice was lost. She was more nervous and frightened than she'd ever been in her life, and her turn was coming up fast.

The girl in front of her sashayed around the room, a frozen smile on her face. Abbie watched, hypnotized. The girl became a blur of dark hair, white teeth, and yellow dress.

Suddenly, someone nudged Abbie. "You're next," the girl behind her whispered.

Abbie woke from her trance, and said softly, "My name is Abbie Dare."

Two of the judges looked up and smiled their encouragement. Abbie felt calmer; their gentle expressions soothed her.

She walked around the room, smiling and holding her head high. She forced herself not to rush, but walked smoothly and easily. She tried to read each man's face as she passed him. Did he like her? Was she doing well? Three of them seemed particularly admiring, but perhaps she was only flattering herself.

After the girls had completed the first part of the competition, they were taken into a dressing room and told to change into their bathing suits. Abbie felt foolish, but silently talked herself out of any apprehension.

In their formfitting, short-legged suits, the girls returned to the conference room, and the parade began again. They lined up and each one took her turn posing for the judges.

When it was Abbie's turn, she focused on the men who had seemed to like her before. She had watched them appraise the other girls and felt they had registered less excitement. Now, upon seeing her again, they visibly perked up, their eyes showing approval. She walked slowly in a self-assured manner. Despite the fact that she was clad only in a bathing suit, she moved with dignity, still every inch a lady.

After the competition, the girls were taken to the studio commissary for lunch and told that the results of the contest would be decided that afternoon.

"May I take your order?" a beautiful brunette waitress—another hopeful starlet—asked Abbie.

"A lettuce and tomato sandwich," Abbie said. She wasn't even hungry for that. Her stomach was churning.

"Will you look at that?" Bonnie Lee said. She nudged Abbie and pointed to the commissary door. "Marie Antoinette just walked in."

Sure enough, an actress in a wig and hoop skirt was looking for a table. The commissary was a wonderland. Actors walked around dressed as trapeze artists, clowns, Indians, pilgrims, and gladiators. Their costumes represented every walk of life from hobo to general, and every period of history. At the table next to Abbie's, Cleopatra and Napoleon were eating hamburgers.

Mrs. Ford, looking out of place in her conservative, modern dress, walked briskly through the door. She came directly to Abbie's table.

"Abbie, would you come with me, please?" she whispered. She took Abbie's arm and the two of them walked out.

Mrs. Ford's eyes were gleaming.

"Abbie, I don't know what it's all about, but a few of the judges would like to see you alone," she said.

Abbie flushed and her heart beat faster. Perhaps they had narrowed the contest down to a few girls and wanted to speak to them before making the final decision. But then why did Mrs. Ford speak to only her?

She thought the winner was supposed to be announced in front of all the girls that afternoon.

Only three men were present, the very ones who had been most impressed with Abbie. It had not been her imagination after all.

"Miss Dare, please sit down." One of them offered her a chair.

"Miss Dare," he continued, "my name is Jonas Klein, this is Robert Kinley and Charles Grady."

Abbie shook hands with the three of them.

"Miss Dare, what we've called you here for—What I have to tell you may come as a mixed blessing," Mr. Klein said.

Abbie looked at him, quizzically. He smiled and paused for a moment.

"I'm not much of a fellow with words . . . but I'll say what I have to as quickly as possible. Miss Dare, I'm afraid you haven't won the contest."

Abbie turned pale, feeling as if she'd just been slapped across the face.

"You see, Miss Dare—Well, the judges decided you weren't really the type they were looking for. They wanted someone who looked like the pretty girl next door or down the street, a more everyday, ordinary sort of look. You're too beautiful."

"Too beautiful?" Abbie echoed, shocked.

"Your features are too classic—too, well, regal," Mr. Grady interjected. "You look more like a princess than the girl next door."

Abbie didn't know whether to laugh or cry. Abbie Dare, from the most ordinary neighborhood, of the humblest family background, looked too much the aristocrat to win a bloody beauty contest.

"But even though you haven't won the contest, we're still very interested in you. We want to give you a screen test," Grady told her. "That's what Mr. Klein meant by a mixed blessing."

Abbie could hardly believe her ears. She brightened immediately. The contest winner would only receive the benefits of a publicity campaign. She would be given clothes, money and her part in the film as promised, but then the studio would bid her farewell. These men seemed genuinely interested in Abbie, which might be even better for her future than if she had won the contest.

"We've arranged a screen test for you tomorrow," Klein told her. "Report to makeup at nine sharp. One of the studio cars will pick you up."

"Oh, thank you!" Abbie said.

That afternoon, she accompanied the other girls back to the conference room to find out the outcome of the contest. With a screen test promised to her, she felt completely removed from the fevered anticipation surrounding her.

Vilma Banky, a lovely actress on loan from another studio, announced the winner—Bonnie Lee Francis.

Bonnie Lee accepted the bouquet of roses Miss Banky held for her.

"Oh, thank you, thank you," Bonnie said, tearfully. It was a well-rehearsed performance. "I just never expected this!"

Chapter 10

ABBIE slept perhaps three hours that night. She woke at six in the morning, and two hours later saw a Stutz Bearcat pull up in front of the hotel. Before the desk clerk had a chance to ring her up, Abbie had come downstairs.

"Miss Dare?" The chauffeur inquired upon seeing her.

Abbie nodded and smiled. Despite her lack of sleep, she looked as fresh as a new day.

The chauffeur drove her to the studios and directed her to the makeup department. A woman named Marie Delillo was scheduled to work on her.

"Just wait here," a secretary told Abbie. "Marie should be here in a minute. She's never late."

Sure enough, Marie entered almost that instant, a tiny, small-boned woman of indeterminable age with a very pretty face. She gave Abbie a generous smile, looking her over carefully at the same time.

"Come with me, dear," she said.

Marie led Abbie to a small, white, well-lit room, and sat her down in front of a bureau with a huge collection of cosmetics on top.

"OK, honey," Marie said. "I don't see you as a vamp. How about something natural?"

Abbie nodded emphatically. A vamp, indeed!

Marie immediately picked up a pair of tweezers. Abbie winced. She had never touched her eyebrows, though the current fashion favored severely thin ones.

"Please," Abbie implored. "I want them left alone."

"Just a touch, dear," Marie said, soothingly. "You'll hardly notice a difference. They'll just look neater when I'm done."

Abbie decided to trust her, and Marie tweezed so skillfully, she barely felt a pinch. Soon, Marie's gentle fingers were applying different creams and makeup. Abbie closed her eyes and relaxed.

"OK dear, all done," Marie said.

Abbie turned around, looked in the mirror, and felt pleased. She still looked like herself, only better; more polished. Her natural beauty had been subtly highlighted.

Presently, Mr. Klein's secretary dropped by the makeup department to fetch Abbie, and led her to the set for her screen test. Messrs. Klein, Kinley, and Grady were already waiting for her. Also present were three men Abbie had never met.

"Hello, Abbie," Mr. Klein greeted her. "You look lovely! Doesn't she look swell, fellows?"

All of them nodded, appreciatively. One she didn't know, a tall, well-dressed, grey-haired gentleman, gave her a penetrating look.

"Abbie, this is Mr. Arthur Shore, president in charge of production at Century Pictures," Mr. Klein said.

Shore smiled and shook her hand firmly.

"And these other two gentlemen are Joe Lamm, one of Century's directors, and Lloyd Farmer, one of our most promising new actors, who will do a scene with you," Klein continued.

Abbie could not recall having seen the indifferent-looking youth in any movies. Maybe he was almost as new as she was.

"Well, I'm going to leave you to Mr. Lamm now, Abbie," said Klein.

He and the three other gentlemen took chairs off-camera. Abbie didn't realize the significance of Shore's presence. She didn't know that only on rare occasions did one of the studio's top executives witness a screen test. However, Klein, Kinley, and Grady were so enthusiastic about the potential star they'd found that Shore had been persuaded to come and see her himself. Actually, they were hoping that Shore would sign her to a contract right away. They were afraid another studio would nab her if they waited too long.

"All right, Abbie," Lamm said, pleasantly. "First I'm going to give you a scene to do with Lloyd, here. Then, I'm going to ask you to do a few things by yourself. I'm going to ask you to express different emotions for me."

Abbie looked puzzled.

"It's nothing to worry about, honey. Just when I say certain words like 'joy' or 'anger,' I want to see how you express those feelings."

Abbie smiled. It sounded easy enough.

"But I want Abbie Dare's interpretation," Lamm warned. "Not Lillian Gish's, not Pola Negri's—Abbie Dare's. No copying. Understand?"

Abbie nodded.

"OK, honey. Now, in this first scene with Lloyd, I want you to pretend he's your fiancé. You're both very much in love. He's just dropped over to take you for a spin in his roadster. Before you leave, though, I want you to spend a little time together. You can talk about the marvelous date you had last evening. He took you to the most expensive restaurant in town. Even though you're both wealthy, it was still a thrill. OK? Everything clear? I'll talk you through the scene, and you just make up the conversation as you go along. I want to see a beautiful, wealthy young woman in love. All right, Abbie, now get on stage."

Abbie moved toward the center of the set.

"Sit down," Lamm told her, "and pick up the book on your chair. Pretend to read it."

She did exactly that. She was so nervous her mind was blank. All she could do was obey that voice.

"OK, roll 'em. All right, Abbie, now Lloyd's knocking at the door—the man you love."

Abbie put down the book and an angelic smile spread across her face.

"Get up to answer the door," Lamm instructed.

She rose to her feet and walked across the room with the same confident grace and elegant carriage she'd observed in the young socialites who had stayed at the Lamont.

"All right, Abbie," Lamm went on. "Now open the door for him, look pleased and kiss him."

Abbie appeared positively delighted to see Farmer. She hugged him in the manner that she used to greet Bill, instinctively drawing on past experiences for her performance.

"OK, kids," Lamm said. "Walk to the chairs and sit down. . . . Now, Abbie, tell Lloyd how much you enjoyed your evening together."

Abbie earnestly told Farmer what a wonderful time she'd had, a sweet smile playing around her lips.

"OK, Abbie, that's beautiful. Cut. Print it."

"What about the emotional expressions?" Abbie asked from the stage. Despite her initial fears, she had begun to enjoy herself.

"That won't be necessary, honey," Lamm said.

Klein, Kinley, and Grady eagerly trailed behind Shore as he came forward to congratulate Abbie on her test. He had decided to offer her a contract without even seeing the developed film.

"Miss Dare, you're a natural-born actress," Shore told her. "And on the basis of what I've seen here, I'd like to offer you a job as a contract player for Century starting at one hundred fifty dollars a week."

Abbie was afraid Shore was being too generous. One hundred and fifty dollars was more money than she knew what to do with.

"Of course, you can take some time to think it over."

"Oh no, I mean yes!" Abbie said, excitedly. "I would love to work for Century Pictures!"

All of the men smiled.

"Very good," Shore told her. "I'll have the contract drawn up this afternoon."

Chapter 11

SHORTLY after signing the contract with Century, Abbie was moved from the La Paloma to the Wellington, a far more elegant hotel on Sunset Boulevard. She was also given an advance on her salary. Klein and Grady had kindly seen to that: the girl had expenses to meet. She made it a point to forward fifty dollars of her first paycheck to her mother along with a letter.

Dearest Mum:

The most wonderful thing has happened! Although I didn't win the contest, I have been hired by the movie studio as a new actress! They signed me to a contract of one hundred and fifty dollars a week. As soon as I'm really settled out here, I want you to come and stay with me. I am looking for a house for us now. Until then, rest assured that I am going to send whatever money I can to you, to make things a bit easier.

Love,
Abbie

Within a couple of weeks after signing the contract, Abbie was cast in her first picture. It was a property Century had bought from another studio, and it had been written by F. Scott Fitzgerald, a great writer who was now working in Hollywood. Abbie was in heaven. Before reporting to work, however, she was told to see Mr. Kinley, who was in charge of Publicity, in his office.

"Come in, dear, come in," Kinley greeted her. "Uh, Abbie, this is my assistant, Doug Storey. Doug, this is Abbie Dare, one of Century's most promising new actresses."

Doug nodded to her.

"This little meeting is just routine, dear," Kinley said. "Just wanted to settle a few things. As a newcomer, you've got a lot to learn. Like how to handle yourself on interviews, who to be seen with, who not to be seen with, where to be seen, where not to be seen." He paused for a moment, as if weary of his own words. "But all that will have to wait for the time being. We have something else to take care of today."

"What?" Abbie asked.

"Your name's got to be changed."

Abbie stared at Kinley, then looked at Storey.

"Why?" she asked.

"It just doesn't suit you," Kinley told her.

"It suits me fine," Abbie said, her anger rising. "It's done well for me until now!"

"It doesn't suit the studio's conception of you," Kinley said.

"Well, what is that?" Abbie asked.

Kinley looked impatient. "My dear, I thought that was understood—you look like an aristocrat, a young socialite. Wait, I have it! Monica . . . Monica Dane!" He seemed very pleased with himself.

Storey nodded his head, eagerly. "That's beautiful, Bob! Beautiful!"

"Yes, it is," Kinley said. "Monica Dane. That's a name that conjures up beauty, breeding, wealth, while

Abbie Dare—" He grimaced. "What does that sound like? Do you see what I mean?"

Abbie didn't answer.

"Look Abbie, almost all our stars have changed their names. I don't know why you find it so objectionable. Of course, off-screen you can call yourself anything you like. You can continue to use your real name." He could barely hide his disdain. "But Monica Dane will be your professional name."

Abbie shrugged and gave in. She was beginning to realize that a good portion of her life would now be governed by the publicity department.

Several days after speaking to Kinley, she started work on her new movie and was introduced to the cast and crew as Monica Dane.

The name of the film was *Lipstick*, so titled because the heroine, a poor girl named Dolly Carroll, discovered a magic tube of lipstick that made her irresistible to Ben Manny, the wealthy college boy she loved. Dolly became the queen of the university prom despite the underhanded efforts of Ben's debutante girlfriend, Mimi Haughton.

The plum role of Dolly went to Ivy Hayes, Century's resident flapper. Abbie was given the small, but important part of Mimi. Abbie didn't identify with Mimi's haughtiness or cruelty toward Dolly, but she managed to give a very good performance. She made Mimi just like every cold, snobbish girl she had ever met at the Lamont.

She could just as well have imitated the snobbish behavior of the actors she was working with. Abbie had become painfully aware that, as a newcomer to Hollywood, she was on the bottom rung of a hierarchy. Many of the established stars she saw around the studios were downright unfriendly and even rude to her, though Mr. Klein told her that once she had proved herself, all of them would shower her with dinner invitations.

During the filming of *Lipstick*, only Ivy Hayes was friendly to Abbie. Ivy was a lively, raffish little blonde and a very successful star, but it didn't take Abbie long to find out that she had one of the worst reputations in Hollywood and was ostracized from the most elite social groups. Ivy's screen image embodied the twenties' "jazz baby," a girl who had broken with tradition and who lived for good times, dreading boredom more than anything else. It was hard to tell the real Ivy Hayes from the characters she played. She drank gin, cursed like a sailor, smoked, and wore daring outfits. She was best summed up in one word—*wild*.

Ivy's friends were mostly assorted hangers-on, who followed Ivy around constantly and seemed to serve no purpose on the set other than fetching coffee for the stars or director. It seemed to Abbie that they were living off her glamor, and she couldn't understand why Ivy let such parasites attach themselves to her. But there was a lot about Ivy Abbie didn't understand. Ivy herself fueled all the scandalous gossip about her love life. She would often tell one of her cronies about the weekend or the night before in the most suggestive terms, within earshot of everyone on the set. Abbie wasn't certain whether Ivy was just flaunting her "emancipation" or purposely trying to shock people.

Ivy talked contemptuously about the "swells"—the other stars who snubbed her. As far as she was concerned, they were phonies, and her crowd had more fun than anybody. She frequently invited Abbie to parties, but Messrs. Klein and Grady insisted she not go. Abbie herself was vaguely afraid and always came up with an alibi when Ivy asked her over.

However, Mr. Kinley decided it was high time that Abbie attend her first Hollywood party. He arranged for her to be present at the premiere of *Scheherazade*, Century's latest extravaganza. The party afterwards was to be held at the producer's Beverly Hills estate. Abbie's escort that night was to be Lloyd Farmer, the actor she had done her screen test with.

The night of the premiere, Abbie was a vision in a powder blue gown and pearls. Makeup artist Marie Delillo had also persuaded her to wear a matching blue headband in her hair. After Abbie finished dressing, she studied herself in the mirror as she had done often since her brief career had started. It wasn't vanity—her beauty was an integral part of her career. Marie had warned her not to take up smoking or drinking and to get nine hours of sleep a night.

"Everything shows on camera; every line, every sign of weariness," Marie had said. "Nothing puts an actress out of work faster than losing her looks."

At eight P.M., the desk clerk rang her up and told her that Mr. Farmer had arrived.

"Send him up," Abbie said, breathlessly.

She took one last, quick look in the mirror before answering the door.

"You look lovely," Farmer said, impressed. "For you." He presented her with a corsage—white orchids.

"Oh, thank you," Abbie said. "They're beautiful."

He pinned them to her gown, guided her downstairs, and the two of them walked through the resplendent green and gold lobby of the Wellington. Everyone was staring.

They got into the studio limousine. Abbie couldn't think of a thing to say to Farmer. He, himself, was making no attempt at conversation. He was looking out the window. He ignored her the entire way to Grauman's Chinese movie theater, but as soon as they stepped out of the car, he flashed a huge smile and put his arm around her tenderly. Photographers started snapping pictures. Bulbs were exploding everywhere. Abbie blinked her eyes in the glare.

There was an enormous crowd of onlookers at the theater roped off from the entrance. Police strutted around importantly. The people in the mob chattered and stared. They pointed at Abbie, their eyes huge, their mouths hanging open, reminding her of hungry children. She did not hold the same attraction for them as the big names did, but they were fascinated by her beauty and her gown and the fact that she was in pictures.

Lloyd led her inside the lobby of the theater, away from the cameras, and became his sullen self again.

The theater was a fantasy dome, a replica of a Chinese palace; a spectacle of whirling colors and lights.

"And here are two of Century's newest contract players, beautiful Monica Dane and handsome Lloyd Farmer!" Someone shoved a microphone in Abbie's face. It was Pattie Grey, one of the town's most powerful gossip columnists, covering the event for a radio station.

"Monica, I understand this is the first motion picture premiere you've ever attended. How does it feel to be here tonight?" Pattie asked, with a smile so wide that every tooth showed.

Abbie had to collect her thoughts. The jarring crowd, the lights, this woman, and the blazing marquee, assaulted her from all sides, but Mr. Kinley had coached her carefully in the expected responses. "I'm thrilled, Mrs. Grey," she said.

"Monica, you're a newcomer to the States, aren't you?" She turned away before Abbie had a chance to answer and talked directly into the mike. "Monica is from England originally, ladies and gentlemen."

If you knew that, why did you bother asking me? Abbie thought, still smiling at Pattie Grey. She knew better than to voice her true opinion: Pattie Grey could make or break careers. She had an enormous following, and her readers believed every word she wrote.

"Monica, what do you think of our town?" Pattie asked.

"Oh, I love it here," Abbie told her, "and I love working for Century Pictures."

"And I'm sure the feeling is mutual," Pattie said. She turned her attention to Lloyd, who had been eyeing her imploringly.

"Monica's handsome escort is Lloyd Farmer, who just finished *Clair de Lune* for Century. When will *Clair de Lune* be released, Lloyd?"

"Probably by December, Mrs. Grey. We just wrapped it up last week," Lloyd volunteered. "It's going to be a great picture."

Pattie was only half-listening to him. Her restless eyes had fastened on Buster Keaton, who had just arrived.

"Well, thank you, thank you so much, Monica and Lloyd, and do enjoy the show," she said briskly.

"Ladies and gentlemen!" she shrieked into the mike, "One of the kings of comedy, Buster Keaton, is here!"

Abbie and Lloyd were guided to their seats by an usher. The theater was filled to capacity, and the crowd glittered. The movie community was there in full force, paying homage to itself.

Ken Bruner, the film's director, suddenly appeared on stage, and the crowd applauded.

"Thank you, thank you, ladies and gentlemen," he

said, graciously. "I don't want to keep any of you from the pleasure this screen holds for you now, so I'll be as brief as possible. It was a privilege for me to direct *Scheherazade*, and it's a privilege to present it to you tonight. Thank you."

More applause. The theater darkened and the wine-colored velvet curtains slowly swung apart.

Scheherazade took its name from the fairy tale, but all resemblance ended there. The screen version served mainly as a vehicle for raven-haired, sultry Maura Wilder, and concentrated on showing her splendid body in a scanty harem costume. The film was a love story between Scheherazade and her captor, and the "tales of the thousand and one nights" were mentioned only in passing.

The picture was well received by the audience in Grauman's, and the studio heads were confident that they had a hit.

"Just the sight of Maura in that Mideastern get-up will have them coming in droves," Kinley told Arthur Shore. His department had already kicked off a promotion campaign, blowing up stills of Maura Wilder and displaying them on billboards across the country.

After the film finished, the crowd poured out of the theater and packed into limousines, heading for producer Lewis Shelby's estate.

Shelby's brick and timber mansion was the size of a hotel, and the interior looked like a turn of the century Parisian salon. Paintings by Renoir and Manet adorned the red walls. The plush chairs were jade-colored and the furniture, black lacquer. White roses were everywhere.

Shelby's wife, Lorraine, was the reigning queen of Hollywood's high society and was responsible for screening new members. The requirements were a combination of money, fame, power, and charm. All four attributes were necessary.

Lorraine Shelby had started out as a Mack Sennett bathing beauty. One day, Shelby spotted her on a set, cast her in a movie and eventually married her. She left her budding career without a single regret, and assumed the role of hostess par excellence.

"So this is Monica Dane," she said, introducing herself to Abbie. She tried to give an impression of warmth, but there was a calculating glint in her eyes, and a vague remoteness in her manner. After all, Abbie was just starting out, and her fate in the film industry was still undecided.

Abbie gave her a distant smile. The woman was obviously trying to pattern herself after a countess and, having been acquainted with the real thing, Abbie could easily spot a copy. The woman's speech and dress were too perfect, too studied. A real noblewoman would have appeared more at ease.

"I understand you've just finished your first movie," Lorraine said.

"Yes," Abbie told her. "It's called *Lipstick*."

"Joseph Lamm directed you, didn't he? I think his work is simply marvelous."

Abbie smiled and nodded. She found the conversation stiff and predictable. She was catching snatches of other people's chatter, and their talk was no more interesting. Most of it centered around the pictures they were doing or different deals that had been made.

Lorraine Shelby excused herself, and Mr. Klein brought Abbie a glass of champagne and an hors d'oeuvre. Although Prohibition was in force, liquor was readily available for those who could afford it, and all the industry czars had private bootleggers.

Klein encouraged her to socialize, but after he left

her, Abbie stood by herself, sipping her champagne. She felt too shy to approach anyone. She observed the other party-goers as if she was watching a film. Scattered throughout the crowd were starlets striking poses, as if in front of a camera. Maura Wilder, the star of *Scheherazade,* appeared as much a vamp off-screen as on. She was dancing a sensuous tango with her current suitor, while a studio photographer snapped their picture.

"May I dance with you?" asked a gentle voice with an accent.

Abbie turned to face the most beautiful young man she had ever seen in her life. His tanned skin had a golden hue, and his blond hair was soft and tousled, free of the pomade that other men used. His features were extremely handsome, yet childlike: a high forehead, large brown eyes, a straight, slightly *retroussé* nose, and a beautifully formed mouth and chin. He was both innocent and decadent; he looked like a sensual choirboy. He was just under six feet tall, slim but strong-looking.

Abbie did not hear the music, she was not aware of her feet moving or of the other people in the room. The young man holding her had obliterated time and place.

The waltz ended.

"Thank you." He offered her a smile that could have made an angel jealous, and slipped away.

Abbie opened her mouth to say something and sighed heavily, instead. Who was he? Where had he come from? Why had he darted off so suddenly? She felt dazed.

Abbie walked outside, hoping that the young man might be waiting for her. There was laughter bubbling from the direction of the swimming pool. Abbie saw figures in brightly colored gowns and walked toward them.

Lloyd Farmer, a starlet named Terra Lane, and some of the crew members were strolling around the pool, giggling wildly. Ivy Hayes and Howard Drake, another young contract player, were on rafts in the pool, fully clothed, and racing each other, using their arms as paddles. Hundreds of roses floated on the water.

"Want to try some?" Lloyd offered Abbie some white powder in a handkerchief. It was cocaine, very popular among Hollywood's young set.

"No," Abbie replied.

Lloyd shrugged and turned back to Terra.

Suddenly, there was a shriek from the pool. Ivy had fallen in and was bobbing up and down, treading water. She swam to a ladder, climbed out and burst into laughter. Her wet silk dress clung to her round little figure.

"Get me a drink, kiddo," she ordered Lloyd.

"I'd better get you a towel," he said. "You'll freeze to death."

"Yup, can't die in the middle of shooting a picture. The studio'll kill me." She smirked.

Everyone roared.

"You stay, Lloyd," Abbie said. "I'll get Ivy a towel."

"Thanks, hon'," Ivy said, "and don't forget that drink, either. Tequila if they've got it, and no salt. Don't need it."

Abbie had only used the towel as an excuse to get away from them. She headed back for the house, still thinking of the extraordinary young man she had danced with. She knew she would see him again. She had to.

81

Chapter 12

*A*BBIE started eating lunch at the commissary every day and visiting every studio haunt she could think of. She took in all the sets at Century on her daily strolls. She was hoping by chance she might see the young blond man, but he was nowhere to be found. She wondered if he worked for another studio; perhaps he wasn't even connected with the movie industry. He might very well have been a friend or relative of one of the guests at the party.

Abbie was too discreet and cautious to ask anyone at Century about him. Studio gossip spread as fast as a cold, and was usually distorted and exaggerated in the process. By the time certain items reached Pattie Grey, they were completely blown out of proportion. A husband and wife who'd had a spat were on the verge of divorce. An actor and actress seen having dinner together were engaged to be married.

Although he was no more tangible for Abbie than a character in a book, not a day passed that she didn't think of the young man. His image added pleasure to her life. She contemplated him before falling asleep at night. He was her first thought when she awoke in the morning. Her happiest moments were spent alone, daydreaming about him. Simply knowing that he was real and there was a possibility of seeing him again was hope enough for her. She had a powerful feeling that meeting him once more was inevitable.

In the meantime, she had been cast in a second picture. It was called *Collegiate*, a film that was hoping to cash in on the national obsession with "flaming youth." *Collegiate* was about the adventures of a group of youngsters at a midwestern university. Like other films of its kind, it included a wild fraternity party, a football game, a romantic boatride on a lake, and a finale at the senior prom. Abbie played a wealthy debutante again. This time she was a sweet character, secretly married to a poor but brilliant medical student.

Unlike *Lipstick*, very little care and effort was put into *Collegiate*. There were too many stragglers allowed on the set and therefore too much noise, making it difficult for the actors to concentrate. Sometimes, the director would actually take a coffee break while the cameras were still rolling.

"You know what happens next," he would tell the actors and simply walk away.

He had a formula for all his films and simply churned them out, showing no concern about lighting, acting, or detail. His sloppy procedure was standard at Century. Only two directors, Paul Hanson and Joe Lamm, could qualify as talents. The other filmmakers were hacks, adept at grinding out assembly-line movies, which were usually completed in two weeks. Most of them were flawed, but they made money. Century was one of the most successful studios in the industry. Instead of concentrating on skilled technicians and good directors, Century depended on sensational stories and fascinating screen personalities. Because so little time and effort were invested in production, Century was able to produce films faster than the other companies, thus having more films on the market.

Lipstick had already been released, and although her part had been small, the reviewers were impressed with Abbie. The critic for the Los Angeles Times had written:

> Miss Dane exhibits more grace and charm than has been seen for some time, and no one on the screen could possibly be more beautiful.

Much to the studio's delight, Abbie had been chosen by *Screen Stars* magazine as a "Star of Tomorrow." However, Abbie was far from pleased when she read the personal information appearing in the article.

> Beautiful Monica Dane hails from London, England. She first visited the States when her father, a surgeon, took the family to New York on a holiday. Monica spent her childhood horseback riding and playing the piano. She even seriously considered a career as a concert pianist, but opted for the Royal Academy of Dramatic Art and movies instead. A marvelous choice for her—and a real delight for us!

Abbie was livid when she read the piece. Terra Lane had shown it to her, thinking she'd be thrilled.

"Why those blokes!" Abbie seethed. "Telling nothing but lies about me!" Her father had been a bricklayer, and she had never been on a horse or played a piano even once. Abbie didn't have to ask who was responsible. She knew Robert Kinley had seen fit to invent a history to match the fancy name he'd forced on her.

"Look, they do it to everybody," Terra told Abbie in an effort to calm her down. "Terra Lane—heck, my real name is Phyllis Schmidt, but that's no name for a movie star. My studio biography says my father's an English professor. Daddy's really a pharmacist, but being a scholar sounds classier. People don't want to think we come from the same backgrounds they do. They want us to be special. Why should they pay money or write letters to someone who could just as well live across the street. Century does this to everybody."

"Well, they're not doing it to me!" Abbie said angrily.

She left Terra and stormed into Kinley's office.

"I want to speak to Mr. Kinley!" she demanded.

"I'm afraid he isn't here," his secretary said, meekly. "May I leave a message?"

"No, I want to see him."

"I don't know when he's coming back. He's at a meeting."

"Well, I'll just wait for him then," Abbie said, unmoved.

She sat down, a determined look on her face. The secretary sighed and returned to her typewriter.

The magazines on the coffee table next to her, promotional pamphlets, and reports on Century's financial status, did not interest Abbie, so she studied the posters of Century's most recent films, which brightened the beige walls of the office. The posters were joint efforts of the Publicity and Art Departments, and Kinley's influence was obvious in all of them. Each print was sensational, focusing on scenes of passion or violence. There was the advertisement for *Scheherazade*, already becoming a classic, with Maura Wilder in a shimmering, see-through harem gown, eyes closed, head thrown back, lying on pillows while her captor hovered over her.

Abbie saw herself featured in the *Lipstick* poster.

WHICH ONE WILL WIN HIS HEART? blazed across the picture in red letters, as if written with lipstick. The picture featured close-ups of Abbie, Ivy, and Howard Drake, the male lead. Howard looked the image of the all-American boy, innocent and unassuming; Ivy was the waif-like blonde, looking at him longingly, her big blue eyes and full mouth wistful. Abbie was the icy beauty watching him, imperiously.

Abbie's eyes wandered from poster to poster and suddenly settled on one that made her heart skip a beat. It was a picture of him! The young man she had danced with! He was gazing into the brown, doe eyes of Terra Lane, and the poster read simply: JEAN-CLAUDE MALLEUX, TERRA LANE IN "DUET."

Jean-Claude Malleux—the slight accent she had detected in his speech had been French.

He was under contract to Century, after all. Evidently he was even more of a loner than she was, since she hadn't seen him around anywhere. Abbie stood up.

"Mr. Kinley should be here shortly," said the secretary.

"I'll see him another time," Abbie said.

She headed for Century's Talent Department and asked to see Jean-Claude Malleux's studio biography. The receptionist returned a few moments later with a huge, bound book.

"Here you are, Miss Dane," she said, handing the book to Abbie.

Abbie sat down, looked through the index, and turned to Malleux's bio.

Jean-Claude Malleux

Jean-Claude Malleux was born on August 14, 1901 in Paris, France to Mr. and Mrs. Pierre Malleux. Pierre Malleux was a descendant of one of France's wealthiest banking families, and Mrs. Malleux, the former Marie-Jeannette Devereux, was a ballerina with France's Corps de Ballet. . . .

Abbie closed the book and sighed. It was probably a fairy tale as false as her own studio biography. She returned the book to the receptionist and left.

She drove the Packard the studio was loaning her to the nearest drugstore, where she quickly leafed through a few screen magazines. One of them, *Movie World,* featured a questionnaire entitled: "Rudolph or Jean-Claude? Who is your Favorite Latin Lover?" Abbie concluded that Jean-Claude Malleux was Century's new threat to Rudolph Valentino.

Abbie returned to the studios and went directly to the commissary, a favorite hang-out of many young contract players when they weren't needed on the set. Terra Lane spent half her life there, and a few of her crowd were sitting at one of the tables. When Abbie asked where Terra was, a young man said she had gone home for the day. He gave Abbie her number.

"Hello?" a groggy voice answered Abbie's phone call.

"Hello, Terra? Did I wake you up?" Abbie asked.

"Oh, just napping. I've got a headache."

"Sorry to hear that." Headache was usually a pseudonym for hangover in Terra's circle.

"What's the matter, Monica?" Terra asked.

"Well, I hate to bother you. But you see some time ago, Jean-Claude Malleux borrowed a beach umbrella from me, and he hasn't returned it yet," Abbie fibbed. "I'm going to the beach this weekend, and I need it. I've looked all over the studio lot for him, and I can't find him anywhere. I don't have his number, either. Would you know how I could get hold of him?"

"Gee, Monica, didn't he tell you he was leaving the country for a while?"

"No, he didn't." Abbie tried to hide her disappointment.

"The studio promised him a vacation after he finished his last picture," Terra said. "He's visiting his family in France."

"Does anyone know when he'll be back?" Abbie asked, casually.

"No. I guess it could be anywhere from six weeks to six months."

"Well, thanks anyway, Terra."

"I would offer you my beach umbrella, but I'll be using it this weekend," Terra said.

"Oh, that's all right. I'll just have to buy a new one, I guess."

"Why don't you try the prop department?" Terra suggested. "They could probably give you one."

"That's a good idea. Thank you, Terra. So long."

Abbie wrestled with her feelings for the rest of the day. Although she worked on the same lot as Jean-Claude, she felt she was no closer to him than the girls who paid to see his movies. He was probably the most sought after young star around, and if he had been interested in her, he wouldn't have left without saying a word. On the other hand, she must have made some impression on him; he had chosen her as a dancing partner.

Abbie shook her head, trying to clear it. For the time being, there was nothing she could do about Jean-Claude, so she decided to concentrate on finishing *Collegiate,* and not think about him so much.

Chapter 13

LIPSTICK had introduced Abbie to the general public and movie-goers were intrigued with her. Fan mail had started trickling in. Most of the letters were from adoring young men who had seen her in her first film. She was flattered by the attention, but many of her fans' assumptions about her were disturbing.

Dear Miss Dane:
  You're so beautiful! I know you can't be as cruel as you seem in "Lipstick." If I were near you, I'd do my best to melt your cold heart.

Abbie thought such sentiments were ridiculous. She couldn't believe that people could take it for granted that she was just like Mimi Haughton in *Lipstick*. Didn't they realize she had only been playing a part, pretending to be someone else? Mr. Klein told her to accept the notes as tributes to her acting ability. Still, she couldn't wait for *Collegiate* to open, so moviegoers could see her in a nicer role.

Once *Collegiate* was released, her salary could double, depending on the public's response. Her part had been much larger than her role in *Lipstick*. Charles Grady had also selected a new property for her called

Holiday. When she read it, she was sure it would establish her as a star.

Holiday was about a high-spirited young countess betrothed to a prince she thought stuffy and dull. She had really been attracted to the chef's dashing son since she had been a little girl. On the evening of her engagement party, the countess persuaded the young man to run away with her, and the two of them spent a night on the town. However, as their holiday drew to a close, Marguerite, the young countess, realized that the chef's son was not for her. He was a charming, exciting companion, but irresponsible and footloose. She had lived out her fantasy. She returned to the prince, appreciating his stability and devotion, ready to become his wife.

Abbie was thrilled with the script and with her role, and when she learned Joe Lamm would be directing her again, her excitement increased twofold. The whole venture seemed nothing short of miraculous when she reported to work her first day, and found Jean-Claude there.

Abbie was rendered speechless when she saw him on the set talking to Joe, with a very serious look on his face. She stared at him for a moment, nearly forgetting where she was. It had been two months since she'd seen him, and he was even more handsome than she remembered.

"Monica! Monica, come over here!" Lamm called, motioning to her. His voice startled Abbie and she became painfully aware that she had been standing there, watching them like a zombie. She walked over feeling very self-conscious. She wasn't sure what to do. Simply saying "hello" suddenly seemed impossible.

"Monica, this is Jean-Claude Malleux; Jean-Claude, this is Monica Dane," Lamm introduced them. He had trained himself to call her "Monica" because Arthur Shore insisted on it.

Jean-Claude's eyes lit up and he extended his hand. "We've met before," he said.

Abbie could feel her face grow warm. She was afraid she was blushing. She shook Jean-Claude's hand.

"Monica, Jean-Claude has the part of Peter, the chef's son, in *Holiday*," Lamm said. "I've already told him you'll be playing Marguerite."

"I'm very happy to be working with you," Jean-Claude told her. "I saw you in *Lipstick* and admired your work so much."

"I'm flattered," Abbie said, shyly.

The day's work went beautifully. In Lamm's hands, Abbie felt confident and enthusiastic. His energy was infectious, and his conscientious work inspired the cast. Lamm compared making a film to building a house. Done with the proper materials and the right amount of effort, the house could be sturdy, beautiful, and durable. If time and care were minimal, the finished product would be shoddy and eventually collapse. No scenes were ever rushed through, no unprofessionalism was ever tolerated.

As soon as Abbie played her first scene with Jean-Claude, she knew he'd be a delight to work with. He was that rarity among Hollywood stars; an actor concerned about his co-stars' performances. He never upstaged actors who played scenes with him and did everything he could to be helpful. He and Abbie were such a smooth, dynamic team, their presence alone guaranteed the picture's success.

Working with Jean-Claude heightened Abbie's interest in him. His incredible good looks were enhanced by patience, intelligence, and humor. He was the most charming man she had ever met in her life. She was completely entranced by him, but could not discern how he felt toward her. It was as if she was enveloped by a mist that did not permit her to see things as they really were. He always seemed attentive, and his smiles were genuine and affectionate. He lingered over their conversations as if he was reluctant to end them, and his actions suggested that he liked her very much, yet he had never asked to see her outside of the studio. Was it possible that one of the screen's greatest heart-throbs was shy?

Abbie was timid herself, but did everything she could to encourage Jean-Claude to invite her to dinner or a play. She was full of smiles and enthusiasm whenever she saw him. Soon, though, Abbie started wondering if he was juggling too many girls already to find time for her.

It was unthinkable for a woman to ask a man for a date, so there was nothing she could do. She felt he was toying with her, enjoying her attention, but not wanting to involve himself. Perhaps he was stringing her along as a future possibility. Abbie became resentful and decided to ignore him, which was next to impossible since they worked so closely together.

Toward the end of shooting *Holiday*, Abbie's love-sickness was compounded by a cold that she couldn't get rid of. Her appetite was poor and she was constantly tired. At the end of a day's work, she usually went directly home and collapsed in bed.

She and Joe Lamm argued over what he called her "bad attitude."

"What do you want, blood?" Abbie wailed.

One ghastly day he forced her to repeat a scene twelve times until she projected the precise mood he wanted. When he was finally satisfied, Abbie ran to her dressing room and burst into exhausted tears.

There was a knock at the door.

Abbie gritted her teeth . . . she was sure it was Joe. She flung the door open viciously, and there stood Jean-Claude. Abbie turned red, and barely caught her breath.

"How are you feeling, Monica?" Jean-Claude asked gently. "I know what a tyrant Lamm can be. He's driven me too hard, too."

"I just feel awful . . . like a fool! I suppose I'm ashamed, really. He is right . . . I haven't been doing a good job lately."

"The picture's nearly finished, you're not feeling well. We're only human," Jean-Claude said and smiled.

Abbie looked up at him. How sweet, how gentle he was.

"You're very kind," she said.

"You look to me like a girl who could use a good rest," he said, "and a few pounds. You've lost weight since we started the picture."

"I haven't been very hungry lately," Abbie told him.

"Do you think your appetite will improve by Friday night?" he said. "I know it's presumptuous of me, but I took the liberty of making dinner reservations for us."

Abbie didn't know what to think. She nodded her head, almost involuntarily.

"We'll be dining at Chez Maurice," he told her.

"I've never been there," Abbie said, dazed.

"How is that possible? How can one live in Hollywood and never dine at Chez Maurice?" He laughed good-naturedly.

Abbie didn't know how to react. She wasn't used to being teased. Bill had always been so sober, and it seemed like years since she had flirted.

"Friday, then," Jean-Claude said. "I'll pick you up at seven."

He left, and Abbie realized that her most fervent prayer had just been answered. She felt alive and alert again. Even her nagging cold seemed to disappear.

She spent the next two days visiting every boutique in town and finally spotted a smart, rust-colored frock that looked as if it had been designed for her. She planned Friday evening down to the last detail. When she wasn't shopping or contemplating what bracelet to wear, she rehearsed possible conversations in her mind, imagining the two of them laughing, herself being charming and witty. She desperately wanted the evening to be perfect.

On Friday, Abbie spent hours arranging her hair. After piling it on top of her head and wrapping it in a bun, she finally decided to let it hang loose in her usual style.

She fretted when Jean-Claude was late, but as soon as she saw him, all annoyance vanished.

"I'm sorry about the delay," he said. "I came by way of the freeway and the traffic is horrendous."

"Oh, that's all right," Abbie said, with a shining smile.

The drive to Chez Maurice was brief and pleasant. For the most part, Jean-Claude discussed *The Sun Also Rises* by Ernest Hemingway. It had made quite a stir in the literary world, and he had just finished it.

"Have you read it?" Jean-Claude asked Abbie.

"No, I haven't," Abbie told him, ashamed. She had never been much of a reader.

"You really should, you know," he said. "I think it's going to be a very important novel."

Abbie nodded and said she'd make a note of buying a copy.

In Hollywood, everything was influenced by the film industry, as if life reflected art. Chez Maurice was a perfect example. It was a French restaurant patterned after an eighteenth century royal court, and the sumptuous interior could have been used as a movie set. The walls were plum-colored, and the Louis XVI chairs and tables were white. Delicate crystal chandeliers shimmered.

The maître d' led Abbie and Jean-Claude to their table. Jean-Claude opened his menu and relaxed, completely at ease in such elegance. Abbie still felt as if she should be pressing her nose against a window and looking in.

The menu was in French, and Abbie didn't understand a word. She decided to let Jean-Claude order for her to avoid embarrassment.

"Are Mademoiselle and Monsieur ready to order?" their waiter asked. With his little moustache and trim figure, he reminded Abbie of a mannikin.

Jean-Claude turned to her with an expectant smile. "Mademoiselle?"

Abbie looked at him nervously. "I just can't decide," she said. "Everything looks delicious. What are you having?"

Jean-Claude looked at her wisely. "May I suggest the *Cassoulet Toulousaine?*" he said. "A mixture of roast duck and roast lamb in vegetables and wine. It is excellent here."

"All right," Abbie turned back to the waiter, relieved and grateful to Jean-Claude.

"And you, Monsieur?" the waiter asked Jean-Claude. "I will have the same."

"Very good," the waiter said and left them.

"This restaurant is beautiful," Abbie said, looking around.

Jean-Claude grinned at her.

"Why are you smiling like that?" she asked.

"I don't mean to embarrass you," he said. "It's just that you're so lovely."

Abbie didn't know what to say.

"How do you like America? It's quite a change from Europe, eh?" Jean-Claude said, to ease her discomfort.

"Hollywood isn't at all like London," Abbie said. "I suppose it's like no other city on earth."

"I like San Francisco much better, myself. It has none of the flash and silliness of this town. San Francisco reminds me of Paris. Quieter, more romantic. Hollywood is not California, you know. Have you ever been to Malibu or Santa Monica? I live in Malibu myself. I'm thinking of renting a place in Santa Barbara or Carmel to escape to on weekends. They're beautiful harbor towns. Have you ever seen them?"

"No, I haven't," Abbie said.

"We'll have to go sometime," Jean-Claude told her.

Abbie felt a thrill. He wanted to see her again! Suddenly, she felt secure enough to relax and enjoy the rest of their meal.

After dinner, they went to see Douglas Fairbanks' latest film, *The Black Pirate*. It was the dynamic Fairbanks' usual swashbuckling fare, entertaining, fun, and very popular with the general public.

On the way back to the Wellington Hotel Jean-Claude parked the car near a secluded beach. It was a soft night, full of the sound of the churning ocean. Abbie had anticipated and feared this part of the evening.

"I really enjoyed the movie," she said nervously.

"I'm glad," Jean-Claude told her. She imagined his smile in the darkness.

He gently touched her hair, then his fingers drifted to her cheek and the back of her bare neck.

"Do you mind?" he said softly. "May I kiss you?"

Abbie shook her head, a shy smile blooming, and she turned toward him. Their lips seemed to melt together. The kiss was long and sweet and full. How many times had she dreamed this moment? How right and complete it was!

Chapter 14

FOR Abbie, being in love was like discovering life's most exciting secret. She felt exhilarated and happy; each day seemed blessed by Jean-Claude's presence. He was a beautiful, spirited creature, hungry for life, eager to experience everything.

He and Abbie frequented every nightspot and speakeasy. Like many Europeans, Jean-Claude was enchanted with the new American phenomenon, *le jazz hot*, and he taught Abbie all the current dance steps like the charleston and the fox trot. His favorite club was "Adeline's" in San Francisco. "Adeline's" was a small, dingy cellar, and Jean-Claude loved its rough, raunchy quality. It was a novelty compared to Hollywood's stale glamor, but Jean-Claude also believed that the uglier the place, the better the music.

"'Adeline's' doesn't bother with pretty paintings and flowers at each table," he told Abbie. "They put their money into hiring artists." And it was true that "Adeline's" attracted the most talented musicians around. Their own regular blues singer was incomparable.

Apart from their flourishing night life, Abbie and Jean-Claude became seasoned California travelers. They hiked through the magnificent Sierra Madre mountains, visited the charming, coastal fishing villages, and marveled at the millionaire showplaces of

Pasadena; mansions so breathtaking that they had become landmarks. Abbie especially loved the tiny, peaceful mission of San Juan Capistrano, just seventy miles outside of Los Angeles, yet completely removed from the rest of the world and seemingly untouched by time.

They spent their weekends sunning and swimming at Jean-Claude's handsome home in Malibu. He was also teaching Abbie tennis and golf.

He was her sweetheart, her friend, her adviser, her critic. He persuaded her to buy her own car instead of relying on the studio for such conveniences. They both decided she should get a little blue roadster that was smaller and easier to handle than the cumbersome Packard.

Jean-Claude had impeccable taste, and under his supervision, Abbie selected more stylish clothes in colors that flattered her complexion and made the most of her figure.

She was playing a princess in a new film called *Queen of Hearts*, and Jean-Claude told Abbie not to depend only on her beauty and grace the way other actresses did. He taught her to use her intelligence to explore a character's personality and motivations; he showed her how to make her performances special.

Although Jean-Claude was very outgoing and loved parties, they both tended to avoid being seen in public together. They knew how detrimental publicity and gossip could be for a new relationship.

Abbie was intoxicated by him, almost unable to think of anything else. When they were separated, she yearned to be near him and reflected on the times they'd spent with each other; she had committed to memory almost every word he'd ever said to her. When they were together, Abbie wanted only to hold him, kiss him, feel his being. His kisses were slow and tender, not rushed or forceful the way Bill's had been. His trim, muscular body thrilled her—he was beautiful. No matter how much Bill scrubbed, there was always the lingering odor of sweat and beer, the mark of a working man. Jean-Claude smelled as sweet as a child, and his skin was smooth, unmarred by roughness or callouses.

Abbie embraced him, caressed him with an abandon she had never felt with Bill. Jean-Claude had made her realize how luxurious, how utterly enjoyable physical contact was. He was always gentle and sure with her, never rough or clumsy. It was very evident that he was a man who knew women—how they wanted to be handled and touched. His easy confidence about the opposite sex made him even more desirable. Abbie wondered how many women he had been with.

As yet, Abbie hadn't slept with Jean-Claude, and he never pressured her. When she felt herself being dangerously carried away by him, she would suggest that they stop. Lately, it was getting harder and harder to stay in control of herself. She craved Jean-Claude—just hearing someone say his name made her glow. At times, she felt she was the more passionate of the two, probably because sexual feelings were new to her, and therefore very strong. Jean-Claude was like a powerful narcotic she could not get her fill of. When they were together she felt drugged. Her reason told her that they devoted too much time to the amorous side of their relationship, but she couldn't stop herself.

She was not ashamed of the excitement she experienced seeing Jean-Claude stripped to the waist, or feeling the smooth firmness of his beautiful shoulders, arms, and chest. Nor had she stopped him the first time he had touched her bare breast; she had been completely overpowered by him.

Jean-Claude's attitude toward sex was so natural that he had stilled most of her feelings of guilt. He was almost innocent in his healthy enjoyment of pleasure. Still, she would not give herself completely to him. She knew Hollywood believed that sex was for enjoyment's sake, a pleasurable release in a frustrating world. But Abbie could not cast off her working-class value system so easily. Sex was sacred, and it was a girl's duty to bring virginity to her marriage. Any girl who challenged that teaching was either a harlot or a fool.

Jean-Claude had never mentioned marriage, and Abbie had never brought it up herself, thinking she might frighten him away. Abbie felt unsure of the ground she was standing on. She believed Jean-Claude when he told her he loved her, but she thought his feelings were not as intense as hers. Love without marriage, for her, was inconceivable.

One recent incident had particularly unsettled her. She had told Jean-Claude about looking for a house even before they'd begun dating in order to start a conversation with him, but she had completely forgotten the subject until she heard his excited voice on the phone.

"Monica," said Jean-Claude, "I'm coming over to see you, and we're driving over to Bedford Drive. Get ready!"

"Why? What's at Bedford Drive?" Abbie asked, startled.

"A house for you!" he said. "One of them has just gone up for sale."

Bedford Drive was a residential area where houses were still relatively inexpensive. Stars like Clara Bow and Buddy Rogers had already purchased homes there.

The house Jean-Claude had selected for Abbie was a one-story Spanish bungalow. It wasn't one of the lavish mansions that Malibu and Santa Monica were famous for, but it was spacious and comfortable.

"Only twenty thousand dollars!" Jean-Claude told Abbie.

Abbie's salary had increased tremendously since she'd started working at Century, and she could certainly afford a down payment on the place. The house was perfect for her needs, but it seemed like a consolation prize. '*A house for you,' Jean-Claude had told her, not a house for us*. Abbie managed to conceal her disappointment.

She clung to the advice a cousin had once given her: if a woman left a man alone and gave him a chance to know her, most of the time he'd propose. Bringing up marriage too quickly was a sure way to drive him off. Abbie had never had to plan such strategy before because Bill had pursued her so hotly.

So she decided to continue seeing Jean-Claude as she had been. They would enjoy each other's company, and she would keep praying that his intentions would become serious. She cared for him too much to give him up.

Chapter 15

EITHER because she was influenced by Jean-Claude's sociability or because she was growing more confident herself, Abbie found herself getting to know more people around the studio. She often went to the commissary with the other stars of *Queen of Hearts*. For the first time in her career, the film's cast and crew almost seemed like members of a family. Most of the actors were newcomers, and Abbie thought that might account for the lack of snobbery on the set.

One day the cast was eating lunch at the commissary. Abbie was telling an anecdote she'd read in a recent issue of *College Humor* magazine, when she was interrupted abruptly.

"I'm telling you, honey, he's the world's greatest!" a raucous voice said. There was a chorus of laughter.

"It's Ivy Hayes telling a story. No one can compete with her mouth," said Leda Moray, an actress in *Queens of Hearts*. "Finish what you were saying later on, Monica."

Abbie smiled and took a bite out of her hot dog. It had been their bad luck to pick a table next to Ivy and her crowd. They were a captive audience.

"Honest, on a scale of ten, I'd rate him a twelve!" Ivy yelped, obviously talking about her latest fling. "I mean it! Jean-Claude's every bit as good as he looks!"

Abbie gasped.

"Rudy might be the Sheik of Araby," Ivy crooned, "but Jean-Claude's the Sheik of Cen-tu-ry!"

Abbie started coughing violently.

"Are you all right?" Leda asked her.

"No, I'm not," Abbie blurted out. "I'm not!"

She got up quickly and ran out to her car, tears streaming down her cheeks. She had to get away from that place, those people, that horrible girl! Angry, despairing, Abbie wept violently as she drove back to the hotel. "How could he?" she murmured out loud. "How could he?"

Once alone in her room, Abbie managed to calm down. Could Ivy possibly have been lying, idly boasting? She was so cheap, so promiscuous. Would a girl like that even appeal to Jean-Claude? How many times had he seen Ivy? Had he gone to her after kissing Abbie goodnight? Abbie couldn't bear to think of him holding another girl.

The telephone rang. She knew it was him and tried to control her sobs. She approached it cautiously.

"Hello?" she said, hesitantly.

"Monica? Hello, darling."

The sound of his voice was too much for her. How bright he was, how golden and carefree—the heel! What a fool he must take her for! She hung up abruptly.

The phone rang again and again, pleading with her. She glared at it and inhaled deeply. She picked up the receiver and said nothing.

"Monica, Monica, what is it, darling?"

His innocent confusion infuriated her.

"What is it?" she cried. "It's Ivy, that's what it is!" Her fury gave way to hurt and she started sobbing again.

"Monica, I'm coming over," Jean-Claude told her.

"No, no!" Abbie cried. "I can't see you, I can't talk to you!"

"Yes, Monica. You must let me explain—" He hung up.

Abbie collapsed on her bed, exhausted.

At length, the desk clerk rang her and announced that Jean-Claude was there. She instructed the clerk to send him up, wiped the tears from her face with a handkerchief, and smoothed her dress.

Jean-Claude rapped at the door. She took a deep breath and opened it. He looked more serious than she had ever seen him, almost grim. He entered the room, his eyes pleading with Abbie, and she knew his clenched hands wanted to reach out for her. She stood away from him, not allowing him to touch her.

"May I sit down?" he asked.

She pointed to a Morris chair near her desk. No lights were on, and the room looked hazy in the darkness of late afternoon.

"What happened, Monica?" he asked her.

"I heard Ivy talking—she was bragging about you and her." Abbie's voice was tense. She was trying hard not to cry.

Jean-Claude sighed. His face looked beautifully tragic. Abbie wondered if he was sincere or if he was merely playing a part? Did his acting career extend off-screen as well? In how many other rooms, with how many other girls had this scene been performed?

"Is it true?" Abbie asked, her voice suddenly sharp. "Have you been with Ivy?"

He nodded and looked directly into her eyes. All at once, he had become as unflinching as she was.

"Do you like her?" Abbie asked him, her voice rising. "Does she appeal to you? Do you prefer her company to mine?"

"I think she is rude, crude, and vulgar."

"Then why? Why?" she cried, aghast.

"What else am I to do?" he said, almost angrily. "When you deny me?"

Abbie looked at him, her eyes huge.

"Do I shock you?" he said. "You think I'm awful? A beast? I'm sorry, Monica, it's the way I'm made. I never claimed to be a saint. It's impossible for me to be celibate—I cannot endure love without sex."

"I don't want to deny you, Jean-Claude," Abbie said, tearfully.

"Then why, cherie, when you know I adore you?"

"Do you adore me enough to be mine forever?"

Jean-Claude smiled, sadly. "So that is it. You want me to marry you. Monica, I'm afraid I have little faith in 'forevers.'"

"I don't have faith in anything else," said Abbie.

He shook his head. "Monica, I have my reasons. Two of them were my own parents. As a young man, my father was a promising artist. Cezanne himself praised Papa's work. Then he met my mother and fell desperately in love with her. Papa was a bohemian. He wanted Mama to live with him, but she refused to be his mistress and demanded that he marry her. Within two years, a pregnant wife and toddler forced Papa to give up his painting and look for something more secure. He opened a bakery shop. He became old, fat, and unhappy. He never went back to his art. And so, Monica, when a woman thinks marriage, I start to tremble."

"Jean-Claude, marriage doesn't have to be that way! It's a symbol—don't you understand? A symbol of two people committed to each other!"

"Cherie, to you it's a symbol—to me, it means you want to cut my wings and put me in a cage," he said.

"Monica, I truly love you. You're a jewel of a girl—beautiful, intelligent, charming. You are my sweetheart, but also a friend, a chum. You would probably make a wonderful wife—but I'm paralyzed with fear. Darling, I wish I wasn't, but that's how it is. If marriage and forever is what you need, there's no way I can give it to you."

Tears rolled down Abbie's cheeks. Jean-Claude folded her in his arms. She nestled there, clinging to him. How could she bear to part from him? Could she endure never being held by him again?

"Monica," Jean-Claude said, softly. "If we continue to see each other, you know I would have to be more demanding. In the future we would have to meet as lovers, not merely as sweethearts."

Abbie shook her head, sadly. "That just wouldn't be possible."

"I know. You won't change and I won't change."

He drew a cigarette from his coat pocket, put it to his lips and lit it.

"I have been in this situation many times before," he said. "I know its outcome from cruel experience. Believe me, I know I am going to sound callous, but I don't mean to be. If we continue to see each other, I think we will only make ourselves miserable—"

Abbie held her breath to ward off the pain.

"I'm sorry, darling," he said. There were tears in his eyes. He held out his arms to embrace her. Abbie stiffened. She took a step backward.

"Please go," she told him. "Go very, very quickly! Now! Immediately!"

He obeyed her. He turned and was out the door. At least he had granted her one kindness. He had not subjected her to the torment of their last kiss.

Abbie stared at the door, her mind numb.

Chapter 16

L IFE resumed. Abbie had obligations to meet, business to attend to, and little time to indulge in self-pity. Her sorrow was private, reserved for times when she was alone. At night, in her bed, she would cry softly and pray. She wanted to forget Jean-Claude, but he was still a painfully real presence in her heart and mind. She wondered how long it would take to cast him out.

Her more perceptive co-workers guessed that something was wrong. Leda Moray thought that Abbie had suffered the death of someone close to her. Though she was thin and her eyes were edged with sadness, she was still very beautiful, haunted, and transparent. Abbie never discussed her unhappiness and people were wise enough not to pressure her.

If not for Jean-Claude, it would have been a very rewarding period in Abbie's life. Just as she had predicted, *Holiday* had imprinted her on the public's consciousness. Her star had risen to dazzling heights. She was a genuinely sweet, youthful presence on the screen. Young men were enamored of her delicate beauty and soft womanliness; women admired the depth of emotion she projected. They identified with her vulnerability and naturalness.

Letters poured in for her in such enormous piles, that the studio hired a secretary to answer them. Columnist Pattie Grey begged Century to grant her an exclusive interview with Abbie. Hostess Lorraine Shelby phoned twice, all sweetness and eager charm, pressing Abbie to come to her next dinner party.

Abbie was reluctant to go, but the studio was pressuring her to do so. She had to improve her social life and to be more cooperative with the publicity department. Knowing how much she disliked Robert Kinley, it was decided to have Jonas Klein speak to Abbie, so they discussed her career over lunch at the fashionable Ambassador Hotel.

"Monica, you ought to consider it an honor that Lorraine Shelby wants to include you in her crowd," Klein said, between bites of his quiche Lorraine. "I could name two people offhand who have gone broke contributing to charities trying to get invited to one of her parties."

It was a well-known fact that philanthropic activities were a plus if one sought admission to Lorraine's group. However, there were charities considered chic one year and passé the next. Right now, Lorraine had her name on the committee of an organization that was planning to build a repertory theater in Hollywood. Donations were pouring in.

"I have nothing in common with those people nor they with me," Abbie said. "I don't happen to like Lorraine Shelby. There's not a sincere bone in the woman's body. She's interested in my celebrity, not in me. And she makes it so obvious, it's disgraceful!"

Klein sighed. "Honey, it's the name of the game. When you're on top everyone wants you—do you think it's different in business, or academics or any other field for that matter? It's the same story everywhere. I guess the game's just more obvious here and played more brutally."

"I just don't see what right the studio has interfering in my affairs so much. Telling me where to go and who to be seen with! It's none of Century's business. I just work there," she said in a huff. "They don't own me. When I signed that contract, it didn't mean I was signing my soul over as well."

"Monica, what can I tell you?" Klein said. "Your career doesn't end after the day's shooting is over. In many ways, your life off-screen is just as important as your life on-screen. Do you get my point?"

Abbie looked at him, irritated and confused.

Klein sighed, like a teacher facing an obstinate student. "Monica, you—movie stars are the closest thing this country has to an aristocracy. A girl who lives in Kalamazoo doesn't want to read that Monica Dane, fabled movie star, spends her Saturday nights at home with a good book. She likes to see a heroine living out her fantasies in exotic places with exciting people, her life one big adventure."

"You owe it to your fans to go to that dinner party," Klein told her. "That's who it's really for. They pay to see your movies; you owe them something."

As a newcomer, she had sworn never to rub elbows with the people who had snubbed her, but Abbie capitulated and accepted the invitation to an "informal" dinner at the Shelby residence. Klein had convinced her.

Marie Delillo warned Abbie that "informal dress" really meant dressing to kill. Abbie didn't relish shopping for a dress since she wasn't all that pleased to be attending the dinner in the first place, so Marie arranged to borrow a gown for her from the studio. It was a beige number with a fringed hemline and roses.

It was imperative for Abbie to have an escort. Most of the elite crowd were married or paired off, and Lorraine was convinced that singles and couples did not mesh well.

The studio decided that Lloyd Farmer was too heavily associated with Ivy Hayes and her wild bunch to fit in decently. The party for *Scheherazade* had been an exception. When the studio unwittingly suggested Jean-Claude, poor Abbie blanched. Finally, a respected young actor named Herbert Raymond was considered suitable.

When Abbie and Herbert arrived at the party, Lorraine greeted her as if she was a long lost sister.

"Monica, dear, I'm so glad you could come," she said, breathlessly. "You look wonderful!"

"Thank you," Abbie said. "You look wonderful yourself." It was no overstatement. Lorraine's black hair was pulled back in a severe bun, emphasizing her sculptured bone structure. Her dark, almond-shaped eyes glittered, and her skin was bronzed. In her exotic caftan, she looked like an Aztec queen.

"Come, dears," Lorraine said, linking arms with both Abbie and Herbert. "Let me introduce you to some people."

The party boasted screen idols like John Gilbert and Dolores Costello, authors Elinor Glyn and Carl Van Vechten. Though Abbie managed to maintain her poise with all of them, she worried about the impression she was making. She had believed she didn't care what people thought of her and was mildly surprised that she did care. Everyone was very gracious to her, congratulating her on the superb performance she'd given in *Holiday* and inquiring about her current projects.

Lorraine was always on the lookout for fresh faces. She needed to pep up her group and keep it vital, and with Abbie's current success and regal image, she seemed an ideal candidate. Hollywood's most prestigious circle had been stagnating. The same stories told, the same people seen. Lately, the press had been more intrigued with the dancing on top of grand pianos and midnight skinny dipping at Ivy's parties. There had even been brawls, bringing the police.

Lorraine Shelby had turned seating people at tables into a science. Because of her English origin, Lorraine sat Abbie across from Charlotte Hodes, a British authoress turned highly successful screenwriter. Abbie was a bit frightened Miss Hodes might discern her working-class roots—supposedly Charlotte Hodes' father was a member of Parliament. However, after a moment or two of conversation, both women smiled knowingly at each other. Miss Hodes was working-class herself.

The dinner's main course was a delectable lobster Newburg prepared by Lorraine's cook, who commanded an astronomical salary. The table was covered with Spanish lace, gold candelabras, and camellias.

Lorraine, who had just returned from a trip to New York, made frequent references to that city.

"One thing I do miss here," she said, "is the quality of theater. That's why a repertory company is so important to our community."

Claire Jameson, a bedizened young matron sitting next to her, whose husband was Century's second largest stockholder, nodded seriously.

"Of course, darling," she said.

"I saw *What Price Glory* while I was there, and I

was simply staggered," Lorraine said, putting a hand to her breast.

"Darling, that was too agonizing!"

"You saw it too, Claire?"

"Darling, but of course! Too powerful!"

Other obligatory topics were touched on—Dorothy Parker's latest wisecrack, an essay Lorraine had read by H. L. Mencken (she couldn't stand him), Ring Lardner's new story in *Cosmopolitan,* the new fall fashions in *Vogue.* But for the most part, the ladies' conversation was rife with gossip and name-dropping. It struck Abbie that their talk was really a sophisticated, more scintillating version of everyday banter on Newbury Street. Much of the gossip involved members of Ivy's group.

"Lewis and I went to Malibu this weekend and saw Lloyd Farmer there," Lorraine said. "Strange how that boy was wearing a suit, even at the beach. He didn't go near the water."

"Oh, he wouldn't dare to take his shirt off," Claire whispered. "Track marks. I hear he can't stand up without a hypodermic!"

"Joe Lax complained that Terra Lane's missed a week's work on *Daphne,* and when she does come in she spends most of her time in the ladies' room vomiting."

"I guess she's got a problem."

"I wonder when it's due—"

"I understand that a bull elephant couldn't tear Maura Wilder away from Howard Drake."

"You're kidding? Does Sherman know that?"

"Darling, I hear he's plotting murder! The joke of it is that Howard's as queer as snow in July. He won't look at a woman, and poor Maura craves him. Isn't that too tragicomic?"

"Insane!"

At least, the next-to-last comment explained why Howard had been so aloof to Abbie during the filming of *Lipstick*.

The ladies drank more champagne, and the talk became racier. It was restrained ribaldry, never exceeding the limits of tastefulness, but Abbie was glad that she and Jean-Claude had kept their relationship secret. At least she'd been spared the indignity of being an item for gossip.

After the chocolate mousse, the group retired to the parlor for a round of charades and a game of "fictionary dictionary," in which players had to distinguish the real definitions of complicated words from false definitions the opposing team made up. Abbie and Herbert left around midnight.

Abbie felt she had not contributed to the conversation at the party and feared she had left a weak impression. But actually, her quietness had worked for her. The next day Pattie Grey would describe Abbie in her newspaper column as "beautiful, refined Monica Dane." Shyness could be interpreted as refinement by Hollywood standards.

After Herbert bid her goodnight and she was alone in her room, Abbie felt utterly desolate. She was becoming highly successful and sought after. She was envied and adored, yet it all seemed to ring hollow. She took no pleasure in any of it because there was no one to share her life or success. People worshipped her, yet she felt unloved.

She needed someone to confide in, someone who would listen to her and offer encouragement and support, but genuine friendships were rare in the competitive movie industry. Mistrust and jealousy lurked everywhere.

Suddenly, Abbie went to her bureau, got out a sheet of stationery and a pen, and started writing.

Dearest Mum:

I have found a house for the two of us. I want you to move in with me as soon as possible. Will have everything ready before you arrive. I miss you more than I can say.

Love,
Abbie

She would buy the house on Bedford Drive. There would be some relief from the loneliness she could no longer bear.

She folded the note resolutely. She would ask Jonas Klein to suggest a lawyer to handle the legal aspects involved.

Chapter 17

WHEN Abbie told Jonas Klein she had invited her mother to live with her, he looked dubious and mentioned his reservations. Mrs. Dare, unmistakably working class, might ruin the publicity department's fabrications about Abbie's life.

"My mother is staying with me or I go to First National Studios," Abbie screamed at him. "I've had all I can stand of your bloody interfering! You have gone too far!"

Klein managed to calm her down and then he apologized. "I'm sorry, honey. I've gone over the limit, I know, but you have to try to see things from the studio's viewpoint. But you can have your mother live with you. I'll take care of everything."

Within a week, all the arrangements had been made; the house was Abbie's. She liked taking drives through the neighborhood and kept envisioning herself and her mother strolling down the sunlit lane past the meticulously kept yards and gardens. She knew precisely the kind of decor she wanted—pastels, woods, and lace. She wanted the interior simple, yet warm and feminine.

She was working hard on a new picture, so she hired a painter and a housekeeper to set things up, giving them specific instructions. Meanwhile, Klein issued a press release:

> Monica Dane's mother, Mrs. John Dane of London, England, is visiting the United States and will be staying with her daughter. She anticipates a quiet, restful sojourn.

They were not to be disturbed. No press conferences, interviews, or photographs. Klein would not even disclose the date of her mother's arrival.

Abbie received a letter from her mother saying that she would come as soon as possible. Since Abbie had left England, Mrs. Dare's sister-in-law had died, and she was helping her brother care for his three young children. She did not want to leave until she was sure the household could function without her. In time, Leonard agreed to hire a housekeeper, and Abbie wired her mother the money for the trip. She anticipated her mother's arrival as eagerly as a five-year-old.

When Mrs. Dare arrived at the train station, Abbie hardly recognized her. She had lost at least thirty pounds and was wearing makeup for the first time in years. She had even bought herself a new dress for the occasion. Abbie smiled with delight.

"Mum, you look marvelous," she said.

"Well, I couldn't come here looking like a drudge," Mrs. Dare said, blushing. "I didn't want to embarrass you."

"You look ten years younger. You've lost so much weight!"

"When you're caring for three young ones, there's not much time to stuff your face."

Abbie laughed and hugged her mother. "How about

something to eat right now? You must be starved," she said.

"That's putting it mildly, dear," her mother said.

They walked into a coffee shop at the station and sat down.

"May I take your order?" the waitress asked.

"What'll you have, Mum?"

"Oh, anything," Mrs. Dare said.

"How about a hamburger?" Abbie said. "A good introduction to American food. I've started living on them."

"All right, love."

"Two hamburgers, please," Abbie told the waitress, who was staring at her intently.

"You're Monica Dane, aren't you?" the girl said, her eyes wide.

Before Abbie could even answer, the girl started yelling loudly. "It's Monica Dane! Monica Dane is here!"

People looked up, pointing, leaving their tables and coming toward Abbie, fluttering pieces of paper in her face.

"May I have your autograph, Miss Dane?"

"Oh, I just loved you in *Holiday*!"

"Isn't she stunning!"

"You look just like you do in the movies!"

Abbie felt suffocated, vulnerable, and frightened. She and her mother had to get away, away from that mass of hands and eyes and mouths. This crowd was like the one at her first premiere, but there she'd been protected by police. Now they hovered over her like hunters over their prey.

Abbie grasped her mother's hand and the two of them pushed through the crowd and bolted out the door. Some of the more persistent fans followed them, but most of the people hung back, and shouted at her.

"All I wanted was your lousy autograph!"

"You're a snob, Monica!"

Abbie and her mother ran to her roadster and got in. Abbie drove off quickly. Neither spoke until they were some distance from the train station.

"Abbie, how often does that happen?" Mrs. Dare asked, breathlessly. She looked frightened.

"It never happened to me before, Mum," she said. Abbie had so wanted the day to be perfect!

When they arrived at the house, both Abbie and her mother tried to soothe each other and make light of the incident in the coffee shop, but it still hung over them like a grim cloud.

Abbie had already made reservations for the two of them to have dinner at Chez Maurice, but now she was almost afraid to go anywhere. Her fame had marked her and set her apart from everyday people. She was now an extraordinary object to be pointed at and fawned over.

"We're going out to dinner later on, Mum," Abbie told her mother, hesitantly.

Mrs. Dare looked worried, and said, "I'd just as soon eat in, love."

Abbie was flooded with anger. She'd be damned if she'd spend her life hiding away in a mansion, afraid of the daylight and the people outside like Hollywood's famous recluses. The people at the coffee shop weren't her enemies, she thought, she had once been one of them, and her name on a marquee hadn't changed her inside.

She went to the phone, called Jonas Klein, and told him what had happened.

"I already know," he groaned.

"How?" Abbie asked.

"That bastard, Charlie Langdon, told me," Klein

said. "Some cop spotted a crowd forming in front of a coffee shop at the train station. He asked them what was going on, and they told him you'd been eating lunch there and had run away when they asked for autographs."

"I was scared to death!" Abbie cried.

"The cop figured he had a scoop of sorts and phoned it in to *Public Eye*, that scandal sheet. Langdon called me just so he could gloat about it, since I'd refused to tell him when your mother would be arriving from England. His story is supposed to appear tomorrow."

Public Eye was one of the many weekly tabloids on the newsstands, a West Coast version of *The New York Daily Graphic*. It was usually bad luck to have one's name mentioned. Jean-Claude had once told Abbie that *Public Eye* reporters could sensationalize anything, and Charlie Langdon was one of the slimiest. "They could turn 'Jack and Jill' into a torrid love story," Jean-Claude had said.

Ivy Hayes was their favorite screen star since her antics made such exciting headlines, but occasionally someone else would fall into their clutches. Now, it was Abbie's turn.

"Nobody reads that trash anyway," Abbie told Klein, trying to convince herself as well.

"No, only half the country."

"Well, no one takes it seriously; people realize most of it's fiction."

"You'd be surprised," Klein told her.

"Well, I'll just sue them if they twist things around."

"It's nearly impossible to do that, honey. They'd have to accuse you of murder. They've got lots of ways to protect themselves, and besides, a public figure has to expect these things. People are curious about you and these stories will circulate."

Abbie was becoming exasperated.

"Well, it's not my fault! I'm sorry that idiot phoned his story in, but what am I supposed to do?"

"Nothing, honey," Klein sighed. She could envision him putting a washcloth to his aching head the way he often did. "It's par for the course for a new star to get worked over by those bastards."

"What in hell can they say?" Abbie yelled.

"Look, just forget it. Don't worry about it; let me handle it."

Abbie sighed heavily. "Getting back to what I called you about. . . ."

"What, honey?"

"I made reservations to have dinner at Chez Maurice with my mother, and now I'm almost scared to go. I don't know how to handle these things."

"Chez Maurice is fine," Klein said, as if going through a lecture he'd given many times before. "Any place exclusive is good. Only the rich, famous, and beautiful frequent those joints. Just watch out for public places. A deli, a coffee shop, a department store, anywhere Mr. and Mrs. John Q. Smith frequent is kind of dangerous. Generally though, a floppy hat, a loose-fitting coat, and sunglasses are all you need to keep your identity secret. If you feel very unsafe, the studio can lend you a wig. Now that you're aware of your new status, you really shouldn't have any trouble at all."

"What about my privacy, Jonas?" Abbie said. "Am I supposed to just kiss it goodbye?"

"If you wanted privacy," Klein told her, "you had no business becoming a movie star."

Abbie was silent for a bit.

"OK, thanks, Jonas."

"Don't mention it and have a good time. And don't worry about *Public Eye*."

Abbie thought he was really trying to comfort himself, but she realized the whole business with *Public Eye* was beyond her control, and suddenly felt much better.

"I talked to the studio, Mum," she said, "and we're eating out tonight, so look your prettiest."

Her mother shrugged. "All right, love. But first a nap and then a bath, please. I feel all in."

"Of course, Mum," Abbie said. "I have some delicious bubble bath."

"Thanks, love," Mrs. Dare said.

While her mother slept, Abbie prepared a tub for herself and luxuriated in the warm, scented water for half an hour. When she got out, she woke her mother and reminded her that they'd be leaving shortly.

After Mrs. Dare had bathed, she put on a lavender frock, and Abbie felt enormously proud of her.

"You look lovely, Mum," Abbie told her. "As pretty as any actress in Hollywood."

Both of them put finishing touches to their hair then scurried out to the car and headed for Chez Maurice.

Mrs. Dare was completely intimidated by the splendor of the establishment. She hardly said a word through dinner and sat very stiffly, staring at the wealthy patrons around her. Whenever Abbie looked at her, she would smile tentatively, but the meal had become an ordeal. Abbie had started to take the luxuries available to her for granted. She had forgotten how overwhelming they were to a person not used to a lavish lifestyle. They left without ordering dessert.

Mrs. Dare was still uncharacteristically quiet on the drive home.

"You didn't have a good time, did you, Mum?" Abbie broke the silence.

"Of course I did, love!" her mother insisted. "The food was delicious, and the place was so beautiful. I was never inside a place like that in my life."

"But you still didn't like it."

"I guess maybe if it had been just a bit homier. . . ." Mrs. Dare said in a tiny voice. "I suppose that's how my taste runs."

Abbie smiled and nodded. She felt like a little girl who'd given her mother a present, and realized her mother was only pretending to be pleased.

Chapter 18

THE next day, when Abbie reported for work and went to her dressing room, the latest edition of *Public Eye* was on her bureau. She was almost tempted to throw the paper in the trash but felt compelled to read what those skilled gossipmongers had written about her. She wondered who might have left the issue there for her. Could it possibly have been Jonas Klein or Marie Delillo?

She leafed through the glossy print newspaper carefully. There was the standard piece devoted to Ivy Hayes, suggestively called "Ivy Takes a Dare." Another spread was titled "Hollywood Scorecard: Who Belongs to Who," about various movie star romances. There was also a sob story written by Nan Britten, President Warren Harding's mistress, who claimed he was the father of her child. Finally, Abbie came across an article that someone had circled in black ink.

WHAT'S THE MATTER WITH MONICA DANE?

by Charles Langdon

This essay is written for all snobbish Hollywood girls, especially Monica Dane.

Monica has scored hits in a few recent movies, most notably "Holiday." Monica started her career playing a stuck-up young thing in "Lipstick" and apparently takes her roles home with her.

Yesterday, at a coffee shop, a few fans spotted Monica and eagerly asked her for her autograph. Miss Dane responded by telling her admirers to leave her alone. Then she stormed out of the restaurant with an older woman, presumed to be her mother.

If Miss Dane did not want her lunch interrupted, she could have graciously asked the autograph seekers to come back after she'd finished her meal. What Miss Dane and others of her ilk fail to understand is that they owe their success to their fans. The very least movie-goers should expect is courteous and considerate treatment by the people whom they have placed on pedestals.

Monica Dane, now that she has tasted fame, money, and luxury, seems to have forgotten that the public can get along without her, but she can't get along without their support. A star, no matter how powerful and bright, cannot afford to ignore their fans or behave as rudely as Miss Dane did.

Monica Dane and others like her would do well to heed this warning: Respect the wishes of your audience lest your star flickers out.

Abbie was horrified. If she had read such an article about another actress, she'd probably never see another film of hers again. Why would this man Langdon write such a thing? He didn't even know her. Abbie burst into tears and hurled the paper against the wall.

There was a knock at her door.

"Monica?" It was Narda Leslie, one of Abbie's co-stars. "Monica, we're waiting for you."

"I can't now," Abbie told her, tearfully.

"What is it, honey? Please let me in. What's wrong, Monica?"

Abbie relented and opened the door. Her face was red from crying.

"Oh, poor kid," Narda said. "What is it—a fellow?"

Abbie shook her head. She picked up the newspaper and found the article about herself.

"It's this," she said and handed the paper to Narda. Narda read it.

"That jerk! Aw, honey, Langdon's a liar and everybody knows it! He'd tell lies on his own mother if it would sell a story. This could have been written about anyone. It was just your crummy luck that he wrote it about you."

"It looks terrible," Abbie said. "I feel miserable about it."

"Anybody'd be furious," Narda said. "It's such a lousy hatchet job."

"What should I do, Narda?"

"I don't think you'll have to do anything. Jonas is probably taking care of it now."

"I'd love to scratch Langdon's eyes out!" Abbie said fiercely.

"You'd have to get on line for that," Narda said.

"Is the article very damaging, Narda? I mean, for my career?" Abbie asked earnestly.

Narda shook her head. "It's to be expected, honey. Everybody in Hollywood has had some lies written about them. Of course when it happens to you, it seems the worst scandal in the world, but believe me, Monica, you were very lucky. This article is nothing compared to the outrages that have been written about other people."

Abbie sighed. She felt slightly better.

"Come on, Monica," Narda coaxed. "We're waiting for you."

"I'm ready," Abbie said, and the two girls walked to the set.

Later, she was interrupted during a scene and told to go to Jonas Klein's office. She ran over.

"Mr. Klein wanted to see me," Abbie told Klein's secretary.

"Yes dear, go right in," the woman looked especially motherly today. News got around fast.

"Hello, Monica." Klein smiled weakly. "Please sit down."

He sat behind his desk staring at his hands. Klein's office was enormous, and made his small frame look almost childlike in the huge swivel chair.

"I guess by now you must have read Langdon's piece of trash," Klein said somberly.

"Yes, I did," Abbie said. "And I'd love to call him up and tell him what I think of him!"

Klein continued to look at his hands and shook his head. "It wouldn't leave a dent, Monica. By this time, that guy's developed a skin thicker than an elephant's hide. Anyway, it's a better idea to lay low with a creep like him. He's a bad enemy to have; he'll just keep picking you apart."

"Can't we do anything?"

"Yes," Klein said. "We're going to counteract his bad publicity with a lot of good publicity. I'm arranging two interviews for you this week. One with Pattie Grey and the other with a reporter from *Movie World*. You are going to have to smile and be charming and polite at all times. You must answer each question, no matter how stupid or personal."

Abbie groaned.

"Don't worry! If you're clever enough you can skirt around questions you really don't want to answer; be vague or quote some philosopher. Be prepared to have them ask you just about anything concerning your personal life; with these ladies, nothing is sacred. And if you don't answer, it's a mark against you. The outcome of these interviews rests with you, Monica. You can come out looking like an angel or a witch, it's really your decision. If you're nice to these ladies and give them what they want, they won't hurt you and will do everything possible to help your career. More than anything, I'm going to need your cooperation."

"You've got it," Abbie told him.

She was more than willing. Dreadful as it was, the Langdon article had made her realize how important her career was to her.

Another surprise was waiting for Abbie when she got home that night. Her mother had peremptorily fired the housekeeper.

"I told her there was no further need for her," Mrs. Dare said, innocently. "And there's not, now that I'm here."

"Oh, for goodness' sake, how could you, Mum? Without consulting me first? I'm going to have a devil of a time getting her back."

"But, Abbie," Mrs. Dare said. "I'm going to take care of the house for you."

"I don't want you to, don't you understand? You slaved away for a lifetime, you've earned a rest!"

"Well, what am I to do here all day then?" Mrs. Dare asked.

"Well . . . you could go shopping or go to the beach . . . take up a hobby, like bridge." Abbie stopped, feeling silly. She could not imagine her mother doing any of those things. Her mother's real pleasure in life was work, and it was nonsense to imagine that she could become a lady of leisure.

"I was planning for the two of us to go shopping tonight, in fact," Abbie said. "Lorraine Shelby invited us to afternoon tea on Friday and, silly as it sounds, we'd do well to look our best."

"Who's Lorraine Shelby?" Mrs. Dare asked.

Abbie laughed. "Around here that's like asking 'Who's Cleopatra?' You could say that Lorraine is the Empress of Hollywood society."

"Oh please, Abbie!" Mrs. Dare begged. "I feel so jumpy around those sort of people!"

"Oh, Mum, believe it or not, they're as human as we are! You'll get used to it. I have."

"I'm older than you are," Mrs. Dare said. "You had to get used to it, but I don't. Please Abbie, I want a bit of peace in my middle years. I feel so out of place with swells."

Abbie sighed. "OK, Mum. What do you say we go to the beach this weekend, then?"

"You know my skin can't stand the sun," Mrs. Dare said.

Abbie didn't know whether to bother suggesting that they dine out later on in the week. The Chez Maurice experience had probably soured her mother on restaurants forever.

"Do you want to play 'hearts'?" Abbie suggested, weakly.

"Fine."

Hallelujah, thought Abbie.

The two of them adjourned to Abbie's bedroom with cookies, and Abbie found a deck of cards. They gossiped about Newbury Street and laughed and played "hearts" till midnight. It was the nicest time they'd spent together since Mum had arrived.

The next morning Abbie put on a white skirt and blazer. She selected her jewelry carefully, hoping to make the very best impression. She felt nervous about the interview awaiting her at the studio.

She was on her way out the door when a call came from Jonas Klein.

"Hello, Monica?" he said.

"What is it, Jonas?" she asked. "I was just getting ready to leave."

"Stay where you are."

"Why, what's the matter?" Abbie asked.

"Pattie's coming over to interview you at the house."

"Why?" Abbie asked.

"She said that's how she wanted to handle it."

"Well, for goodness—"

"C'mon, Monica, don't get ruffled," he said. "Adds a more personal touch to the story, I guess. After all, fans are curious about what stars' homes look like."

Abbie shrugged. "I suppose so."

"She'll be over about noon," Klein told her.

"That means she'll need lunch," Abbie sighed.

"It wouldn't hurt to have something for her. They take note of those things."

"All right, I'll prepare something."

"Good girl, Monica! And good luck."

"Thanks," Abbie said.

"Who was that?" Mrs. Dare asked.

"It was Jonas Klein from the studio. I'm afraid a woman is coming over here from a fan magazine to interview me."

"Well, I'll just make myself scarce," Mrs. Dare said.

"Oh no, Mum. This is your house, too," Abbie told

her. She was thinking about what to serve Pattie Grey for lunch, when she remembered that her mother had dismissed the housekeeper.

"Oh goodness, I've got to have lunch ready for this woman and you had to get rid of the housekeeper!"

Her mother brightened.

"No problem at all," she said. "I'll make lunch." For the first time during her stay, she seemed genuinely excited. "I'll make omelets for us!"

"Oh, Mum, you can't cook and serve! You're a star's mother. It will look bad."

"Oh bosh! You just rest easy. I'll take care of everything."

Sure enough, by the time Pattie Grey arrived, everything was ready.

"Please come in," Abbie greeted her warmly. "You're just in time for lunch."

"Oh, you needn't have bothered for me," Pattie said.

"No trouble at all. Our housekeeper's gone on a holiday, so my mother and I just whipped up some omelets."

"You do your own cooking?" Pattie asked, startled.

"If you can call that cooking," said Abbie.

"It's more than most stars do," Pattie assured her.

Abbie introduced Pattie to her mother, who was wearing a becoming print.

"I hope you're enjoying your stay here, Mrs. Dane," Pattie said.

"Every minute," Mrs. Dare told her. She had made a gallant effort at disguising her cockney accent so that an American would not be able to detect her working-class background.

The three of them had a congenial lunch, discussing movies and the latest fashions. Mrs. Dare didn't say very much, and Pattie just assumed it was because she was a stranger to the goings-on around town. After lunch, Mrs. Dare politely excused herself.

"My afternoon nap," she explained.

Abbie gave Pattie a short tour of the house, and then the two of them sat down with tea in the living room.

"Such a sunny, cozy place," Pattie said.

Abbie thanked her, secretly pleased that she liked the house.

"And you decorated it yourself?" Pattie asked.

"Yes."

"Lovely job." With those words, Pattie put her tea down and settled back in her chair. She took out a notebook and pen from her leather briefcase.

"Shall we start now?" she asked.

"All right," Abbie replied.

"Monica," Pattie said. "You're such a beautiful girl and so obviously nice and bright—I'm sure you make heads turn each time you enter a room and yet there seems to be no man in your life. Why aren't you married or affianced? Or rather, how is that possible?"

Abbie was speechless for an instant, then decided to answer as honestly as she could.

"I suppose it's because I haven't met a man yet that I couldn't live without," Abbie said. "I couldn't marry a man unless I was absolutely sure we were right for each other. I've been in love, but romantic feelings aren't the only foundation for a marriage."

Pattie looked impressed by her candor.

"What is necessary for marriage, Monica?"

"I think it's probably maturity. A certainty about the choices you're making. The most important thing for me is that I marry the man I want to stay with for the rest of my life."

"What kind of man will that be?"

"A man of courage and integrity. A man I can trust.

137

A kind man. I don't think those are unreasonable demands. I would try to live up to those same standards if I cared for a person. What he looks like isn't important to me. I just want him to be considerate and attentive."

"What about money?"

"I really don't care if he's wealthy or not."

"But a girl of your background, Monica. I would think you'd want to be supported in a way you've always been accustomed to."

Abbie smiled demurely. If she only knew, she thought.

"A lot of money is not important to me," she said firmly. "I have enough to take care of myself. But it would matter to me that my husband have his own career. If he were living off my earnings, I doubt that he'd have very much self-respect, and I'm sure that sort of situation would eventually ruin our marriage."

"Would you continue to work after you were married?"

"Yes, I'm sure I would. I think I'd probably miss making movies, otherwise."

"What if you had children?"

"I'd retire for a while," Abbie said, softly. "Until they were school age, I'd want to look after them myself."

There were a few more questions about upcoming projects and then Pattie gathered up her briefcase.

"Thank you so much for your time, Monica," she said. "I've enjoyed this."

"Thank *you*," Abbie replied, confident that she had done well.

Her second interview the following day, with a reporter from *Movie World*, was practically a replica of the first one; the same fascination with her personal life and her views on love and marriage. She rephrased her answers a bit to avoid sounding exactly as she had with Pattie Grey.

Pattie released her interview with Abbie in her daily newspaper column and much to everyone's delight, it was a winner.

Titled "Monica Dane: An Aristocrat of the Screen," it began:

> When I say that Monica Dane has breeding, I don't necessarily mean it's because she has a bevy of titled ancestors. There is an innate refinement of the heart and mind that marks her character.
>
> When I call her an aristocrat it isn't because she has blue blood flowing through her veins, it's because she has the dignity, grace, and kindness we often associate with Kings and Queens. At the same time, this is the most unspoiled and natural young lady one could ever hope to meet.

"It's great!" Klein said of the interview. "Monica, you should be very pleased."

Abbie was flattered by Pattie Grey's praise, knowing full well that Pattie was rarely this generous with young actors and actresses. Pattie was far more powerful as a journalist than Langdon was and had far greater readership. Her glowing words would break Langdon's cudgel in half.

Abbie went home that evening prepared to celebrate. Maybe she would even drag Mum to a restaurant. But her mother's greeting shattered her good mood.

"Abbie, dear, I've decided to go back to England," her mother announced, almost as soon as she walked in the door. "I had to tell you straight out and get it over with. I've been thinking about it all day."

139

"Why, Mum? I don't understand. Has something happened to Uncle Leonard or the kids? Is there some sort of emergency?"

"No, dear, no emergency. Oh, Abbie, love—it's so many things. This blasted heat, for example. And well, more than that . . . I feel so useless here."

"Oh, Mum!"

"No, it's true, dear. I don't serve any purpose. You go to work, and I just sit here and read magazines or listen to the radio. At home with my brother and his children, I'm busy all the time. I'm needed."

"I need you, Mum," Abbie whimpered.

"No love, not the way they do." Her mother smiled, sadly. "Abbie, as soon as you begged me to come stay with you, I knew it was because you'd been hurt in some way. A young man, wasn't it?"

Abbie didn't reply.

"I won't press you about it, dear," her mother said. "Not if you don't want to talk about it."

She stroked her daughter's hair.

"Abbie, you were like a child who'd fallen and wanted your mother to make things well again. I'm right, aren't I?"

Abbie was crying, softly.

"Abbie, you're so young and beautiful," her mother said. "Very soon, this unhappiness will be far behind you."

"But what about now?" Abbie cried. "I need someone to care for me now!"

"I do care for you, love, but you're a grown up girl now. You're too big to only be happy with your mother's concern—you need a husband's love."

Abbie sighed.

"And it will happen, Abbie," Mrs. Dare assured her. "You'll see."

"When are you going?" Abbie asked quietly.

"Probably by the end of the week, dear." Mrs. Dare kissed Abbie. "Thank you for having me."

"I'll miss you, Mum."

"I'm afraid I've been a bit of a nuisance for you, Abbie. I know I'm hard to please in my old age. Set in my ways, I suppose."

Abbie hugged her, a little ashamed at the relief she felt.

Chapter 19

$\mathcal{A}$ short time after her mother had left for England, Abbie received a memo from Paul Hanson, one of the industry's most distinguished directors. Even more demanding than Lamm, he was ranked with Erich Von Stroheim and Cecil B. De Mille. His painstaking work resulted in classics.

The memo read:

Dear Miss Dane:

For some time, I have admired your work on the screen. I sense in you sensitivity, intelligence, and a fine dramatic gift.

I must confess it strikes me that your parts fall short of your ability. You are not being shown to your best advantage nor being given a chance to develop your powers as an actress.

I have recently been given the job of directing Gustave Flaubert's "Madame Bovary" and I would like to invite you to test for the leading role.

I would appreciate it if we could confer beforehand. Would it be possible for us to meet next Tuesday, October 10 at 1:00 P.M.? Please call my office if you'll be able to keep our appointment.

I look forward to seeing you then.

Sincerely,
Paul Hanson

Abbie glowed from head to toe. It seemed that Hanson, watching her on the screen, had looked into her soul. She felt truly understood and appreciated as an artist by a man she'd never met.

She immediately called his secretary to confirm the appointment.

After work Abbie stopped off at a bookstore and bought a copy of *Madame Bovary*. She felt almost too excited to eat the dinner she prepared, and soon retired to her bedroom with the book.

Abbie felt Emma's sorrows and joys, she wept, she smiled, she lived Emma's life as she read. Any woman could identify with the naive and romantic Emma Bovary, who was disappointed in marriage, but retained her passionate and idealistic yearnings. When Abbie finished the book, it was one in the morning, but she felt inspired. She had to play this part! It had stirred her deeply and she blessed Paul Hanson for thinking of her.

Of all the directors at Century, only Hanson was allowed to handpick his cast. And he wanted her! Abbie had never felt prouder in her life. She hugged her pillow, not knowing how she would manage to survive until she met Paul Hanson.

The following Monday, however, Hanson's secretary called to tell her he had been called out of town on an emergency—an urgent business meeting concerning production costs.

"Well, when will he be back?" Abbie asked.

"I really couldn't tell you, Miss Dane. I'll have him call you when he gets here," the secretary said cheerfully.

Two days passed and the call never came. The third day, Abbie phoned his office.

"I'm afraid he's in San Gabriel doing some location

shots for his latest picture," the secretary said. Her insincere sweetness made Abbie's frustration more acute.

"He could have called me," Abbie said, sharply. "Didn't you leave word?"

"Yes, I did, Miss Dane. Things just happened all at once."

Abbie could sense the situation was hopeless. The next day she read an article in *Variety* announcing future projects. Century's section read: "Jessica Palmer has been cast in the title role of the forthcoming production of *Madame Bovary* under the direction of Paul Hanson."

Abbie burst into tears of rage. She called Hanson's office immediately.

"I want to speak to Paul Hanson!" she cried.

"He's still on location." The secretary sounded a bit frightened.

Abbie slammed the telephone down. It was useless. Why had Hanson done such an underhanded thing? Or was it his doing? Jessica Palmer was Century's "cinematic Bernhardt," and pressure may have been put on Hanson to give her the starring role.

She decided not to talk to Jonas Klein about it. Jonas was primarily a buffer between the studio powers and the employees; his main function was to calm frayed nerves and keep the peace. She would go directly to Arthur Shore, himself.

She marched over to his office. She knew he was almost impossible to see, but she'd speak to him if she had to shoot the lock off his door.

"I want to speak to Arthur Shore," she shouted at his secretary.

"Have you got an appointment?" the girl asked, trying to hide her nervousness behind formality.

"No, I haven't!" Abbie said, "But I'm going to see him and I'm going to see him now!"

The secretary quickly rose, knocked at Shore's door and went into the inner office. She was there for perhaps a full eight minutes. When she came out, she told Abbie that Shore would see her.

Abbie went in, proud and erect, ready to meet this studio titan face-to-face.

Shore's office was filled with flowers and plants of every size and shape. They seemed to swallow up everything in the room except Shore himself, an impressive-looking man, poised behind his desk. He was tall, gaunt, and grey-haired, with a neat moustache and the most electric blue eyes Abbie had ever seen in her life. He always gave the appearance of being in complete control of a situation, and there was an undercurrent of tension present whenever he was around.

"Sit down, Miss Dane," he said, calmly.

Abbie did.

"I understand you're quite anxious to speak to me. What exactly is the problem?"

In Shore's formidable presence, Abbie's fury subsided into shyness. "Well, it's about the new Hanson picture," she said, almost apologetically.

"Yes," he said. "*Madame Bovary.*"

"Last week, I got a memo from Hanson. He was seriously considering me for the part."

"Yes?"

"And when I was supposed to meet with him to discuss it, he was called away for a business conference, then he had to leave to shoot some location shots, and the next thing I knew Jessica Palmer had been chosen to play Emma."

"From what I understand," Shore said, "Jessica had the part from the very beginning."

"Then why did he want to see me?" Abbie asked.

"I have no idea," Shore told her. "Perhaps he and Jessica had a misunderstanding, and he considered trying someone else. I really don't know."

Abbie sighed. Maybe he was right. Hanson might have just been playing with the idea. He may very well have been using her to threaten Jessica Palmer.

"What interests me is your eagerness to play this role," Shore told her.

"What actress wouldn't leap at the chance to play that part or to work with Paul Hanson?" Abbie had forgotten her shyness. "And besides that, I'm awfully tired of the parts I've been getting."

"You are?" Shore's eyes narrowed.

"Countesses and princesses and duchesses and debutantes," she said, wearily. "I guess I'm tired of being the 'Aristocrat of the screen.'"

Shore smiled. "I don't think I have to list the advantages you have over other actresses, like Maura or Ivy or Terra. You're never expected to pose in a bathing suit or go through the other indignities of Wampas' Baby Stars." Wampas stood for the Western Association of Motion Picture Advertisers, and girls they considered potential stars were obliged to pose for cheesecake shots.

"I suppose that's so," Abbie said, "but I'd like to try a different kind of part for a change. I just feel stifled."

"Monica, don't think you're the first actress who's ever complained about her roles and her screen image. In a few cases, I was forced to give in. Do you recall an actress named Selena Winfield?"

Abbie shook her head.

"I suppose everyone's forgotten her by now," he said quietly. "Selena was the most beautiful girl of her day; she outshone every other actress on screen. Hair the color of a cornfield, sea-green eyes, pink skin, a full, voluptuous figure. She was Century's goddess of love and beauty. What else was she fit for?" Shore shook his head, sadly.

"But Selena wanted to show off her dramatic talents. She was tired of playing Helen of Troy—she wanted to be an ordinary woman, she wanted realistic roles. It was laughable. Every ordinary woman wants to be Helen of Troy, but Helen wanted to be average. Finally, we went along with her demands. The results were disastrous. The public felt cheated. They didn't give a damn about Selena's acting ability, which was only adequate at best. They felt they'd been robbed of the fantasy goddess they worshipped. Instead of Aphrodite, they were confronted with Sally-across-the-street. Selena's popularity faded, and she suffered a nervous breakdown."

"What happened to her after that?" Abbie asked, almost frightened.

"She married a wealthy man, but it didn't work out," he said. "She made an attempt at suicide, and when she was released from the hospital, she broke down again. After her second mental collapse, she never recovered. She's been in an institution for years now."

Abbie lowered her eyes and didn't say a word.

"You see, Miss Dane," Shore said. "When a star's screen image changes drastically, movie-goers are befuddled and confused. They feel betrayed. It's as if you fell in love with someone for certain reasons and then your sweetheart changed completely. A woman may love a man for his kindness and intelligence. If he suddenly becomes mean and stupid, do you think she would remain his? Of course not. She would reject him just as your audience would reject you if you lost the things they loved about you. And I'm afraid one of the characteristics your fans admire most is your regality."

Abbie sighed. "Still, I'd love a chance to play a *real* woman."

"How about Anna Karenina?" Shore suggested. "She was wealthy and upperclass, but every bit as real as Emma Bovary."

Abbie brightened immediately.

"Oh, I'd love that!" she said.

"Perhaps we could discuss the idea further. In all honesty, it just came to me now."

Both of them laughed.

"How about tomorrow, over lunch?" Shore asked Abbie.

"I'd like that," she answered.

Chapter 20

SHORE took Abbie to his luxurious home in Santa Monica for their luncheon date.

"I hope you don't mind—it's just that I loathe restaurants," he told her.

"I feel the same way," Abbie told him, fascinated by the meticulous elegance of his house. The furniture was Spanish Medieval, the marble floor was covered with Oriental rugs, and the El Greco paintings accentuated the majestic gloom. Faultless as the decor was, Abbie felt a lighter touch was needed.

"It's such a glorious day," Shore said. "Why don't we have lunch outside?"

"That's fine," Abbie said.

A butler served them shrimp cocktails on a terrace overlooking the ocean.

"Would you excuse me for just a moment?" Shore said to her suddenly.

He went inside and put Beethoven's *Pastorale* on the victrola.

"Who are your favorite composers?" he asked Abbie when he returned.

"I don't know much about music," she admitted.

"How fortunate for you," Shore said. "So much to learn; so much to look forward to."

"That's a nice way of looking at things."

"I'm sorry I've led the conversation astray. We were going to discuss business, but I hope you'll understand if I tell you I'm not in the mood."

Abbie smiled. "I understand."

"Do you know you're a pleasure to look at," Shore said. "And to be with?"

"Thank you," she said.

"No need. I wasn't giving you a compliment; just making an observation."

"I'm not much of a conversationalist," Abbie said quietly.

"You mean you don't rattle on foolishly the way so many here do. You listen and you think, which is quite a rarity."

Abbie smiled shyly. He made her feel special and important.

"I hope the afternoon wasn't a total waste for you," Shore told her.

"Not at all," Abbie said.

"About your music lessons," Shore said. "It just so happens that Mozart's Symphony No. 29 is being performed at the Hollywood Bowl this Friday evening. It would give me great pleasure to accompany you there."

"Thank you," Abbie said. "I'd be pleased."

Abbie found herself intrigued by this powerful man. He was in his forties, old enough to be her father, but his age and experience only added to the attraction. He knew precisely the right things to do and say; he seemed to possess a mastery over situations acquired over a lifetime, that was lacking in younger men.

Abbie started seeing him on a regular basis, and their relationship was strangely soothing for her. His subdued manner was a change from the flashy style of Jean-Claude and the others like him. There was no driving compulsion to take in every nightclub or new opening in town. On the contrary, Shore seemed to hate public places and preferred long drives in the country or quiet afternoons spent in his garden. On weekends, they would camp out in the desert, since he felt the solitude helped him to forget the pressure of his workday. Often he and Abbie would be silent together, and it was a welcome relief for her not to feel obligated to keep a conversation going. She felt comfortable with him.

Another quality she admired was his total respect for her. A goodnight kiss was all he expected. There was no fending off the passes that Abbie was subjected to with younger men.

Their romance became public when they attended David Oakley's birthday party together. Oakley owned Century, but stars from all of the studios turned out in his honor. Lon Chaney, Norma Talmadge, Tom Mix and of course, the finest that Century had to offer, Jessica Palmer, Maura Wilder, Jean-Claude, who came with Terra Lane on his arm.

Abbie managed to be remotely polite to Jean-Claude, though strangely enough, the sight of him with Terra did not upset her. For one thing, she hadn't thought of him since she'd known Shore. If anything, Jean-Claude seemed a bit unstrung at seeing her again, especially as the companion of one of the industry's most important figures. The usually suave Jean-Claude fumbled for words and accidentally spilled his drink while speaking to her. It occurred to Abbie that he was merely a very young, good-looking, but superficial boy, with none of Arthur's depth.

The celebration was held at the swank Ambassador Hotel at one hundred dollars a plate. The grand ballroom had been decorated with blow-ups of Century's stars and stills from its most famous pictures. The cake was ten feet high and had taken three days to decorate. Lewis and Lorraine Shelby were the official host and hostess, and a good part of the evening consisted of speeches in Oakley's honor, some resembling eulogies. Robert Kinley's maudlin comments prompted Ivy Hayes to ask her escort, "Does Oakley have cancer or something?"

The women present seemed to be competing for a best-dressed title, each one at her sequinned loveliest. Lorraine's gold and opal necklace was the show-stopper. Supposedly, it had belonged to the Egyptian queen, Nefertiti and had cost Shelby over half a million dollars. When he had purchased it for his wife, the news had made international headlines.

The party provided the national papers and magazines with enough material for weeks to come. They wrote about the spectacular aspect, the personalities, the beauty and fashion. The party was also a target for social criticism. Some thought that such costly nonsense in a world full of disease and starvation was criminal.

Abbie and Arthur Shore struck gossip columnists as being a very newsworthy couple; a twentieth-century version of Caesar and Cleopatra. Pattie Grey dubbed Shore and Abbie, "The most exciting couple of the year! His brains, her beauty; his experience, her youth; his wisdom, her charm."

The publicity bothered Abbie. She felt as if the whole world was watching them, and resented the fact that her private life seemed to be public property. But Arthur seemed to be used to it.

"Ignore it," he advised her. "Laugh at it. I think the

idea of these dunderheads trying to guess what's on our minds or what we'll do next is pretty funny."

However, the dunderheads' predictions of wedding bells turned out to be quite accurate. On Abbie's twentieth birthday, Shore took her to an impressive Spanish restaurant. The restaurant was a converted villa, and Shore had reserved the entire veranda for the two of them. Abbie could almost taste the sweetness of the evening. Candlelight, roses, lace, the hushed strains of guitars.

Before they ordered, their waiter appeared with a tray holding a small jewelry box.

"Miss Dane, for you," he said. He smiled and placed the box on her plate.

Abbie opened the small card attached to it. It read: "For the fairest flower that ever saw the light. . . ."

Abbie blushed.

"Open the box," Arthur urged.

Inside was the most elegantly cut diamond Abbie had ever seen in her life. She stared at it in fascination. She knew it was an engagement ring.

"Oh Arthur," she said, breathlessly.

"I'm a patient man," Shore said. "I don't expect you to make your mind up this minute, but I'd like an answer from you sometime in the near future."

"I—I don't know what to say," Abbie truly had not been expecting a proposal of marriage so soon. They had only known each other a little over a month.

"There isn't a doubt in my mind, Monica," Shore told her. "There wasn't from the moment I saw you."

"I need time," Abbie said, dazed. "This is all so unexpected."

"I'll give you all the time you want," Shore said quietly.

After Shore left her at her house that evening, Abbie spent most of the night pacing the floor.

She knew well that Shore was probably one of the world's most eligible bachelors. Wealthy, handsome, powerful, brilliant—women who'd never even met him would probably say 'yes' with no hesitation whatsoever. What was stopping her? Was it the feeling that she didn't know him well enough? He was a difficult man to know; there seemed to be whole areas of his life that he kept hidden from her, and yet this mysterious quality of his enticed her.

Did she love him? How could anyone be sure that they loved another? In retrospect, her love for Jean-Claude had only been physical desire. She did not feel that passionately about Shore, but in a way, she was glad, because she felt more in control of herself. With Jean-Claude, there had also been the overwhelming sensation of being in love for the first time. She had really been in love with love. Perhaps true love was really a partnership between a man and a woman.

She and Arthur were certainly compatible. She tried to envision the two of them married. Herself, a devoted wife and helpmate, listening, sympathizing as he told her about the rough day he'd put in at the studio. The two of them vacationing together in a European capital. Abbie saw herself as a mother holding a beautiful infant.

Her career suddenly didn't seem to matter very much. Perhaps it had seemed so important to her in the past few months because it was all she had.

She glanced at the clock on the night table on her bed. It was 2:15 A.M. She called Arthur to tell him her decision.

"Hello?" he answered, immediately. She knew that he hadn't been sleeping.

"Arthur, I've made up my mind."

"Yes?" he said.

"I've decided to accept your proposal of marriage."

"You're a very intelligent girl," he told her and they both laughed.

Chapter 21

THE two of them decided to keep their engagement secret for a while. They didn't want to announce it publicly until they decided when, where, and how their marriage would take place.

Abbie wanted as small an affair as possible. She had even suggested elopement, but Arthur told her both ideas were out of the question. It would mean snubbing too many people he knew in the industry.

"I'm afraid a wedding is really for people other than the bride and groom," he said. "And we both have a lot of people to consider. For example, imagine what Pattie Grey would do to us in the press if we got married without telling her—or worse, if we had a wedding and didn't invite her."

It was true. Abbie knew that Pattie considered herself to be her fairy godmother since the favorable article she'd written.

Still, Abbie was a bit surprised that Shore wanted a wedding. She knew he had been married before, some years ago. He had touched on it once very briefly, but had given her the distinct impression he didn't want to talk about it. She had never pressed him about the matter. It was, after all, part of his past, his private business. He knew nothing about Jean-Claude or Bill. The marriage had simply "not gone well," and he and his wife had gone their separate ways. As far as Abbie knew, they were not even in contact with each other now.

The fact that he was divorced didn't bother Abbie. In Hollywood, a single divorce was very modest, indeed. People could afford to end marriages easily so they married more often.

Finally, Abbie reluctantly went along with Arthur's plans for a large wedding to be held at his private estate. They decided to plan it as soon as she finished the movie she was working on.

The picture was called *The Sisters O'Neill* and she was working with Ivy Hayes again. They played two sisters separated as children. One grew up rich and elegant, the other, poor and sassy. They met again by accident, when the wealthy one hired the poor one as a maid.

Abbie was no longer angry with Ivy about Jean-Claude, and the two of them got along very well. Despite Ivy's brash manner, Abbie thought she was basically warm-hearted and never forgot that Ivy had been the first Hollywood star to offer her friendship. Abbie was now established enough not to have to care whether or not Ivy was "suitable" for her to associate with. Indeed, Abbie even felt a little sorry for her. Despite her hordes of friends, there seemed no one she could really confide in. She was always touchingly eager to talk to Abbie and was grateful for her understanding and willingness to listen. She could confess to having problems instead of eternally playing the good-time girl.

One evening, about seven o'clock, Abbie was preparing to spend the night with a good book when her telephone rang.

"Hello," she answered.

"It's me, Monica. Ivy," a frightened voice said.

"What is it, Ivy? You sound scared."

"I am, honey. Scared as hell! I've got some guy real mad at me, and he's not just playing around. I got a phone call from him just before that made me lock all my doors!"

Abbie shook her head. Ivy seemed to have a talent for getting herself into awful situations.

"Why don't you call the police if you're so frightened?"

Ivy groaned. "They're just plain useless, that's why. They wouldn't do anything until he did me physical harm. Anyway, I don't trust cops for nothin' . . . I was just wonderin', kid. Do you think you could just come over and keep me company 'til my housekeeper comes?"

Abbie sighed. "When will that be?"

"Well, she's not due till ten tonight, but I think I can reach her before then. I been tryin' to get her, but she's not home. Oh please, Monica! I'm scared to death!"

"OK, Ivy. Just stay calm, I'll be over."

"Oh thanks, kid! You're really a friend. When do you think you could make it here?"

"I'll leave now."

"That's great. I'll make it up to you, I promise!"

It was pouring out, so Abbie put on her raincoat and hat. She dreaded having to drive all the way over to Ivy's place in the downpour, particularly since she was using an unfamiliar car. Her own roadster was in the repair shop, and Arthur had lent her a Winton from the studio. She had only driven it for a week and found it harder to handle than her own little car.

She got in and headed out toward the boulevard. Sure enough, traffic was an awful mess. She spent most of the time simply sitting and waiting until traffic started flowing again. By the time she got to Ivy's house, it was eight-thirty.

Abbie parked her car in the driveway of Ivy's cottage. The place was pink and white and looked like a sugar box, with hearts carved on the shutters and door. A publicity stunt, Abbie was sure.

Abbie got out of the car and ran to Ivy's front door. In her haste she had forgotten to bring an umbrella. The curtains were drawn and it looked for all the world as if no one was home. She would have expected Ivy to be at the door waiting for her.

Abbie pressed the buzzer several times, but no one answered. She knocked at the door and even tried to open it, but it was securely locked. The whole situation was a little curious. But Ivy was notorious for her lack of responsibility and might have just decided to leave the house and visit someone, neglecting to let Abbie know in the meantime. Perhaps she had tried to call Abbie back after she had left. Perhaps the fellow she'd had the tiff with had stopped by and the two of them had made up and gone somewhere to celebrate their reconciliation. From what Abbie had heard, getting men angry was a hobby of Ivy's.

Abbie shrugged and decided to leave. She pulled the car out of the driveway and headed for home. By the time she reached her house it was nine-thirty, and she was ready for bed. She just prayed that Ivy didn't disturb her with another phone call, apologizing and coming up with some fantastic story about where she'd been that evening.

Abbie undressed, went promptly to bed and slept very soundly.

The next morning, she rose, went downstairs and started breakfast for herself. Sausage and eggs. The paper had arrived on her doorstep, and she went out to fetch it. She read the day's headline with horror.

IVY HAYES FOUND MURDERED

Lovely movie actress, Ivy Hayes, 22, was found strangled at 10:00 P.M. last night. Norma Buttram, Miss Hayes' housekeeper, discovered the body and called police.

A coroner's report revealed that Miss Hayes was probably murdered between the hours of seven and ten P.M. Police are gathering information and questioning intimate acquaintances of Miss Hayes.

The only tangible evidence in this case was reported to police by a neighbor of Miss Hayes. She told Lieutenant David Brooks that at approximately 8:30 P.M. last night, she saw a grey Winton pull out of Miss Hayes' driveway. So far, the information has not been particularly helpful since Wintons are such popular cars.

Abbie dropped the paper, sick with fear. The neighbor had seen her driving away from Ivy's house. Abbie wrung her hands. She was too frightened to go to the police, mistrusting them as did most of the English working class. She called Arthur. He would know best. She tried his house, but apparently he had already left for the office. She called him at the studios and his secretary answered the telephone.

"May I speak to Arthur Shore?" she said, as casually as possible. "This is Monica Dane."

"I'm afraid he's conferring with a police lieutenant right now, Miss Dane. I guess you must have heard about the terrible tragedy by now."

"Yes, I have," Abbie said. "It's monstrous."

"Isn't it, though? And I thought all those awful incidents were behind us."

The girl was referring to the grisly murders and deaths in Hollywood's very recent past. Fatty Arbuckle, a comedy star, had been implicated in the death of starlet Virginia Rappe. Wallace Reid and Barbara La Mar (billed as "the girl who was too beautiful") had both died of drug addiction before they'd reached the age of thirty. Director William Desmond Taylor had been found dead and his murderer never apprehended. The scandals had caused widespread public criticism. The clergy condemned Hollywood as a city steeped in sin, and women's groups vowed never to see another motion picture. The United States Senate threatened the industry with federal censorship. To remedy the situation, industry heads had hired former Postmaster General Will Hays to keep a watchful eye on the studios and its employees, and morals clauses had been written into film stars' contracts. Abbie could well imagine the tension now building over Ivy's murder.

"Would you please have Mr. Shore call me when he's through?" Abbie asked. "I'm at home."

"Certainly, Miss Dane."

After Abbie hung up, she sat waiting for Shore's call, her mind frozen with panic. Last night when she'd reached Ivy's house, poor Ivy had been already dead. Abbie started to cry from grief and fear.

Finally, after what seemed like hours, Shore's call came.

"Monica," he said. "You wanted to speak to me."

"Oh, Arthur, I'm so frightened! You must come over immediately!" she cried.

"Monica, Monica, it's the Hayes murder, isn't it? But there's nothing for you to be afraid of. There's no mad fiend running around killing movie stars. I'm sure what happened to Ivy is an isolated case."

"No, no, Arthur! That Winton that was reported at Ivy's house," Abbie sobbed. "It was me!"

"What are you talking about?"

"Ivy called me last night . . . she begged me to stay with her. Some man had threatened her over the phone, and she was afraid to be alone. I drove over to see her. When I got there, no one answered the door. I guess she was already dead!" Abbie sobbed.

"Monica, get a grip on yourself," Shore ordered gruffly. "You're overreacting. You're telling me nothing of any consequence."

Abbie was taken aback. "Should I go to the police?" she asked.

"Certainly not," he told her.

"But you don't understand—"

"Monica, I want you to make yourself a drink and calm down. I'm going to be over there as soon as I can."

He hung up. Abbie sighed heavily. She went to her liquor cabinet and made herself a whiskey sour. It went down smoothly and she felt more relaxed.

In a short while, the doorbell rang. She got up from her chair and let Arthur in.

"Are you feeling better?" he asked. He looked tired and grim. She knew he had spent the morning answering questions for the police.

"Yes," she said.

He guided her to the couch and sat down next to her.

"I'm going to take the Winton back to the studio," he told her. "And I want you to forget you ever borrowed it."

"But you don't understand, Arthur," Abbie said. "I

think I might have been the last person to speak to Ivy. She told me that some man was mad at her and had threatened her."

"You consider that some sort of revelation?" he said, disdainfully. "I think what happened to Ivy speaks for itself. You wouldn't be telling the police something they didn't already know."

Abbie felt confused. "Then you don't think I should mention it to the police?"

"Monica, it would do more harm than good. This is going to be a very murky affair, and I don't want you or your good name involved in it at all. I have a feeling this is going to be an unsolved crime like the Taylor murder, and I want you to stay out of it completely."

"All right," Abbie said, a bit relieved.

"Of course, you're going to have to answer a few routine quesitons," Shore told her. "You're one of her co-workers. You'll tell the police that you didn't know her very well. If they ask you where you were the night of her murder, you'll tell them you were at my house, visiting."

Abbie nodded.

Shore got up and kissed her. "Now I don't want you to worry about a thing. Where's the car?"

"In the garage," she whispered. She gave him the keys and went outside with him.

"I'll see you tonight," he said.

As soon as he left with the grey Winton, Abbie felt infinitely better.

Chapter 22

FOR weeks, the papers were crammed with accounts of the sensational murder. Lloyd Farmer and Jean-Claude Malleux were both brought in to police headquarters for questioning. A cigarette lighter with Jean-Claude's initials inscribed on it had been found in Ivy's home, and Lloyd's alibi as to his whereabouts that night sounded flimsy. Insane confessions came in daily to the police from men claiming to be Ivy's secret sweethearts. Mediums and psychics volunteered their services to the police, and their theories about Ivy's murderer appeared in the tabloids. When there was no new information from police headquarters, publicity focused on Ivy's amorous life-style.

Actor Howard Drake was quoted in all the papers. When asked by police if he could name any fellows Ivy had known intimately, Howard had replied, "Why don't you just question every other man in town?"

Abbie was revolted by the way the press was handling the tragedy, as were most of the people in the film industry.

"It's horrendous," said Marie Delillo.

"How long is it going to go on?" Abbie asked.

"As long as it sells copy," Marie answered.

Finally, interest in the murder started to wane. There were no new revelations about Ivy's personal life, and the police had reached a dead end in their search for the killer.

The public's attention now shifted to a news item announcing the engagement of Monica Dane to Arthur Shore. Abbie, herself, was surprised at the round of congratulations that greeted her one morning at the studio. Arthur had neglected to tell her that he had made their engagement official.

"Why didn't you tell me, Arthur?" she asked when she saw him that day.

"I'm sorry, Monica," he said. "It was on impulse. I just felt the time was right, so I called the papers before I had a chance to speak to you."

Abbie suspected that he had announced their forthcoming marriage when he did, partly for the good of the studio—to divert public attention away from the Hayes murder. She resigned herself to the fact that the studio would probably always be a third party in their marriage. She might be Arthur's wife, but his work would be his mistress.

A flurry of engagement parties were held in their honor, and the affairs took the spotlight in the society columns. The country eagerly awaited Abbie's "fairy tale" wedding.

Abbie didn't even know how to begin to plan for such an extravaganza, and she was happy to realize she wasn't expected to. The matter was put in the hands of professional caterers, decorators, and designers. The wedding was still another production in Abbie's life.

Abbie paid little attention to the publicity being churned out on her account. She rarely read screen periodicals, and the only movie column she ever looked at was Pattie Grey's, since Pattie had been good to her and was also Century's favorite gossip columnist.

However, one day, while waiting in her dentist's office,

Abbie stumbled across a vintage movie magazine, a collector's item: a 1920 copy of *Screen Stars*. She leafed through it for fun and settled on an article entitled "The Inside Story of Hollywood's Divorces." She was stunned to discover that one of the divorces described was the break-up of Arthur Shore's year-old marriage to Selena Winfield. *Selena Winfield* . . . Abbie recalled the name from somewhere. Of course, she was the actress Shore had mentioned during their first conversation. Abbie read on:

Although Arthur Shore has gallantly claimed "incompatibility" as the reason for divorce, it is common knowledge that the beautiful, but highly neurotic Selena Winfield is most likely a terror to live with. Her mental condition has disintegrated during the past few years and no man, no matter how great his love, could be expected to stay married to a woman in her mental state.

After the divorce is final, Selena is expected to leave Hollywood and reside with her widowed mother in her native state of Oregon.

"Poor Arthur!" Abbie thought. No wonder he had never been able to speak about his past marriage! Selena Winfield had been his wife! The article hadn't touched on Selena's attempted suicide or permanent institutionalization. Arthur had somehow managed to keep the news from the press and shield poor, mad Selena from further humiliation. *It's common knowledge that Selena is most likely a terror to live with.* . . . If Abbie had not appreciated Arthur's courage and strength of character, she did now. Her eyes filled with tears. He had never discussed it with her, not wanting to burden her with his personal tragedy. Probably he was still supporting

Selena in the insane asylum. Abbie decided not to tell him that she knew the truth. She would never bring it up.

She vowed to herself that she would be as kind and understanding as she could be; she would make up for the time he had suffered with Selena.

Chapter 23

$\mathcal{A}$BBIE's "storybook wedding" was a new daydream for every young girl in the country.

It was held outdoors on Shore's sprawling estate. The weather was so glorious that Shore might have ordered the day himself. The sky was blue and calm, and the sun shone victoriously. Tables and chairs were set up for the guests under the shade of magnificent oaks and weeping willows. A small orchestra had been hired for the day, and the cellos and flutes played serene background music. Roast duckling in brandy sauce was the main course, and waitresses dressed in blue-and-gold uniforms darted here and there to serve the guests.

Abbie's three bridesmaids, Terra, Narda, and Leda, dressed in lavender silk, surrounded her on a dais, their beauty serving as a backdrop for hers. Abbie looked exquisite. Her black hair was piled on top of her head, loose tendrils softly framing her cheeks and forehead. Her veil was gathered with blue violets and was so long it touched the ground. Her ankle-length lace gown had an embroidered bodice and a high neck. Her necklace and earrings were mother-of-pearl, and her gown's full skirt emphasized her tiny waist. Three little girls with ribbons in their hair carried her train.

Abbie's mother had come to the States for the occasion and spent most of the time talking to Marie Delillo,

171

the only person besides her daughter that she felt comfortable with.

The reception was elegant, but restrained. The only numbers played for dancing were slow waltzes. Drinking was moderate, laughter and chatter somewhat subdued. People seemed cautious about having too good a time, as if no one dared to disturb the placid effect that Arthur had created so painstakingly.

The reception was neither too long nor too short. No one left too quickly or stayed too late. Abbie and her new husband had enough energy afterwards to pack a few odds and ends for their trip to New York the next day. They had a nightcap of champagne to toast their marriage.

The very next morning, Abbie, Arthur, and her mother took the train to New York. Mrs. Dare had to catch the boat to England from New York, and Abbie and Shore would honeymoon on the East Coast. Arthur also had to attend a business conference concerning the studio's distribution plans.

The trip to New York was vastly different than Abbie's journey to California. This time she was traveling first class; she might as well have been staying in a hotel. She and Arthur had their own suite, and Mum had a room to herself as well. Abbie could not help but notice how much faster the time went when one had such comforts.

Shore had made reservations for them at the unostentatious, but exclusive Algonquin Hotel. The hotel was famous for its "town and country" atmosphere. It was also renowned for its dining room, which literary talents such as George S. Kaufman, Alexander Woollcott, and Dorothy Parker had made legendary.

Abbie fell in love with New York immediately. The

city was at its zenith—vibrant, electric, promising excitement at every corner. It seemed a place where all dreams could be realized, where anything was possible. Unlike the languorous Californians, New Yorkers were keyed up, highly charged. The pulse of the city was always racing.

While Arthur attended his meetings during the day, Abbie spent her time shopping and sight-seeing. The latest Paris designs had just arrived in all of the Fifth Avenue shops, and Abbie purchased a satin coat and opera cape at Lord and Taylor's.

She discovered the power of live theater and felt that movies dimmed in comparison. Abbie wondered if she would ever have the courage to perform before an audience; she could not envision a greater challenge.

Abbie and Arthur made the rounds of the city's social events, and she noticed immediately how proper and sedate New York social gatherings were compared to those in Beverly Hills. Instead of the showy, chic glamor of the California showplaces, the New York mansions and townhouses were austere and classical—each article of furniture meant to endure for several generations. The groups of guests were smaller and more select. There was no low-minded gossip. No one misbehaved or drank too much. All of the women were discreet and elegant in their use of makeup and jewelry.

Abbie knew that New York Society considered the Beverly Hills elite "barbaric," and now she understood why. These people seemed free of the pretensions of the nouveau riche on the West Coast. They had no need to flaunt their wealth; it had always been part of their identities. Their impeccable manners were second nature to them, not newly acquired along with their fortunes. They didn't have to impress anyone.

Still, their harsh judgment of other people disturbed

Abbie. Family and established wealth was everything to them; innate worth seemed to count for very little.

After two weeks, Abbie and Shore returned to California and business continued as usual. Arthur resumed his twelve hour work day, and Abbie spent time vacationing, reading, gardening, and playing tennis. They were one of the country's most influential and envied couples. To outsiders, their marriage seemed ideal.

It wasn't. There was one aspect of their married life that Abbie could not mention to anyone. She was confused and frightened. After six weeks as Arthur's wife, she was still a virgin. What made the situation even stranger was Arthur's behavior. Absolutely no reference was made to the fact that they'd never slept together. He acted as if everything was completely normal.

When they had stayed in New York, Abbie had usually fallen asleep by the time Shore had returned to the hotel from his after-hours business meetings. In their home in California, they had adjoining bedrooms and retired to their rooms separately.

As a new bride, and a girl who had been raised in a home where discussion of sex had been forbidden, Abbie didn't know what to do. She had heard of only one case similar to Arthur's. When she was in her teens, she'd eavesdropped on a conversation between Mum and another woman. They had talked in hushed tones about the woman's son-in-law who had been hurt in the war. Had something happened to Arthur that he couldn't bring himself to tell her about? Abbie had hunted for information about the problem, and finally found a library book written by a doctor, that discussed sexual problems and their causes. In defining impotence, the doctor had attributed psychological as well as physical causes. Could Selena's madness have rendered Arthur impotent? Had she created a fear of all other women in him?

There was no one with whom Abbie could discuss something so intensely personal. Finally, in desperation, she sought professional help. She arranged to see a Dr. Joseph Manheimer, one of the finest physicians in the country. She was ready to see a psychiatrist if he recommended it.

With much difficulty, she told him about her situation.

"By keeping quiet," Manheimer said, "I think you're only making the situation worse. This problem is a lot more common than most people think and in most cases, absolutely curable."

"I just don't know how to broach it to him," Abbie said. "He never brings it up at all."

"I'm not surprised. It's probably too delicate a matter for him to handle. I think he might secretly be relieved if you helped him confront the problem. In the meantime, the both of you are needlessly suffering in silence. I'm sure with the proper help, patience, and understanding on your part, his impotence can be overcome."

Bolstered by Dr. Manheimer's advice, Abbie decided to speak to Arthur, and that night, when he announced he was going to retire to his room, Abbie held her breath. He gave Abbie a customary goodnight kiss. She gently took his hand.

"Arthur . . . dear, there's something I'd like to discuss with you," she said, softly.

"What is it?" he said.

"It's us, Arthur," Abbie said. She found she was at a painful loss for words. "Darling, it's just that we're . . . well, we're not very affectionate, physically, with each other."

He was silent. He studied her, a stony expression on his face.

"Arthur . . . I saw a doctor today and . . ."

"What are you talking about?" he demanded, brusquely. "Seeing a doctor?"

"Oh, Arthur." Abbie groped helplessly for the correct thing to say. "Arthur, I—well, maybe—I mean, I understand and I want to help—and maybe, if you spoke to him."

He slapped her sharply across the face. She stared at him, stunned.

"I knew you reminded me of her somehow, and I was right," he said, grimly. "That's why I haven't been able to touch you."

Abbie was horrified. "I'm nothing like Selena!" she screamed.

Shore's eyes widened. "So you know. Yes, very like her, secretive, conniving. . . ."

"I've known for a while now," Abbie said.

"Yes, in the same mold," Shore continued, mercilessly. "Constantly dissatisfied, high-strung, complaining, neurotic. That's why I can't bear to hold you. You're too much like her."

Abbie knew he was lying, using it as an excuse, blaming her for his impotence.

"If you thought I was like her, then why did you marry me?" Abbie cried.

"Because every man wants you," he replied coldly.

Abbie's eyes narrowed in horror. She was a status symbol, one more testimony to Arthur Shore's power.

"I want this marriage annulled as soon as possible," Abbie said.

"That's out of the question," he replied, calmly.

"Out of the question!" She didn't know whether to laugh or cry. "Are you out of your mind? Any court in the country would grant me an annulment! You married me under false pretenses. This marriage hasn't even been consummated yet!"

"But I don't want to divorce you," Shore said. "And I'm not going to." There was an ominous certainty in his voice.

Abbie sneered. "You don't want to! Are you trying to threaten me?"

"That's precisely what I'm doing, Monica. And I make good my threats. I can't tell you to ask my enemies, because I don't have any enemies. I annihilate all of them."

How hateful he was, how ruthless!

"What can you do to me?" she cried.

"Anything I want to, Monica. I can see to it that your career is finished and your reputation a shambles. I can do even more than that."

"What?" she cried.

"Well, there's quite a bit. Let me illustrate my point. There is the regrettable Hayes incident, for example, and the matter of the grey Winton that went unreported."

Abbie gasped. She had played right into his hands.

"Withholding evidence, Monica." Shore feigned an expression of mock reproach. "Quite serious."

"I'll go to them now!" Abbie screamed. "I'll tell them you told me not to report it to them!"

"And what if I deny that?" Shore asked. "And there is the touchy subject of Jean-Claude Malleux, you know. You and Ivy were both seeing Jean-Claude, weren't you? I'm sure that didn't sit well with you at all, having to share your *amour* with another woman, particularly a strumpet like Miss Hayes. I wouldn't be surprised if you hated Ivy; maybe even hated her enough to—"

"Stop it, stop it!" Abbie screamed. "You hateful liar! How did you know about Jean-Claude?"

"My dear, I must keep track of all my 'children.' That's what all of you are to me, you know. I have to watch out for your welfare and know what you're all up to. Goodness knows, the trouble you all get yourselves into."

Tears slid down Abbie's cheeks. "I'll tell the police the truth," she sobbed. "They'll believe me."

"Will they, Monica? Don't tell me you've begun to believe your own publicity, my love? Let's not forget our humble beginnings. I doubt that the police would take very seriously the words of a guttersnipe parading as a great lady."

Abbie tried to slap him, but he caught her arm and roughly pushed her back on the sofa.

"I wouldn't advise that, my dear. I'm a peaceful man, but as you must have gathered by now, once trifled with, I strike to kill."

She spit at him, and he slapped her again.

"I'm warning you, dear. Behave yourself."

"What if I leave you?" she cried. "What if I just walk out of here."

"If you do, rest assured that there will be a warrant for your arrest by the time this day is over. I will immediately call police headquarters and tell them everything I know about you, the grey Winton, Ivy Hayes, and Jean-Claude."

Abbie wept helplessly.

"Now, now," Shore said. "I'm not a complete monster. I intend to treat you very well." He motioned to the furnishings surrounding them. "This isn't exactly a prison. I assure you I won't use a whip so long as you're tame. You're allowed all the spending money you want for clothes, vacations, anything your greedy little heart desires. Of course, I demand a few favors in return."

"What?" Abbie stared at him.

"You have to earn your keep, my dear. Now that I'm a married man, I intend to do a lot of entertaining. And now that you're ostensibly my wife, you are to supervise our social life. This is your career now, Monica . . . my very own live-in hostess, Lorraine Shelby's new rival. Together you and I will seize the kingdom from the Barbarian Queen and her philistine friends."

"Don't tell me that's the only reason you married me," Abbie said. "To supervise the parties you plan to throw here."

"No, no, Monica. I've already told you. You're one of the world's most desired women. And whatever there is to desire, I feel compelled to make mine. It's a quality that defines a powerful man." He smiled at Abbie. "But then I don't expect you to understand what I'm talking about, Monica. You're more intelligent than most beauty queens, certainly more than Selena was, but you are primarily a beauty queen with a decidedly mediocre mind to match."

"I understand every word you're saying," Abbie said, her eyes steely. "But nothing I've heard is worth commenting on."

"Suit yourself," Shore shrugged. "But be honest, Monica. It isn't really such a brutal proposition I've presented you with, is it? I feel I'm being very fair. And tell me truthfully, Monica, if I granted you your freedom with the stipulation that you forfeit your career, could you really return to the life you led before you came to Hollywood?"

His question hit her hard. No, it would be impossible to go back to Newbury Street. She had grown too accustomed to wealth and luxury.

She didn't answer him. She stood and ran up the stairs to her bedroom.

He called after her, "Monica, I no more deceived you than you did me. After all, I never told you I loved you. And you never told me."

She slammed the door of her room in reply. She had never spoken of her love to him, because the truth was she had never loved him. His power and importance had been the genuine attraction for her, she realized that now. Was she any better than he was? She cupped her face in her hands and started crying. She was in an elegant cage, entrapped by her own greed.

She had never even loved him enough to be hurt by his cold manner. His lack of consideration had always been obvious, from his announcement of their engagement without consulting her, to the callous way in which he had planned their honeymoon to coincide with his business trip to New York. He had always regarded her as an object, something incidental. If she had loved him, she would have been cut to the quick by his behavior, but she had always been indifferent.

She sobbed uncontrollably. The performance of her life, as Mrs. Arthur Shore, was about to begin. She would maintain her part of the bargain; she had no other choice.

Chapter 24

$\mathcal{A}$T least Abbie's new vocation as socialite and party-giver kept her occupied. The work was mindless but that was all to the good, since it kept her from thinking too deeply.

When not overseeing caterers, decorators, and servants, Abbie was obliged to cavort with the likes of Claire Jameson, Victoria Bruner, and other young Beverly Hills matrons. Claire invited Abbie over to play tennis and soon Abbie joined Claire's exercise class and found herself taking polo lessons. Claire and her friends had always reminded Abbie of hamsters on treadmills. Expending frenetic amounts of energy for no earthly reason, they gave the impression of not having a moment to themselves, perpetually busy with dancing instructors, art lessons, charity work, or batik. Abbie had always regarded such activities as a means of staving off boredom for idle, rich women, and now she was caught up in them herself.

Claire did fail in trying to interest Abbie in psychic phenomena and the occult. Claire, herself, didn't make a move without consulting fortune-tellers and spiritualists. She wanted to refer Abbie to her astrologer, who called herself Soraya.

"I know she'd just love you," Claire said. "She adores Virgos!"

Abbie politely declined.

Although Abbie no longer worked at the studio, she followed a disciplined routine. She usually rose at ten and breakfasted on whatever the maid had prepared. After her bath, Claire usually called to tell her where they'd be having lunch. Claire also spent the early part of her morning checking Pattie Grey's column for any mention of her name. She dutifully reported to Abbie any item about Arthur and her. It was always variations on a theme of marital bliss.

That Monica Dane and Arthur Shore are well-mated and happy cannot be gainsaid. . . .

Rumors have it that Arthur Shore talked his new bride into giving up her career so she could devote herself to home and hearth.

'Nonsense,' says a friend. 'Monica's as happy as a lark in her new life. She's a perfect wife, and from what I understand retiring from pictures was her decision.'

The women met for lunch daily at either Chasen's or La Pomme, two posh restaurants in town. Usually, lunch was a leisurely three hours, spent sipping wine, eating salad (dieting was a hobby among Abbie's circle), and trading snatches of gossip. After lunch the ladies returned to the chauffeur-driven automobiles waiting outside for them and visited a shop or boutique that one of them suggested. Clothes were purchased as often as groceries, necessary for the constant parties, luncheons, dinners, and cruises.

Next on the agenda would be an appointment with Miss Evelyn or Francois, the group's star hairdressers. After that, manicures, pedicures, facials, and massage.

Along with supervising Arthur Shore's social life, the upkeep of her beauty had become Abbie's full-time career, and, like her companions, she invested much time, money, and work into her looks. The ladies seemed confident that their efforts would defeat time itself. It occurred to Abbie that the obsessive pursuit of youth and beauty was a desire for immortality, though their wealth could buy them anything but that.

After finishing up at the salons, they would return home, and bathe and dress for dinner that evening.

Because Abbie's popularity as hostess had swiftly eclipsed Lorraine's, the latter had stepped down. It was wiser to bow out graciously than battle over the throne, suffering defeat and possible exile. Now, Lorraine functioned as Abbie's first lady-in-waiting, sharing the responsibilities of being the group's social leader, advising Abbie on what hors d'oeuvres to serve, what decorators to hire, which members of the circle to drop from grace.

Abbie only saw Arthur Shore at parties or dinners, when the situation was similar to playing a love scene with an actor she detested. However, she found that she no longer hated Arthur Shore. Although Abbie had become adept at presenting a warm, vital appearance to the world, she was emotionally drained, incapable of feeling joy or sorrow, love or hatred. It was a blessing of sorts. Her emotional numbness spared her the pain of hating herself.

She wanted as little to do with Arthur as possible and found it surprisingly easy to do so. He was usually at the studio, and she was usually out with her social circle. On rare occasions when they were both at home, the house was so enormous that she could occupy one wing and he another. He was more a shadowy presence than a human being.

In an attempt to break the monotony of her life, Abbie went to Europe for a personal holiday. By some miracle, she was not afflicted with seasickness on this trip, but she did not enjoy the cruise. She joined the ship's captain for dinner several times, and although he was married, he made no effort to conceal his interest in her. She was shocked by his aggressiveness and felt compelled to refuse all further dinner invitations.

Several other male passengers, all of them distinguished men, requested the pleasure of Abbie's company for dinner, but she was suspicious of all of them. She had come to realize that being the wife of a powerful man made her an especially worthy conquest to some people.

She did become somewhat friendly with a Dr. Gustave Springer, an eminent Austrian physician. Springer was a kind and gentle man, and she felt he liked and respected her for herself, not because she was Monica Dane or Mrs. Arthur Shore. It was especially nice to be given credit for having a mind by someone as brilliant as he was.

Dr. Springer had been a classmate and personal friend of Sigmund Freud's, and through their association, had developed an interest in and knowledge of psychiatry. Psychoanalysis was the revolutionary new science of the mind, a controversial and explosive topic that usually reduced grown men to shouting at each other like children. Abbie was fascinated by her discussions with Springer. At times, she was almost tempted to bring up Shore's impotence, but restrained herself. From their conversations, she gathered that her husband's hunger for power was a compensation for his unfulfilled sexual life. She couldn't help but pity him.

"Freud's theories are so shocking to many people because they force us to confront parts of ourselves we don't want to know," Springer told her. "Instead of accepting the darker side of human nature, we're taught to deny it. I see so many people running away from themselves, as if they're terrified of who they are."

His words did not sit well with Abbie. For the first time in months, her mental numbness had given way to moodiness. She was feeling things again, and she didn't want to. If she started dwelling on her life with Arthur Shore, she wouldn't be able to bear it. Everything was easier when she didn't think, so she curtailed her friendship with Dr. Springer.

Abbie's first stop in Europe was Rome, a magnificent jewel of a city. Abbie loved the warmth of the Italians she met and their reverence for beauty. The fountains, the coliseums, the soft majesty of the city at night, moved her almost to tears.

Paris was a city of lights and romance, as vital as New York was, but enhanced by a deeper appreciation of the joys of life. Each meal was an event, each sip of wine something to be savored. Dancing, singing, music was everywhere. On the Left Bank were innovative artists, writers, and musicians. Many of them were American expatriates in love with the bohemian life-style they'd found in Paris, living with a freedom impossible in the States. Abbie met the Gerald Murphys, heirs to the Mark Cross Leather Goods fortune, Americans who had settled in Europe and were close friends of the F. Scott Fitzgeralds and Ernest Hemingways. They invited Abbie to their splendid home and were charming and gracious hosts. They urged her to see something of Paris' sparkling nightlife before she left. They both raved about Josephine Baker, a gorgeous black woman, currently dancing at Place Pigalle, a nightclub. Abbie hated to leave Paris. She felt she could have lived there forever.

Marvelous as the European cities had been, they'd filled her with a sad yearning. The reality of her situation had prevented her from enjoying them completely. Arthur had granted her the illusion of freedom, but she felt bound by invisible chains, unable to partake of life like other people. Her destiny had been decided for her; there seemed little to hope for.

Her last stop was Graham Street in London, where her mother was now living with Leonard and his children. Abbie had asked her mother to keep her impending visit a secret from all outsiders. She couldn't bear welcoming parties, and, although Mum had never said a word, Abbie was sure that her working-class neighbors resented her screen image as Monica Dane. 'Gone and given herself airs,' she imagined them saying.

The three children, Mandy, Andrew, and Stephen, could not stop gawking at their Aunt Abbie, the famous movie star. Often, when she tried to talk to them, they didn't even answer. They just continued to stare. Their behavior unnerved her, especially when she would turn around and find one of them following her.

"Oh, love, it's hero worship," her Uncle Leonard would rebuke her when she complained. "They idolize you."

Mrs. Dare suggested several times that Abbie call her old friend, Flora. "Sometimes I bump into her in the market, and she always asks about you. I think she's hurt that you never wrote her."

"She never wrote me," Abbie said, sharply.

"Oh, can't you see it her way? I guess she didn't know what to say, seeing you were a star and all. Maybe it made her shy. Maybe she'd thought you'd changed a lot."

"I have changed, Mum," Abbie said. She looked her mother directly in the eye.

"Still, I think she'd be tickled pink if you saw her. She still works at the hotel. You could drop in on her."

"No, Mum," Abbie said. "I've got my reasons."

Too much time had passed. Too many things had happened. If she saw Flora, she would have to pretend to be cheerful and well, and Abbie was tired of acting. Her bright performance with Mum and Uncle Leonard was enough of a strain.

"Well, Abbie, I think you should see her. After all, Flora was responsible for all your good fortune. She was the one who persuaded you to enter the beauty contest."

Abbie didn't reply. All the more reason for not seeing Flora.

One evening, Abbie felt she had to be by herself. She took a walk down Newbury Street for the first time since she'd arrived. The neighborhood seemed foreign to her, so distant, like a place she'd read or heard about. Had she really lived there? She could hardly believe it, though it was exactly the same as she remembered it. Children were playing street games. People sat on their front stoops, talking and drinking ale. Some passed near enough for her to get a close look at them.

Abbie was amazed at their lack of concern for their appearance. She had come to believe Lorraine Shelby's credo: Beauty wasn't everything; it was the only thing. She was unaccustomed to seeing plain, working people with ragged hair, blemished skins, and scruffy clothes. Even the prettiness of the young girls was flawed. They looked as if they'd patched themselves together; their hair carelessly brushed, their lips too red, their stockings torn. Abbie had been like that herself, once. Most of the middle-aged women were fat and dowdy. She might have turned out the same if she'd stayed on Newbury Street.

"Bill, wait up, eh?"

"Come along then, Nancy."

Abbie turned around. A young woman wheeling a baby carriage caught up with the man she'd called to.

The man was Bill Reid, Abbie's ex-fiancé. He had put on perhaps twenty pounds. She recognized the woman as Nancy Winters, Helen Winters' older sister. They must have married and had a child since she'd left.

They didn't notice Abbie, but continued on their way. Abbie walked back toward Graham Street. Seeing Bill had been like seeing any other strange man. It was incredible to think she'd nearly married him, that she might very well have been in Nancy's place. How would life have been if that had happened? Would she have been happier?

She mentioned the incident to her mother.

"Yes," her mother said, quietly. "Bill married Nancy Winters shortly after you left."

Abbie smiled ironically. So much for Bill's undying love. And she had felt guilty for hurting him.

"I didn't know whether to mention it to you or not," her mother said, slowly.

"Why?" Abbie asked.

Her mother shrugged. "I thought the news might upset you a little."

Abbie had to laugh. "Don't be silly, Mum," she said.

When Abbie left for New York, her mother cried even more than she had expected her to.

"What is it, Mum? Something wrong?" Abbie asked.

"No, nothing, love," Mrs. Dare insisted. "It's just that I'm going to miss you so."

Mrs. Dare did not know how to mention that she was troubled by a bitterness, a coldness in her daughter. Mrs. Dare didn't know what the cause was, and she felt helpless to do anything.

Chapter 25

THE Christmas season was the high point of social activity in Abbie's circle. One could almost liken the frantic atmosphere to final examinations and the anxious ladies to panicked students. Each woman put painstaking work into her Christmas party, each one knew her gathering would be judged severely by the others; each one realized how much the future of her social life depended on success.

The tropical climate did nothing to injure the spirit of Christmas. The Jamesons doused all their palm trees with fake snow and lined their mansion with cotton batting. Hollywood Boulevard was christened Santa Claus Lane for the holidays. The annual Christmas Day parade featured Santa Claus in a sleigh, with actress Mabel Normand sitting beside him. Homegrown poinsettias clustered in a field at the corner of Hollywood and Sunset Boulevards.

The Jamesons gave the first party of the season on December 22. Claire fancied her home a meeting place for the moneyed, continental set, and her party was in honor of her houseguest, Princess Elfreda Von Goeller, a member of European royalty. A visitor from the East Coast, Sheila Inness, was also staying at the Jamesons. Beautiful, blonde Sheila was the debutante of the year and Newport society's current darling. She struck Abbie as being a rather nice cross between a princess and a flapper, refined enough to be considered well-bred and witty enough to be fun. Abbie had heard that Sheila was toying with the idea of a motion picture career despite her parents' disapproval. Princess Von Goeller was traveling without her husband (it was rumored that there was trouble). She was the thinnest woman Abbie had ever seen, and with her somewhat severe features, she looked like a frail bird. She refused to touch a morsel of the lavish spread Claire had prepared.

The studio party followed Claire's two days later. It was an annual gala meant to boost morale, patch up rifts, and bring new employees into the "family." Lorraine insisted that the Century chieftains and their wives have lunch at the Beverly Hills Derby before rubbing elbows with the commoners.

When they arrived at the studio, the group visited Jonas Klein's office, and Abbie quickly discovered that office parties were the same everywhere. Emboldened by alcohol, a boy who worked in the mailroom made a pass at Maura Wilder; Maura slapped him across the face. Secretaries and script girls competed with each other to sit on Jonas Klein's lap. Robert Kinley's office was filled with champagne and caviar, and he, too, was being pursued by receptionists and wardrobe girls. Lloyd Farmer, who was dead drunk, was crawling around on all fours, nipping at ladies' feet. Finally, a starlet named Paula Grant put a stop to his antics by kicking him in the nose.

Abbie was disgusted to overhear a sodden Jean-Claude offering a pretty and naïve young hairdresser stardom if she accompanied him home that night. It was too much for her. She left the party early, feigning a headache.

Two days before New Year's, Lorraine hostessed a luncheon at her house with her usual finesse. She was at heart a frustrated artist, who adored the company of creative people and envisioned her parties as soirées, her home, a salon. Her gathering was festive and cheerful, incomparably chic.

On December 31, it was Abbie's turn. The party of the year was to be held at Mr. and Mrs. Arthur Shore's estate.

When guests arrived, the mansion was ablaze with lights. Everyone congregated in the ballroom, where, among the El Grecos and Goyas, there was a new portrait of Abbie, resplendent in a red satin gown. It had been painted by Coles Philipps and had recently adorned the cover of *Vanity Fair* magazine.

Dancer Irene Castle was present and floored everyone with a remarkably spirited Charleston. Irene, a trendsetter, had introduced American women to short hair. Seeing how becoming the style was on Irene, Abbie was tempted to have her own hair bobbed.

Abbie spent most of the evening dashing here and there, catching each guest as he or she entered, introducing people to one another and trying to be as charming as possible. She wasn't the conversationalist Lorraine or Claire was, so she depended on a friendly and open manner to take her through the night. She gave each guest the impression that she was sincerely interested in whatever he had to say.

Presently, a headache threatened, and Abbie took some aspirin. She wanted to be alone for just a moment, to breathe some fresh air outside, but Arthur wouldn't allow it. There were more people to talk to and more faces to see, until it seemed to her that all the guests talked with one voice and all their faces were the same.

She was talking to Bob Kinley's wife, Edna, when she saw Charles Grady motioning to her emphatically.

"Will you excuse me please, Edna?" Abbie said, touching the woman's arm.

"Of course, dear," Mrs. Kinley told her.

Grady was standing with a man Abbie had never seen before. He was quite tall, and while not conventionally handsome, he was finely built and sensitive looking, with dark hair and candid grey eyes. He had a long face, an aquiline nose, and a firm mouth and chin.

"Monica, I don't believe you've met Paul Hanson yet, have you?" Grady said.

Abbie stiffened. So this was Paul Hanson. She still hadn't forgiven him for *Madame Bovary*.

"No, I haven't," she said, coolly polite.

"Well, it's no wonder," Grady said. "He's one of the biggest hermits in town. I think David Oakley had to promise him a raise to get him here tonight."

"How do you do, Mrs. Shore?" Hanson said. He seemed a bit remote himself. Abbie would have thought he'd shrink at the sight of her.

"Well, I hope you two will excuse me," Grady said. "I see Edna's alone and Bob asked me to keep an eye on her and make sure she doesn't misbehave."

Grady left and Abbie and Hanson were silent, smiling at each other warily.

He certainly is good-looking, she thought. It seemed ages since she'd noticed a man that way.

"You know, I saw *Madame Bovary* recently," Abbie said.

"Really? What did you think of Jessica's performance?"

"I think I would have been better," Abbie said, without batting an eyelash.

"I think you would have been, too," Hanson replied.

"Then why didn't you give me the part?" she asked, stunned.

Hanson looked totally confused. "I thought you didn't want it," he said. "That's what I was told when I tried to get in touch with you after coming back from San Gabriel."

"You did try to get in touch with me?" Abbie said.

"Yes, I did," Hanson told her. "I tried to reach you by phone via your husband's office. His secretary told me you were tied up with other projects and had lost interest. I just decided to drop it. Don't think I wasn't disappointed when I'd heard you changed your mind."

Abbie shook her head, befuddled.

"I've heard rumors that David Oakley and your husband see copies of all the correspondence that's typed up," Hanson said. "I never took it seriously, but I suppose it's true."

He didn't elaborate. He was too much of a gentleman to give his opinion of Shore's spying methods. Abbie recalled Shore's words: *I look after all my children.*

"Well, why not?" Abbie said, smiling ironically. "If they can interfere in our lives outside of the studio, controlling us while we're there must be child's play. Arthur saw the memo you wrote me, conveniently invented some business trip to occupy you the day of our appointment, intercepted your call when you got back and instructed his secretary to lie to you and yours to lie to me—isn't he clever?"

Hanson didn't know what to say. He looked at her uncomfortably.

"I'm awfully sorry," she said, "I didn't mean—"

"No problem," he said, gently. "At least, it's nice to find out that you did want to work with me. I have to admit it was a blow to my ego when you turned me down."

"I wanted to work with you more than I ever wanted anything!" Abbie exclaimed. Hanson smiled shyly and lowered his head. Abbie blushed.

"Oh, I'm sorry," she said. "Sometimes I get carried

away." The truth was that Abbie could not remember the last time she'd felt such enthusiasm.

"I'm flattered," he told her. She looked at him, admiring his sweet, open smile.

"Would you like to go for a walk?" he asked her. "Frankly, I get nervous in crowds. I'm not a man for parties. That's why I never go. After a half hour, I'm ready to leave."

"I'm the same way," Abbie said.

"Well, I'll be damned!" he said, surprised. "The hostess of the season—the lady who took it away from Lorraine Shelby? I would imagine you'd love parties."

"I'm a very good actress," Abbied said, smiling.

"Well, I've known that since *Lipstick*."

"Let's do go for a walk," Abbie said, eagerly. "I want to go outside."

He took her arm, and they went out into the garden. There were a number of people on the grounds, and she didn't want to speak to any of them, so she and Paul walked along the beach, some distance from the house. She knew Arthur would be angry when he discovered she'd left the party, but she was feeling happy, excited for the first time in what seemed like years. Arthur and the gloom he'd shrouded her life in seemed a million miles away, as distant as the stars overhead.

"Where are you from?" she asked Hanson. She wanted to know everything about him; she wanted to tell him everything about herself.

"Nebraska," he said. "Little Falls, Nebraska."

Abbie laughed. "Little Falls, Nebraska?"

"What's so funny?" Hanson said in mock indignation.

"It's just such a perfect name for a small town," Abbie said. "I've never known anyone from Nebraska before."

"Well, you do now," he said. "I guess I've never quite

adjusted to being transplanted out here. I never have managed to fit in very well."

"That says a lot for you," she said sadly.

"No," he said. "I don't believe people here are really any different than anywhere else. They make more money and have more time, and I suppose that's what sets them apart from the people I knew as a boy."

"What did you do in Nebraska?" Abbie asked.

"My dad was a dairy farmer," he told her. "I was planning to follow his path the way my brother had, until I saw my first movie."

"How old were you?" Abbie asked.

"I was twelve years old. It was called *The Violin Maker of Cremona*. It was Mary Pickford's first picture." He laughed. "It changed my life. I spent most of my time in movie theaters after that. Couldn't get enough of them. I was addicted. That same year I vowed I'd be as great a director as D. W. Griffith."

"Your dream came true," Abbie said, smiling.

"That's nice to hear. How about you? What made you decide to be an actress?"

Abbie sighed. "I'd rather not go into it."

"You know, you're awfully lovely," he said. "I wish you were happier."

He looked at her, sympathetically.

"I am happy—talking to you," she told him.

"You're very beautiful," he said, quietly. "And very fine. You're also married."

She looked at him, undaunted. There was almost a defiant spark in her eye.

"Do you know what I wish?" she said.

"No, I don't."

"I wish you would kiss me."

"I wish I could too, but. . . ."

"Please, Paul," she said softly. She closed her eyes. "Oh, please."

He stroked her cheek, tenderly. She could feel his sweet presence near her, she felt his breath on her face. She rested her weight against him, and he enclosed her in his arms. She pressed against him, feeling so happy, so secure and protected. She was safe in his arms; nothing and no one could hurt her.

Paul cupped Abbie's face in his hands, admiring her tender beauty. Slowly, he bent his face toward hers. His warm lips brushed softly across her eyelids, her cheeks, and then settled on her mouth. Paul's arms encircled her firmly, almost lifting her off the ground. She caressed his hair, his broad shoulders, his back. She felt heady, overcome by Paul's sheer manliness.

His lips found Abbie's ears and neck, her bare shoulders. He was mesmerized by her loveliness, and she was thrilled by his obvious desire for her. How long had it been since she felt herself womanly and beautiful?

Their lips met again, passionately. Paul gently brought her down to the soft, cool sand beneath them. The two of them lay together as the surf beat quietly on the beach and turned the air to perfume.

Abbie unbuttoned Paul's shirt and slipped her hand inside, feeling the smooth warmth of his skin, the taut firmness of his arms and chest. She shivered with eagerness. She slid closer to him, until their bodies were so close she could feel his heart beating.

"I want you, Monica," Paul whispered.

"Yes, darling," she told him.

No further words were needed. The time was now. She felt ready and sure. She wanted Paul more than she'd ever wanted anything. His fervent kiss assured her he felt the same as she....

Cries of glee came from the direction of the house in the distance. Firecrackers and sparklers exploded in the air and lit up the sky. It was midnight. The new year had brought new hope and had blessed Abbie with a miracle. For that moment, Abbie did not dare question her happiness or gauge its future. She was in love and that was all that mattered. Her love was something worth believing in, finer, greater than she could ever have imagined.

"Happy New Year, Monica," Paul said, gently.

"Happy New Year, darling," she whispered, tears in her eyes.

"Monica, dear—you're crying." He touched her cheek.

"It's just that I'm so happy," she told him. "And I'd nearly given up hope."

Her words touched him deeply and he drew her close.

"I love you, Monica," he said. "I know it's incredible —we've only just met, but I do love you."

Abbie wept with joy and gratitude. Life had not abandoned her.

Chapter 26

"WHAT happened to you last night?" Arthur confronted her the next morning before he left to spend the day at his gentlemen's club.

Abbie was still in bed, drenched in sleep and thoughts of Paul and their time together. Had it really happened? The soft night, the beach, the two of them alone, the closeness, the dearness of him— It seemed dreamlike to her now, that they had loved so swiftly and fully.

"I was around," she said.

"Where? I couldn't find you. People were asking about you."

"I went out by myself for a while," she said, irked. She turned over in bed so she wouldn't have to face him.

"With a house full of guests? Deserted your own party?"

"I wasn't feeling well!" she cried. "And I'm not feeling well now! Leave me alone!"

"Well, we are being difficult this morning, aren't we? I sincerely hope our behavior improves later on—it had better, I might add."

He left her room, making sure to slam the door.

As soon as he was gone, she returned to thinking of Paul. It was all true; it had really happened. Before they had parted, just before dawn, he had promised to call her later that day, and plan where to meet.

It would be wise for her to go downstairs and tell the maids that she'd answer all calls that morning herself. If Shore tyrannized his secretaries and forced them to spy for him, he probably involved the servants in his schemes, too.

Blanche had already prepared French toast and eggs downstairs.

"Blanche, I'm expecting a call this morning and I want to answer it myself," Abbie said, casually. "It's my uncle in England. He wrote and said he'd be calling me."

"Certainly, Madame," Blanche replied.

In the middle of breakfast, the telephone rang. Abbie jumped up. "I'll get it," she called.

"Hello?" she said into the receiver, breathlessly.

"Hello, Monica dear? You'll be pleased to know the whole town is singing your praises!" It was Claire Jameson with a full report on what the columnists had said about the New Year's Eve party. "You ought to read what Pattie Grey said. It couldn't be more glorious!"

"Oh, thank you, thank you for calling, Claire," Abbie said, impatiently.

"Don't you want to hear?"

"Not now, dear, I'm in the middle of something. Let me call you back."

"Of course, darling. Don't forget: lunch today at the Derby."

"I'm afraid I can't, Claire."

"Why not, angel? Is something wrong?"

"Oh no, just an appointment."

"My, we're certainly being mysterious, aren't we?"

Damn Claire, Abbie thought. Maybe she worked for Arthur, too. Claire had the biggest mouth in town, and it was wise not to trust her too far. Lorraine had once warned Abbie that Claire could be "lethal."

"Very well." Abbie laughed lightly. "If you must

know, it's a dental appointment. I lost a filling, and it's the only time my dentist can take me."

"How interesting," Claire said. "You have a dentist who works on New Year's Day."

Abbie paled. "Oh Claire," she began. "It's really—"

"Very well, Monica. Don't tell me. Anyway, sweets, I've got to start dressing for lunch. Toodles."

She hung up. Abbie sat down and sighed deeply. That woman. Another intruder on her happiness.

The phone rang again. Abbie grabbed it.

"Hello?" she said.

"Monica?" It was his low, resonant voice.

"Hello darling," she said. "How are you?"

"I'm great," he said. "And I love you."

"I love you too, Paul," she whispered. "How should we arrange this, darling? Where can we meet?"

"There's a small luncheonette near my house. Very inconspicuous and out of the way. Why don't you take a taxi there, Monica? It's on 55 Perry Street. It's called the Cracker Box. Not very classy, I'm afraid."

"Who cares?" she told him. "I'll be over right away."

"OK dear. I'm leaving now, too. I'll race you."

Abbie laughed and hung up, feeling as if she could fly there. She called a taxi service, rushed through her shower and hastily put on a dress. The only makeup she had time for was lip rouge. By the time she was ready, the taxi had arrived.

"55 Perry Street," she told the driver. "The Cracker Box Luncheonette."

Abbie wrapped a scarf around her hair so she wouldn't be recognized that easily.

On the drive over, she was filled with anticipation. How would she feel seeing Paul again? By herself, she felt radiant with love for him, but what would happen when they met each other once more, face to face?

Perhaps she had been too impetuous the night before. She had been so lonely and unhappy; perhaps she would have been vulnerable to any handsome, sensitive man.

When she walked into the Cracker Box, Paul was waiting, and all her doubts vanished. She sat in the booth across from him.

"My feelings haven't changed toward you, Paul," she said softly.

"Neither have mine." He gently took her hand.

"What are we going to do, Paul?"

"I don't know, Monica," he said quietly. "I only know I've never felt this way about another woman. I never thought I could. I'm awfully particular, you know. I never dreamed I'd find one who could meet my standards. You're a treasure, Monica."

Abbie smiled at him.

"What do you want to do, Monica?" he said. "The way I feel now, I'd marry you this instant." He shook his head. "I guess I must sound very adolescent. I can imagine what you must think. Of course, I know—"

Tears suddenly rolled down Abbie's cheeks. "I can't divorce Arthur Shore," she said, almost inaudibly.

"Is it for religious reasons?" he asked unhappily. "Do you feel obligated to him in some way? I can certainly understand, Monica. After all, you are his wife."

"No, no," Abbie shook her head, miserably. "I wish those were the reasons! I wish it could be as decent as that!"

"Why then, Monica?" Paul asked. "Do you still feel you might care for him?"

Abbie shuddered. "I hate him! I hate him more than I thought I could ever hate anyone!"

"What is it, darling?" he asked, taken aback. "What has he done to you?"

Abbie looked around furtively.

"Can we go somewhere more private?" she asked anxiously. "I'm sorry. Living with Arthur has made me so afraid of everything."

"Let's go to my place," Paul said. "I have a bungalow just a few blocks from here. We can walk over."

"What if someone sees us?"

"Don't be afraid," Paul said gently.

They left the Cracker Box and headed for Paul's bungalow on Minnetta Lane. Once inside, Paul offered Abbie something to drink.

"I have some great wine here," he said. "Please join me?"

"All right."

He disappeared into his small kitchen. Paul's living room was traditional, with sturdy oak furniture and seascapes by Turner on the walls. Abbie had to smile in spite of herself. The home was so very like him—rustic and American.

"Here we are," he said, returning with drinks. "Feeling better?"

"Yes," she said. She felt much calmer and also a bit foolish. She must have overwhelmed poor Paul. It was just that she had carried those dreadful secrets in silence for so long and had been grateful to be able to speak freely to someone who listened and cared. Still, though they loved each other, they had only just met, and it wasn't fair to burden Paul with her problem. Her hatred for Arthur might poison her love for Paul, and she couldn't bear that.

"Now, what is it, Monica? What is it you wanted to tell me?" Paul asked earnestly.

"Nothing," she said softly. "It doesn't matter."

"Are you sure? It was something about you and Arthur. Why you couldn't divorce him."

"I don't want to talk about him," she said. "I want to talk about you."

He kissed her. "You know, I've got something to confess," he said.

"What?" she asked.

"One of the reasons I asked you to do *Madame Bovary* is because I've had a crush on you since *Lipstick*."

She laughed. "I hope I haven't let you down."

He shook his head. "You've surpassed all my expectations."

She put her head against his chest and held him. "Let's just enjoy each other for now, darling," she said. "Let's just be happy for what we have. Please?"

"Yes, Monica," he told her. "Whatever you want."

Chapter 27

*A*BBIE's life became more complicated after Paul entered it. She was still responsible for organizing parties and dinners for Arthur, and she was still obliged to socialize with Lorraine and Claire. The elite circle did allow a period of grace before dismissing someone from the group. If a person was out of town for a limit of six months, they might be welcomed back when they returned; part of the decision was based on the quality of the gifts they brought their hostesses. But as a rule, the ladies tended to have short memories. The same principle applied to regular members of the group who began to break too many luncheon appointments or shopping dates. Abbie had to balance her days, dividing her time between Paul and the duties of being Mrs. Arthur Shore, and the more she came to love Paul, the harder it was.

She felt guilty, sure that she was being unfair to him. She couldn't marry him, and she prevented him from meeting someone else. Still, he insisted that he was helplessly in love with Abbie and was grateful for whatever time she could grant him.

They met secretly, avoiding any situation that could draw attention to themselves. Most of the time, they went to his bungalow, found a deserted beach, or took long drives to San Juan Capistrano, the mission site that Abbie loved so much. Neither of them had any desire to frequent public places, but they were tired of being careful, of arranging their meetings, of having to hide from the world as if they were ashamed of their love. Abbie felt that she was married to Paul. They had made a moral commitment to each other. But in the eyes of the law and the Church, she was Mrs. Arthur Shore.

Finally, the inevitable day came when Paul said, "Darling, I just can't accept the relationship on these terms anymore! I'm losing sleep!"

"What then, Paul?" she said, trembling. "You think we should stop seeing each other?"

Paul looked horrified. "Monica, how can you say that knowing how I feel about you? My God, I can't live without you, don't you realize that?"

Abbie smiled through grateful tears. "I was hoping you'd say that, darling. You're the only man I've ever known who's never disappointed me!"

"Monica, we have to get married," Paul said. "There's no other choice. I can't continue this charade any further. I hate skulking about this way as if we were criminals! Darling, I want you here, in my house, in my arms, as my wife! I can't bear to think of you going back to another man every time we part. Can't you understand that?"

"Yes, darling, yes! Don't you think I feel the same way? Oh, if only I'd met you before!"

"Monica, we can't regret what's done. We can't make the past over, but we can take hold of our lives now. Monica, I want to marry you. I want you to tell Arthur to grant you a divorce. We'll both tell him, together."

"No, Paul," Abbie sobbed. "It's impossible. He'll never let me go."

"Why, Monica? Please tell me why! I just don't understand it. You told me once you hated him more than anything. How can a man keep living with a woman who despises him?"

"Because he's sick," Abbie said tersely. "That's putting it the kindest way I know how."

"Then why won't you leave him? Why have you stayed with him all this time? What can he do to you?"

Abbie looked at Paul gravely. "More than you could ever imagine."

"What, Monica?" Paul said, confused. "Please tell me. I want to understand."

She sighed deeply.

"Monica, I have a right to know."

It was true. He was in love with her: she owed him an explanation.

"The only reason Arthur married me was because I represented prestige for him. He never loved me . . . he's never even made love to me . . . he's impotent," she said.

Paul looked shocked, then his face filled with pity. "Oh, Monica! You've lived with him all this time, poor darling."

He drew her close and held her. "Why, Monica?" he asked. "Why have you stayed with him?"

"He—he can harm me, Paul. He can ruin me. You have no idea of how dangerous he is. He's a monster."

"Monica, he isn't superhuman— God knows, he isn't."

"Paul, he finds things out about people and threatens them with what they fear most. I've seen him do it, casually, with guests in the house. He finds their weaknesses, their hurts, their doubts, and he picks on them. He knows Lorraine Shelby's been trying to have a baby, so he makes insinuations about her childlessness. Or he'll say something subtly anti-Semitic in front of Jonas Klein. He's horrible!"

"All right, dear, he's a bastard, but what has he been torturing you with?"

"Oh Paul, he's—he's blackmailed me to keep me from leaving him."

"With what?"

"Paul, I was the last person to speak to Ivy Hayes. She called me on the phone and told me a man had threatened her. She was frightened and begged me to keep her company until her housekeeper came. I drove over, but—I guess poor Ivy was dead by the time I got there. No one answered the door. I just assumed she had gone out somewhere and drove home. The next day, the newspapers reported her murder and said that a grey Winton had been seen leaving her house. It was me in that car! I got so panicked when I read that, I didn't know what to do. I called Arthur, and he told me not to tell the police. I stayed out of it. I was just frightened of having my name dragged into it and being questioned by the police."

"That's understandable," Paul said.

"Anyway, when I found out that Arthur was impotent, I mentioned that he should see a doctor. He refused. We got into a fight, and he told me if I tried to have the marriage annulled, he'd tell the police that I'd withheld evidence. He'd also tell them that Ivy and I had both been seeing Jean-Claude Malleux."

"Had you?"

"Yes, for a short time. Oh Paul, can't you see how incriminating it would all be?"

"Yes dear, but still—trembling under the shadow of Arthur Shore's threats—Monica, that's no way to live! Monica, I really think we ought to confront him."

"But, Paul, I'm so frightened! I know he'd tell the police!"

208

"What if he does? You and I both know you're innocent, and the court will find out the truth. Monica, justice is a lot more intricate than you think it is. All Arthur has is very superficial evidence."

"But I even lied to the police!" Abbie cried. "He told me to tell them I was with him the night of the crime."

"Then you'll tell them he told you to lie. Human nature is human nature. You were scared, and did what he said."

"Would you stand behind me if I went to the police?"

"Monica, would I be suggesting this if I wasn't prepared to? As far as I'm concerned, this whole matter is as much my problem as it is yours."

She put her head on his shoulder. "Paul, did you know Selena Winfield?" she asked.

"No, I didn't. I have heard certain things, though. I know it's a subject that's hardly ever mentioned now."

"What things have you heard?"

Paul sighed. "You know, Jonas Klein was once in love with her."

"He was?" Abbie said, in surprise.

"Oh, it was a fairly brief romance. I don't know all the details. I guess it just wasn't meant to be. Still, he carried a torch for her for years. One night, he and I had a few drinks and he started talking about her."

"What did he say?" Abbie asked.

"I had just arrived," Paul said, "fresh from Nebraska. It was about the same time poor Selena's whole life was fading. She and Arthur Shore were getting divorced around then, and her career was finished."

"That must have been six or seven years ago," Abbie said.

"Yes. The town was buzzing with rumors about Selena's insanity and what a sainted martyr Arthur was for putting up with her."

"I wonder!" Abbie said vehemently.

"Poor Jonas wondered, too. He had had quite a few drinks, and he just started telling me how sick the talk about Selena made him, how unfair everyone was being to her. People were assuming the worst since she couldn't defend herself. He was nearly in tears."

"Poor Jonas," Abbie said.

"He talked about Selena, and he blamed Century for what had happened to her."

"Century?"

"Yes. He told me she'd been one of the sweetest, nicest girls one could ever hope to meet. She sincerely wanted to be a good actress, and she was damned tired of being a showpiece in roles that only required her to bare her legs and smile mysteriously. She wanted better roles, and the higher-ups resented the waves she made. To teach her a lesson, they threw her into parts that required too much of a girl who hadn't been adequately prepared. The outcome was awful—a girl with no training can't be expected to do Mary, Queen of Scots her first time out. Of course, the critics were merciless, and Century played on poor Selena's insecurities. They thought if they kept putting pressure on, she'd gladly go back to wearing bathing suits again. Instead, she persisted, desperate to prove herself, and she had a nervous breakdown in the process."

"Poor girl!" Abbie said, her voice hushed.

"Her career was smashed and when Arthur Shore proposed marriage, I guess it was like a drowning woman being thrown a lifesaver. I remember Jonas said to me, 'No one knows what goes on behind locked doors.' I didn't pay attention then, but I suppose he meant that Selena might very well have been the injured party, although everyone felt sorry for Arthur Shore."

Abbie shook her head. "I feel so awful for her."

"I guess Selena wasn't strong enough to help herself," Paul said. "But you are, Monica. And you have my full support."

Abbie impulsively embraced Paul, grateful for his strength and courage.

Chapter 28

ARTIE and Carol have to decide when small
Arthur should begin music lessons there tin

Chapter 28

$\mathcal{A}$BBIE and Paul did not have to decide when to tell Arthur about their plans; fate gave them the opportunity.

Pattie Grey had recently announced in her column that the Lewis Shelbys were expecting their first baby in September. Abbie's circle was absolutely thrilled for Lorraine, who had been trying to have a child for several years, and Abbie was elected to throw a surprise champagne party for her and Lewis. It was held on a Saturday evening under the pretext that the Shelbys were meeting the Shores at their home for dinner.

When the Shelbys arrived at the Shore residence, they were greeted by Century's VIP's. All of the studio heads and most of the producers and directors were present, since Shelby was the studio's most influential producer.

Lorraine was more radiant and serene than Abbie had ever seen her.

All of the guests departed by midnight except for Paul Hanson. In the course of the evening, Abbie and Paul had both decided to speak to Arthur.

After Abbie bade Lorraine and Lewis a warm goodbye, she returned to the parlor. Arthur was seated on the divan, nursing a highball. Paul was leaning against the fireplace, his drink in his hand. They gave Abbie the distinct impression of two adversaries, squaring off and sizing each other up. Arthur was so cunning, he'd probably guessed what was in store.

Abbie sat down. The air in the room seemed frozen; no one uttered a word. Abbie found herself concentrating on the steady tick of the huge grandfather clock.

Arthur was the first one to break the silence.

"Well, Paul," he said amiably. "You really ought to attend more parties. You must enjoy them, seeing as you're the last guest to leave."

"That's not the reason I'm still here, Arthur," Hanson replied. "There's something I have to speak to you about —or rather, something Monica and I both have to speak to you about."

Abbie was nearly faint from tension. Arthur, still the picture of composure, turned to her with a curious smile.

"Oh?" he remarked. "What have you two been conspiring? Don't tell me—you want Monica to star in your next picture. I'd prefer she didn't, but of course the final word rests with her."

"No, Arthur, no pictures. There's no need to play games; I have a feeling you already know what it is," Paul said. "Arthur, Monica and I are in love. We want to be married. I don't know how else to say it."

"You've said it very well, plainly and simply," Shore said. "I appreciate your frankness, but I'm afraid what you ask is quite impossible. You see, I have no intention of giving Monica up."

"It isn't just a matter of your intentions," Paul said. "Monica is extremely unhappy with you."

Shore turned to Abbie with an expression of mock confusion and hurt.

"I think you ought to let Monica speak for herself in this matter. Have I slighted you in some way, Monica? Hurt you in some fashion? Let me assure you it wasn't deliberate, and you have my complete apology. Your satisfaction and well-being are my primary concerns."

"Oh, stop this farce, Arthur! Our marriage is no marriage, and you know it!" she cried, unable to contain her anger. "You don't love me, and still you're too much of a snake to let me love someone else! I want to marry Paul!"

"And does Paul know everything there is to know about his would-be bride?" Arthur said. "You know, Paul, Monica isn't quite as sweet and uncomplicated as she appears. On the contrary, she's quite a woman of mystery. I guess you could call her a lady with a past."

"I know all about Jean-Claude," Paul said, disgusted. "I'm also familiar with her involvement in the Hayes business. Monica told me all about that herself, and I don't really give a damn!"

"You're very understanding, I must say," Arthur told him. "I suppose you love her truly. You have my heartfelt condolences, but I'm afraid the lady is and will remain my wife."

"You really think so?" Paul said. "I doubt that. You're overestimating yourself, Arthur. You see, your venom doesn't hurt me the way it does some people. You might have been able to terrorize Monica, but now she and I are prepared for the worst you can do. I've already assured her that all you *can* do is call the police and try your damndest to incriminate her by offering them some pathetic tidbits. Why don't you face it? You're going to look like the biggest fool in the world when the cops find out what fluff you've handed them. I can just imagine what Langdon will have to say about it. 'Jealous Hubbie Lies to Send Wife to Jail.' Pattie Grey will make you out to be the villain of all time. You see, Arthur, in the long run, you'll lose."

A glimmer of rage crossed Shore's immobile features.

"I'm afraid you don't leave me any choice, Paul. You've forced me to give you an ultimatum. Either you stop seeing my wife or the whole country finds out that one of Hollywood's most gifted filmmakers is an ex-con. Paul, Century would drop you faster than a time bomb and no one would pick you up!"

"What is he talking about, Paul?" Abbie asked anxiously.

"Well, so it turns out that *you're* the man of mystery!" Shore chortled. "And I thought you were so direct and straightforward! If anything, I thought our Monica was the sneak."

"Monica," said Paul, "when I first came to Hollywood, I couldn't find a job in pictures. So, I waited tables, moved furniture, did construction work, anything. Even menial work was hard to come by. During one dry spell, it got so bad, I couldn't make the rent on my room. I was staying in a boarding house, and the landlady asked me to leave. I got myself a sleeping bag secondhand, and camped out on some land I assumed was deserted. I'd figured wrong. The owner spotted me sleeping there, reported it to the police, and I was charged with trespassing and vagrancy. I was alone, broke, and friendless. I couldn't pay the fine, so I was sentenced to thirty days in prison. It should have been longer, but the judge took pity on me. Shortly after my release from prison, I met Ken Bruner. He liked me and took me on as an assistant. I didn't see any reason to tell him about my time in jail. Until this moment, I didn't see any reason to tell anyone. That's why I didn't tell you. I was wrong. I'm sorry."

"Paul, you have nothing to be sorry about," Abbie told him. "And I have nothing to forgive you for."

"Isn't that touching!" Shore interjected. "I wonder how deeply the public would be moved by Paul's impassioned confession? I wonder how forgiving they would be after all the scandals in this New Babylon? And I wonder how the industry would react to their disapproval?"

"I'm willing to take my chances and find out," Paul said. "If only for the satisfaction of knowing that you don't have a thing on me!"

"No, Paul, please! Paul, I couldn't marry you under those conditions. I couldn't live with the thought that you'd ruined your career on my account!" Abbie said, frightened. She knew Shore was right.

"She's giving you good advice," Shore said. "You don't want to pull the trigger, do you, Paul? After all, what I know about you is a loaded gun. It's probably Hollywood's best-kept secret."

"Oh no," Paul said, shrewdly. "It's Hollywood's *second* best-kept secret. I think the three of us know what the first is."

For perhaps the only time in his adult life, Arthur Shore was caught off-guard. Abbie had never seen him look frightened before.

"I don't believe I have to supply you with details," Paul said, meaningfully. "Monica's too much of a lady to ever consider using it against you, but I know the only way to handle someone like you is by using your own methods."

Shore stared at him grimly. "I'm warning you, Hanson—"

"And I'm warning you—You've got Monica and me deadlocked, but you're in it too. We're all sitting on a keg of dynamite. You can ignite it, Shore, but keep in mind that you'll blow yourself up, too."

Shore stared at Hanson murderously. He had been outsmarted.

"Monica won't marry me because she's afraid of the harm you can do," said Paul, "but you're not going to stop us from seeing each other. And if she ever tells me that you've mistreated her in any way, I'll not only have the pleasure of slamming the hell out of you, personally, I'll call every paper in town and tell the secret that Arthur Shore married and victimized two innocent women to hide. So help me, I'll find out the name of the madhouse where you've put Selena and I'll talk to her too!"

Paul was trembling with rage. He gently put his hands on Abbie's shoulders. "Darling, will you be all right here?" he asked.

"Yes, Paul," she answered, overwhelmed.

"I'm leaving now," he told her. "I'll call you tomorrow. You're tired, go to bed."

He kissed her, glared at Shore, and took his leave.

Chapter 29

SHORE and Hanson's animosity soon extended into their public lives as well.

A new phenomenon had appeared in the motion picture industry: sound. Sound was still in its infancy, relegated to newsreels and shorts, and Warners was the only studio using sound in full-length films. It had released *Don Juan*, starring John Barrymore, with a synchronized musical track. The Warners' publicity department was ballyhooing *The Jazz Singer*, their first official "talking" picture that was due to open in October featuring the song and dance star, Al Jolson.

Most of the major studios weren't taking the new innovation seriously. It was a gimmick, they thought, a fad that would briefly capture the public's attention and then fade away. For one thing, the soundtracks were tinny and crude, disconcerting for audiences to listen to. Vitaphone microphones were so sensitive that they picked up any noise on the set. The rustle of a dress could drown out lines of dialogue. Microphones were stationary, hidden in vases or other props on the set, so actors had to stand strategically near the hidden mikes to deliver their lines. The sight of an actor reciting his words of love for his sweetheart into an artificial rosebush looked unreal, and the actors' freedom of movement was completely lost when they had to work on a small, cramped sound stage. The restrictions were both stifling and frustrating. Both directors and producers were afraid of the power the sound technicians could exercise over a studio.

But worse than any other problem, switching to sound would mean enormous expense. The cost of hiring sound technicians and installing equipment in studios and movie theaters would be staggering. It might also present a problem with foreign distribution. Silent films were universal; English-language films would have no market in Europe.

As far as the majority of filmmakers and executives at Century were concerned, the advent of sound was about as welcome as a snake at a picnic. However, David Oakley insisted that Shore and his assistants investigate this new development, find out how other studios were responding, and present their findings to him. Almost all the directors including Joe Lamm were dead set against talking pictures. Sound would make everything they knew obsolete and force them to take a backseat to the new sound technicians until they learned other directing methods.

The stars were also terrified. Romantic screen personas often belied dreadful voices and diction. Foreigners like Jean-Claude Malleux could be hindered by their heavy accents.

Still, there was a minority of movie people who were beginning to view sound as the next frontier of the industry. Producer Lewis Shelby was one and Paul Hanson was another.

Although Shore assured David Oakley that the idea of talking pictures would be forgotten within two or three years, and *The Jazz Singer* was bound to be a disaster, Hanson presented Oakley with an opposite point of view. Granted the present sound equipment was crude, but the silent movies had also been primitive in the beginning.

Hanson sent Oakley a letter stating that by the next decade, "talking pictures will have eclipsed silent films. What courage and foresight Century might exhibit in being a pioneer in this area!"

Unlike the other directors, Paul Hanson saw sound as a new challenge, with tremendous creative possibilities. He tried to encourage people to sign a petition asking to meet with Oakley and discuss the idea of introducing Century to sound, but just about everyone was reluctant to give their signatures. Sound was too threatening. However, Hanson's reputation was enough to interest Oakley in what he had to say. He and Paul conferred privately.

Shore was incensed when he found out that Hanson had gone over his head to meet with Oakley, and he soon called for a showdown. A meeting of Century's top producers, executives, and directors was arranged by Shore and held in Oakley's office.

"Since there seems to be so much dissension over the prospect of equipping the studio for sound, I think both cases for and against should be heard and a vote taken," Arthur Shore proposed, knowing full well the vote would be in his favor.

"That's fair enough, Arthur," Oakley said. "You gentlemen can decide which of you wants to speak first."

"Paul?" Shore said politely, knowing that the last words spoken usually carried more impact.

"Thank you, Arthur," Hanson said. "I've stated to David Oakley personally that I believe talking pictures will replace silent movies, probably within the next ten years."

Everyone looked aghast.

"Silent films were one phase in the creative destiny of the motion picture industry," Paul continued. "If Century looks to the future and decides to take a major step and switch to sound, we could be the leading studio by

1930. I feel we should at least invest in this new equipment on a small, controlled basis. That's all I have to say. Thank you, gentlemen."

There was scanty, obligatory applause.

Arthur Shore rose, smiling. "Mr. Hanson displays the bold recklessness of youth in his predictions. It is far easier to prophesy when one is young and fairly inexperienced. Anything new or different dazzles and entices. However, those of us who are older and wiser have witnessed much that was new and different come and go. I can't help feeling that sound pictures are a fad that will attract the public's attention for a short time and then disappear. To revamp our entire studio or even a small portion of it because of the romantic visions of a young man, would be irresponsible and possibly dangerous. I have investigated this new development and nothing makes me believe that any money should be invested in sound technicians and equipment at this time."

Everyone applauded heartily.

"Thank you very much, gentlemen," Oakley said. "And now, it's my turn. I'm going to leave the decision with everyone in this room. All those in favor of installing sound equipment into the studio as an experimental venture, say aye."

Paul and Lewis Shelby delivered the only "ayes" there.

"Those against, say nay," Oakley said.

Shore led the other men in defeating the idea.

"Very well," Oakley said. "The nays have it."

The men applauded, congratulated each other, and filed out of the office.

"Well, that finishes that," Shelby told Hanson.

"I don't give up so easily," Paul said.

"Nice try, Paul." Arthur Shore grinned from ear to ear.

"Not nice enough," Paul grinned back. "I'll just have to try harder."

He and Shelby left, and whisked off to a local speakeasy for a drink.

"What else can you do?" Shelby asked Paul, when they sat down.

"I'm going to read everything I can about sound pictures; everything that's written. And I'm going to methodically cut it out and mail it all to Oakley. I'm going to keep tabs on all the new studios springing up and find out what they're doing."

"Look, Paul, it's not only Century. It's MGM and Fox, too. None of them wants sound."

"Of course, their castles are being threatened. It means the end of their dynasties. Only the smaller, less-established companies like Warners are taking the risk. Warners is going to leave them all behind."

"It's their problem," Shelby said.

"But as long as we're with Century, it's our problem, too," Paul told him.

Shelby shrugged. "Look, it's not an urgent situation—" he said.

"Yet," Paul interjected.

"Why don't you just sit tight for now, Paul? After all, for all we know, *The Jazz Singer* could be a real bomb."

"No," Paul said. "I'm going to move Oakley's hand, or I'm going to get out. I don't believe in going down with a sinking ship."

"Paul, you're getting melodramatic! Century's in the black; 1926 was one of our best years ever!"

"In this business, six months can make the difference between being on top and being in the garbage can. The overlords like Shore would rather see the studio crumble than forfeit the positions they've got. I mean it, Lewis, they'd happily take the rest of us down with them."

223

"I know, you're right, Paul. Oakley's just a rich man who thought it would be fun to own a movie studio. He's a figurehead. What is it they say: 'Oakley makes the final decisions, but he gets his orders from Arthur Shore.' Shore's a master of manipulation."

"Everyone resents him, but no one ever challenges his authority. All he really is, is Oakley's hatchet man."

Lewis smiled. "You sound like you want to make things tough for him."

"Tougher than they've been," Hanson said, downing his drink. "I'd just like to show that bastard that what he says doesn't necessarily go, that Oakley will listen to other people. I pity the studio staff if he doesn't. Oakley can afford to lose Century, but a lot of jobs hang in the balance."

"I still say you should wait until *The Jazz Singer* opens before you start launching your attack."

"Don't worry, Lewis. I know what I'm doing. It's too early for an all-out battle. I'm just loading the cannons."

Chapter 30

THE professional rivalry between Arthur and Paul took its toll on Abbie, helplessly caught in the middle.

Not a day passed when Paul Hanson didn't drop by Oakley's office to leave a news article on the latest developments in motion picture sound technique, or a report from a new studio specializing in talking pictures.

The daily reports started Oakley thinking that perhaps Century was making a mistake by not giving talking pictures a try. He started questioning Shore's actions, something he'd never done before, and Shore became uneasy.

To protect his position, Shore was forced to clip negative reports on talking pictures and think up arguments as to why they would inevitably fail. The ceaseless battle of wits with Hanson started to wear him out.

Shore always took the office home with him and now the largest problem in his workday was Paul Hanson, his wife's lover. Shore became more and more openly hostile toward Abbie. Before, they had rarely spoken to each other, each one occupying their private territory in the mansion. But lately, Shore would come home, find Abbie, and try to antagonize her by lashing out at Paul.

"You know, that lover of yours is getting to be a damned nuisance," Arthur announced after a particularly harrowing day. Hanson had shown Oakley an article emphasizing how eagerly most movie-goers were anticipating the premiere of *The Jazz Singer*.

Shore poured himself another straight bourbon; he was drinking a lot lately.

"I don't know what I'm going to do to pin the bastard's ears back, but I'm sure my inventive nature won't fail me," he said.

There was a pause. "Tell me, Monica. How would you like to see Europe again?"

"No, thank you."

"Well, I'm afraid I'm going to have to insist."

"Leave me alone, Arthur," Abbie said hotly. "I'm not going."

Shore left the room abruptly. Suspicious, Abbie followed him. He was in the library, making a telephone call.

"Who are you calling?" she demanded.

"Wouldn't you like to know?" He grinned. "Hello?" he said. "*Public Eye*? Is Charles Langdon there? I have something to tell him about Paul—"

Abbie ran over and knocked the receiver out of his hand.

"Stop it, Arthur, stop it!" she cried.

Despite the threat that Paul dangled over Shore's head, Abbie felt that in the long run, Shore could do more damage to Paul. Shore's secret was a matter of personal pride, while Paul's past could affect his career and reputation.

"Are you going to Europe or not?" Shore said.

"I'm not, but I'll see less of Paul if that will make you happy!" She and Paul had been together every day since they had confronted Shore. She wondered how she could bear being separated from him.

Shore seemed appeased by her words and retired to his room.

The next afternoon, Paul dropped by unexpectedly. He wanted to take Abbie to the movies.

"I can't today," Abbie lied nervously. "Arthur and I are expecting houseguests and I'm going to have to spend time preparing things for them."

"Houseguests? Who are they?"

"Oh, some sort of European royalty—a baroness or something. I really don't know."

"You seem upset," Paul told her.

"Just anxious about all this bother. How have you been?"

"Nothing much has happened in the last twenty-four hours," he told her. "I'm mostly busy leading the battle for talkies."

"I think the whole thing is rather premature, myself," Abbie said carefully. "I can't understand why everyone's getting so heated up."

"How do you know people are getting heated up?"

"Oh, it's in th_ papers and Arthur mentions it, sometimes."

"What does he say, Monica? Has he mentioned that I'm his greatest opponent at the studio?"

"Oh, I don't know. I really don't listen to him . . . I just think people should see how *The Jazz Singer* fares before they make decisions."

"That way, Warners has the jump on everybody else. And the studios who wise up now get the jump on Century. So where does that leave us?"

"Oh, who cares?" Abbie suddenly blurted out. "I'm sorry, Paul, I just get so tired of hearing about it!"

"What is it, darling? Has he been bothering you?"

"No, no! I mean, of course, I hear him talking about it—it is his work, but—I guess I'm just worried about these guests I'm having and all the fuss involved."

"Monica, something's wrong. You're not yourself at all," Paul said, worried.

"No, I'm fine. Listen, Paul, I'll call you next week."

"Next week!" Paul said, dismayed.

"I'm sorry, Paul. I'm just going to be tied up until then."

Paul looked at her. "Monica, something is wrong," he said. "Have I done something to hurt you?"

"No, Paul, nothing . . . Oh, will you look at the time? I have to meet my lady friends for lunch. I really must get ready."

"Monica, you sound like Claire Jameson, for God's sakes! What is the matter with you?"

"The matter with me!" Abbie cried. "What's the matter with you? You're so obsessed with the idea of talkies and the studio and Arthur, you can't think straight! You don't even know who I am anymore."

She started to cry.

"Oh, Monica, darling!" Paul folded her in his arms. "Don't you know you're more important to me than anything else? I guess I have been babbling on about it too much."

"No, Paul, it's your work. I'm sorry. I guess I just get jealous, sometimes."

"Monica, you have every right."

"No, I don't. I was just being selfish. Do you forgive me?"

"You know I do. Do you really have to meet those peacocks for lunch?"

"Yes, Paul. You know I'd rather be with you."

"Then why are you going?"

She shrugged. "They'll be here any minute."

"Monica, you're still afraid of Arthur, aren't you? I have a feeling he insists on those friendships. You're so different from Claire and Lorraine."

228

"Paul, I've got to have friends, and these women are the best this town has to offer. Really, they're not so bad. I've actually grown very fond of Lorraine."

"You really can't see me until next week?"

"No, love," she said. "But I'll be thinking of you every minute. Will you think of me?"

"Yes, Monica, I will. God knows, I'll miss you."

They embraced, reluctant to let go.

"It's only a week," Abbie said. "I can endure that as long as I know I'll see you again."

"Are you sure I can't call you tomorrow?" Paul asked.

Abbie couldn't help herself. "Yes, do. Please," she relented.

They kissed once more, slowly, dreamily.

"Goodbye darling," she told him softly.

Chapter 31

$\mathcal{A}$ few days after Abbie's self-imposed separation from Paul, an ugly line appeared about them in a gossip column known as The Loaded Question: *Which director has been seen around town with which studio head's actress wife?*

Abbie's old foe, Charles Langdon, was more direct.

It seems that director Paul Hanson sees the boss's wife after hours. He and Monica Dane (Mrs. Arthur Shore) were spotted holding hands at a local eatery.

Abbie had realized this bilge was bound to surface. In Hollywood, such secrets were impossible to keep hidden from the reporters for long.

It was also true that she and Paul had relaxed their discretion after their showdown with Shore. They openly attended concerts together and frequented places they had been careful to avoid before. It was inevitable that people would gossip, but Abbie had not expected so much of it all at once.

Unfortunately, the items had hit the newsstands all on the same day; a journalistic blitzkreig against Abbie's reputation, and, although Claire Jameson called Abbie daily to report what was said about her in whose column, she didn't dare tell Abbie this news.

That morning, Abbie wondered why Claire hadn't called her as usual, but was distracted by a number of household duties that had demanded her attention for some time. The dining room walls needed painting, so Abbie got in touch with someone Lorraine had once suggested to her. Abbie also caught up on her letter writing.

Alone, with the whole day to herself, she had to fight a powerful urge to call Paul. She missed him terribly. Finally she gave in and phoned his office.

"Hello?" Abbie said to his secretary. "Is Paul Hanson there?"

"No, he isn't," the girl answered. "May I leave a message?"

"No," Abbie said quickly, and hung up. She was still ashamed of being married and involved with another man. It was a feeling she couldn't discard easily, although she knew Arthur had forced her into that position. She was still in the habit of telling the servants that she would answer the telephone whenever she expected Paul to call her. She realized she was being foolish; the servants were probably aware of what was going on.

Abbie was in her bedroom reading a book when Arthur came home that evening. She knew he was in a foul mood; he was slamming doors and making noise all over the house. The long halls in the mansion tended to reverberate with any sound. She could hear Arthur fumbling around in the bar and the clinking of bottles. He probably wanted attention, she thought.

At length, he sauntered into her room, a drink in one hand and some newspapers in the other and glared at her hotly. She pretended to be engrossed in her book.

"Interesting book?" he asked with acid sarcasm.

She didn't answer.

"I've been doing some rather absorbing reading myself. Want to have a look?" He hurled the newspapers and magazine at her.

Abbie angrily closed her book.

"What's the matter with you?" she cried.

"Go on; pick them up and take a look at them."

She gritted her teeth, gathered up the papers and started leafing through them. The articles he wanted her to read were circled in black ink.

She felt repulsed. She didn't know what to think or say. If Arthur didn't make her situation as impossible as he could, the rest of the world did. She felt too miserable to shed tears.

"Maybe you don't give a damn that everyone thinks you're a harlot," Shore said. "But how dare you drag my name through the mud with you? Brazenly parading your affair around in public for everyone to see!"

He hovered over her menacingly.

Suddenly, the telephone rang. They looked at each other.

"Don't answer that phone!" Shore yelled. Blanche, who was out in the hall, ready to pick up the receiver, scurried away like a frightened squirrel.

"I have had more pitying looks today than I can stand!" Shore hollered.

More than with Selena? Abbie was tempted to ask but stopped herself. How ironical that Arthur Shore, the victimizer, somehow always appeared to be the victim! Abbie knew well that everyone's sympathy was probably with him. They thought Arthur Shore a devoted, middle-aged husband who adored his young wife, and Monica Dane an ungrateful, spoiled little minx who spent her husband's money and spat in his face by seeing other men. Now she understood why Claire hadn't called that morning. The ladies had probably discussed the situation at lunch.

"I'm expecting David Oakley will probably want to talk the matter over with me," Shore said. "It's a disgrace for the studio as well."

Abbie said nothing.

"I've already decided how to minimize some of the injury," he said, more calmly. Evidently he had just gotten one of his brainstorms. "You are going to call Pattie Grey and write an open letter for her column, defending yourself and stating that all these accusations are lies and vicious slander. You and Paul Hanson are merely friends —you were seen together discussing plans for a movie."

"What movie?" Abbie asked, unable to resist. "*Anna Karenina?*"

"That's enough of that!" Shore said. "You will do what I say! You are going to denounce this filth for my sake!"

"It's going to give the gossip more attention if I do that," Abbie said. "That garbage isn't worth getting upset about."

"It is if a person has any pride!" Shore said. "My reputation has been blameless in this town, and I intend to keep it that way. You write the open letter—or I will. But the contents of mine would be markedly different than yours. If I let the world know that Paul Hanson is a jailbird on top of being a gigolo—"

"How dare you!" Abbie screamed. "A gigolo! Why, you rotten-minded—"

Shore raised his voice. "If I told the world about Hanson's prison record in the heat of this scandal, there'd be no mercy! He'd be fried alive! I suggest you write that letter—I think you'd prefer it to mine."

"This is asinine!" Abbie said.

"So is your behavior!" Shore told her. "Your evening's work is cut out for you. I'm going to come back at nine and see what you've written. You have two hours to bail yourself out. Now get yourself a pen and some stationery and start writing—immediately!" He left the room.

The idea of writing an open letter disgusted Abbie. It was like going for the bait the reporters were dangling in front of her. How they would relish the fact that they'd pressured a star into taking their nonsense seriously! And once she wrote the letter, who was to say if it would stop there? She might be making herself an open target for any idiot who wanted to make a name for himself by attacking her. She sighed. She had to do it. She had no other alternative.

She went to her desk and took out a pen and a few sheets of monogrammed paper. How she wished she could speak to Paul! Poor darling, he had been hurt by those vicious jibes too, probably even more than she had. After all, his position with Century could be threatened. Oakley prided himself on running a respectable studio. She had to write this letter to spare Paul from further harm. If only she could tell him that, before he stumbled across it in Pattie Grey's column. It might appear to him as if she was denying their love.

She sat down with the blank sheet of paper in front of her, feeling like she was in school again, faced with a boring essay to write. Presently, the words came to her.

Dear Pattie:

I would like to take this opportunity to condemn the malicious cycle of Hollywood gossip. It causes heartbreak, ruins careers, and destroys the faith that husband and wife should have in one another.

There has recently been some vicious slander directed at me, linking me romantically with a noted young director. I understand how this gossip started. I have been thinking about returning to the screen, and this director and I met strictly as business acquaintances.

It is not unusual for people discussing business ventures to meet over lunch rather than in an office. Executives sign deals over cocktails all the time. However, when the people involved are a man and a woman, suddenly all sorts of insinuations crop up.

I don't know the people who have written these dreadfully cruel articles about me, but apparently they are untalented journalists who must manufacture gossip and untruths to sell stories.

Thank you for allowing me the chance to speak my mind, Pattie. Perhaps this letter will encourage other stars who feel their reputations have been maligned to speak out and defend themselves.

> Sincerely,
> Monica Dane

"That should satisfy everyone," Abbie thought. And what a first for Pattie—a star using her column to lambast her competitors!

Abbie left her room with the letter. She glanced at her wall clock on the way out. It was seven thirty. She'd completed the chore in a half hour. She descended the stairs.

Arthur was in the living room.

"I'm done," she said curtly. She deposited the letter in his lap, then marched upstairs again, and retreated to her room. If only he would leave so she could get in touch with Paul. Arthur had refused to install a telephone in her room, so she could only place private calls when he was out of the house.

She heard the telephone downstairs ring. Someone answered it. Blanche came up and met Abbie at the top of the stairs.

"Telephone call for you, Madame," she said.

Abbie went down to answer it. Had her letter soothed Arthur enough that he would let her speak to Paul?

"Monica, dear, I just had to call you to find out how you were!" It was Claire Jameson, her voice dripping sympathy.

"I'm just fine, Claire," Abbie said calmly. "Considering."

"I read that horrible slander about you and Paul Hanson, and I just didn't have the heart to call you until now. All of us sympathize with you completely, dear, and we don't believe a word of it. I just had to call to tell you that."

"How sweet of you," Abbie replied.

"Poor Arthur—I can just imagine how upset it must have made him."

"Well, why don't I let him tell you himself?" Abbie took the receiver from her ear and called out. "Arthur! Would you come here a moment? Claire wants to ask you something."

On the other end, Claire was sputtering. "Monica— please, it's not necessary! I mean—"

"Here he is, Claire."

Arthur got on the line. "Hello?" he said.

Abbie walked into the living room, half-listening to Arthur. Evidently, the tone of the conversation had changed. Arthur sounded congenial and pleasantly involved in some small talk—probably Claire had changed the topic to the weather.

The gall of that woman, calling out of morbid curiosity! She was probably hoping that Abbie would break down and pour her heart out, so she could tell the other women all the details.

Arthur hung up, and said, "I don't know why Claire Jameson wanted to speak to me. She had nothing to say."

"I hope you're satisfied with the letter," Abbie said.

"Not quite," he told her. "I've added something."

He handed the note back to her, and she saw that a few more lines had been added to the closing paragraph.

I was especially unhappy about the harm that was done my husband. He was wonderful about it, comforted me and said it didn't matter.

Abbie felt sick. She handed it back to him without a word.

"I'm going to call Pattie Grey now and take this over to her later," Shore said. "I want it in the morning paper."

Abbie went upstairs to her room and lay down on the bed. She heard Arthur speaking to Pattie on the telephone downstairs. Maybe he'd leave soon, if only for a short while. It would be time enough to reach Paul and tell him how much she loved and needed him.

Abbie concentrated on every sound coming from the living room downstairs. She heard Arthur replace the receiver, then open the coat closet. He said something to Blanche, and then the front door slammed.

Abbie quickly ran downstairs. She picked up the phone and dialed Paul's number.

"Hello?"

His voice immediately filled her with new hope, new life. "Hello, Paul, darling!"

"Oh, Monica, I've been trying to reach you all night!"

"I know, Paul. Arthur wouldn't answer the phone."

"Monica, he hasn't hurt you—he hasn't threatened you in any way?"

"Oh no, no. I'm all right. He just made me write a ridiculous open letter saying the gossip wasn't true."

"Oh, Monica, why did you do it? I don't give a damn what other people think!"

"No, Paul, it does mean something. Think of your work at the studio, your professional reputation."

"Monica, I don't care! Things like that are whispered about everyone."

"Yes, Paul," Abbie said, sadly. "But in our case, it happens to be true."

"I'm not ashamed," Paul said. "I know we're right! Monica, I couldn't live without you!"

"Nor I you," Abbie said. "Paul, you're more important to me than anything else!"

"That's why those fools' opinions shouldn't matter to us."

"But they count, Paul. What if David Oakley took that gossip seriously? He could fire you!"

"No, Monica—when it comes to business, Oakley puts his personal morality second. He knows I'm talented and he needs me."

"Oh, Paul, I really can't stay on much longer. Arthur went out for a while, but he'll be back soon."

"What does that matter? Monica, I thought I'd set him straight. Why do you still let him threaten you?"

"I'm sorry, dear. It's just so awkward when he's around, and I don't like him listening in on the most precious part of my life."

"How are your houseguests?" Paul asked, wisely. Abbie could tell that he knew she had been lying. Still, he was too kind to reprimand her.

"They're leaving soon," she told him.

"I hope so," he said. "I'm dying to see you."

"So am I, Paul, so am I!"

Chapter 32

*A*BBIE's open letter appeared in Pattie Grey's column the next day, and the public reaction to it was very favorable. People admired Abbie's courage and integrity and tended to believe her side of the story.

Claire Jameson called Abbie and gushed over the brilliant way she'd defended herself. She insisted that Abbie join the ladies for lunch, a sign that Abbie had won her way back into their good graces.

At lunch, no reference was made to the recent gossip or Pattie Grey's column that morning. The ladies seemed a bit too deliberate in the way they steered the conversation to safe subjects, such as baby names that Lorraine was thinking of.

"I've seriously been considering Chandra for a girl," Lorraine said. "It's Sanskrit. It means 'she outshines the stars.' "

"Darling, don't you think that's a bit much?" Claire said, disapprovingly. "I'm telling you, dear, exotic names are dead. How about Ann or Joan or Jean? They're simple and classic. Always fashionable."

"But those are so simple, they're dull!" Lorraine fretted. "I want something more exciting than Joan!"

"I love the name Olivia," Victoria Bruner said. "My cousin just named her daughter that."

"But I want a name no one's *ever* used before," Lorraine said, like an author thinking up a title for a book.

"Then you'll just have to invent a name," Claire said, brusquely.

"What if it's a boy?" Abbie asked.

"Lewis, Jr.," Lorraine said.

The ladies were as gracious as ever toward Abbie, but the atmosphere had changed subtly. She was sure they didn't believe the letter she'd written for the newspaper, though she knew they were not morally offended by her affair. It was common but unspoken knowledge that Lorraine had once been involved with a young leading man, and the year before, there had been unvoiced suspicions that Victoria was carrying on with her tennis instructor.

But the ladies did object to Abbie's indiscretion. She had handled her affair gracelessly and had been caught. Such carelessness diminished her in their eyes. Of course she would still be a social ruler and a Queen Bee, but she had her husband's wealth and position to thank for that.

At the studio that day, Shore was offered his share of supportive smiles. In a gesture of camaraderie, David Oakley called Shore into his office and lauded his wife for having the character to deny such slander. Shore's public image was as sterling and untarnished as ever.

Paul Hanson, on the other hand, suffered a rather disconcerting experience that afternoon.

He went into Oakley's office with an envelope stuffed with clippings about the talking pictures that a budding movie company, Standard Productions, was planning to make, but instead of accepting the material and promising to give it to Oakley as she always did, the secretary said, "Mr. Hanson, Mr. Oakley says it won't be necessary for you to leave any more of these reports with him. He's made up his mind. He's going to stick by Arthur Shore's opinion until he sees *The Jazz Singer*."

"Can I talk to him?" Paul said, surprised.

The secretary sighed heavily, got up and knocked at Oakley's door. Oakley popped his head out.

"Hello, Paul," he said. "What can I do for you?"

"Your secretary told me you don't want to see any more of the reports I've been bringing you."

"I'm afraid that's so, Paul. Arthur's just convinced me to wait. What else can I tell you?" he said, smiling.

"Mr. Oakley, forgive me for speaking so plainly, but as the owner of this studio, I think you ought to read whatever literature there is about new developments in the film industry. I think it's your duty."

"Paul, I hired you as a director, and I wish you'd remember that," Oakley said. "I don't know how you've gotten it into your head that you're my advisor, but you're not. Paul, you've been pretty blunt with me, but I'll be even more blunt. I know what I'm doing and I don't need your advice. You're a fine director, the best there is, and you know I want you to keep working for me, but please don't venture into areas where your services aren't wanted. Good day, Paul."

Oakley closed the door of his office. Paul stood there, staring.

"Anything else, Mr. Hanson?" the secretary asked triumphantly.

"No, no, nothing," Paul said, dazed.

He turned to leave, then changed his mind.

"Wait a minute, there is something," he said, suddenly.

"Yes?"

He put the envelope in front of her.

"Take this and put it in the circular file," he told her.

"What's that?" she asked.

"The trash can! And you'll learn to type faster if you're smart! When all these silent movie empires go down the drain, there's going to be a lot of competition for jobs at Warners!"

He stormed out of the office, leaving the girl with her mouth wide open.

Paul was stunned by Oakley's attitude. He couldn't understand it. Was the man so terrified of change that he'd rather risk ruining Century than take a chance on talking pictures?

Paul almost asked Lewis Shelby to join him for a drink, but changed his mind. The only person he really wanted to see was Abbie. He was desperate for her gentleness, her sweet manner.

He was tempted to drive over straight from the studio, but he didn't want to startle her. Shore might be there, and he wanted to spare her another traumatic scene. He wondered why she had invented the story about houseguests? She was so vulnerable and delicate, such an easy target for Shore's ruthlessness.

Paul called her from his office.

"Monica, can I please come over and see you?" he pleaded. "I've got to talk to you!"

Abbie had just returned from lunch. It was three thirty. Arthur would be home for dinner in another hour and a half.

"Oh Paul, I don't know, I—"

"Monica, I've really got to talk to you."

"What is it, Paul? Is something wrong?"

"Yes, actually there is."

"What, Paul?" she asked, frightened. "Is it what the papers said about us?"

"No, no. Nothing to do with that."

Abbie instantly felt relieved.

"Please, Monica," Paul said. "I'd rather tell you in person."

"All right, dear. Come quickly."

Paul hung up, went to the studio parking lot and got his car.

When he reached the Shore estate, Abbie was waiting for him in front of the house, wearing a white sundress. He hadn't seen her for nearly a week, and she looked like a dream come true.

She got into the car and they embraced. Abbie kissed his face all over; his ruddy complexion was so warm and smooth. He always looked as if he'd spent the day outdoors. She held him close, realizing how much she had yearned to be with him.

"I'd almost forgotten how lovely you are," he told her, admiring her porcelain skin and enormous dark-blue eyes.

They drove to his bungalow, even though they knew the danger of someone spotting them. But no place was any safer than another. The sight of the two of them was enough to cause stares and whispers anywhere in town.

Once inside, Paul started making coffee for the two of them.

"What is it, Paul?" Abbie asked. "What you had to tell me about? You seemed so upset."

"Oakley seems to have completely rejected my opinions about talking pictures. He just refuses to hear me out or discuss it any further. His whole attitude changed overnight."

"Maybe he's just stubborn," Abbie said. "You know, a gentleman of the old school."

"It might be my imagination, but he seems to have cooled toward me. I don't know—maybe, I'm taking the whole thing too personally."

"He's a fool," Abbie said.

"I just can't figure out what would make him change so suddenly."

Abbie looked at Paul, but said nothing. She suspected Oakley had turned against him because of their love affair. David Oakley was fifty and his wife was twenty-five. The rumors had intensified his sympathy for Arthur and had suddenly made him see Paul as a threat; a younger, more desirable man.

"What is it, dear?" Paul said to Abbie. "You look so sad."

"I'm just sorry that you're unhappy," she told him.

Paul smiled. "I'm not now. Not with you here. Do you know you make life an absolute joy for me?"

"In spite of everything?" Abbie asked.

"In spite of everything," Paul told her.

He came forward and embraced her gently, firmly, pressing his lean, tall body against hers.

She would tell Shore she'd been shopping. She would tell him something, but she would not give up this time with Paul for anyone or anything.

Chapter 33

*T*HE *Jazz Singer* would have its world premiere at the Warners theater in New York on October 6, 1927, and Century sent several representatives to attend the opening.

At the studio, little reference was made to *The Jazz Singer,* but there was a fever in the air. As Paul intimated to Lewis Shelby, although the bigwigs at Century appeared unruffled in public, they were probably sweating it out behind closed doors.

Both Paul and Lewis had wanted to go to New York for the opening, but Paul couldn't afford to take time off from the film he was working on, and Lewis was busy attending to his wife and new daughter, Raina Simone. Lorraine's most pressing headache since Raina's birth was how to handle the awkwardness of inviting Mr. and Mrs. Arthur Shore and Paul Hanson to the baby's christening.

"If only she could have had an affair with someone at Paramount," Lorraine moaned.

"That's quite enough," Lewis told her.

Paul solved Lorraine's problem by refusing the invitation, inventing an excuse about visiting his ailing sister in Pomona. Paul looked for any excuse to avoid unnecessary contact with Oakley and Shore; having to associate with them at the studio was more than enough.

Raina's christening was just two days before the premiere of *The Jazz Singer* and, though Lorraine insisted that the party in honor of her new baby was not the place to discuss studio business, a few of the men had to talk about the new movie.

"I think Warners is going to have the flop of the century on its hands," was Shore's opinion.

Oakley nodded in agreement.

As it turned out, both of them were dead wrong. *The Jazz Singer* opened to critical acclaim and enthusiastic public response. The film ushered in a new age: motion pictures would never be the same again.

Amazingly enough, the major studios were still trying to deny the success of talking pictures, frightened of the enormous amounts of money involved. With movie-goers flocking to see *The Jazz Singer* in record numbers, Oakley was finally forced to call an emergency conference.

"All right, gentlemen," Oakley said. "We're at an important crossroad—that is, does Century take a shot at talkies or don't we?"

Shore immediately spoke up. "I still say we should proceed with caution, the way Schenck and Mayer are doing. Fox and MGM haven't installed any sound equipment in their studios simply because one talking picture got some attention. I think it's merely a novelty. Anyway, I refuse to give my approval to a venture that would involve spending millions of dollars when we're not sure whether talkies will last or not."

"What do you want?" Paul blurted out. "A chorus of angels to tell you? The handwriting is on the wall—can't you see that?"

Shore's face turned crimson. "I will close with this quote," he said, glaring at Paul. "The world's greatest silent screen actor, Mr. Charles Chaplin, said: 'People

don't want their entertainment splitting their eardrums
—silents are a tranquil haven in a chaotic world.' "

The men's pleased expressions approved Shore's response. Paul suspected it was not necessarily Charlie
Chaplin's aesthetic viewpoint that had swayed them.
Perhaps it was even more than a question of money; it
was politics and principles. The industry czars did not
want their kingdoms toppled by the new breed of filmmakers. They would rather go down struggling than
yield to the demands of the young men like Hanson
who worked for them and now challenged their authority.

Paul did not leave the meeting angry. He was sad,
disillusioned, and frustrated. He felt himself to be one
of the few vital parts of a dying organism. He didn't have
the heart to continue the movie he was working on; it
seemed a fruitless venture. He was aching to learn how
to direct a talking picture and there wasn't a chance of
that at Century.

Instead of returning to his office, he drove over to
Annie O'Days, his favorite "speak." Unlike most cold,
shabby speakeasies, Annie's was a warm, friendly looking
place, resembling someone's living room. The cozy atmosphere induced the clientele to stay for hours, and
the place was always crowded with customers, which included many directors and producers.

Paul sat down with his drink at his usual table in the
corner. Sean McCracken, a director with Preferred Pictures, was sitting with a noisy group in the middle of the
room. He waved wildly at Paul and, when Paul waved
back, Sean got up from his chair and pushed his way
through the crowd to his table.

"Hey, Paul," McCracken said, brightly. "Let me buy
you a drink! What are you having?" McCracken was a

chubby, blond fellow who looked much younger than his thirty years.

"Not much fun," Paul answered glumly.

Sean sat down opposite him. "What's the trouble, old man?"

"I don't know what the situation's like at Preferred, but—"

"Well, neither do I, chum, because I don't work there anymore."

"You don't?" Paul asked. "Since when?"

"Since about three months ago. I'm with Standard Productions now."

"Really? How is it?"

"Great! Couldn't be happier. Of course, the pay's nothing to speak of. It's a new company—"

"What made you leave Preferred?"

"Let's just call it a personality clash and leave it at that," Sean answered.

Paul smiled. "I think I understand."

"But tell me, are you having troubles at Century?"

Paul grinned. "Let's just call it a personality clash and leave it at that."

McCracken laughed. "Whose personality, Paul? Shore's or Oakley's?"

"Both of them. I'm outnumbered. They don't want to hear about talking pictures."

McCracken shook his head. "Sounds familiar. But I'm surprised you don't have more influence with them. After all, you are one of the industry's wonder boys. I would think they'd listen to you."

"No," Paul said. "Trying to talk to them is a waste of time. I just feel helpless."

"Have you considered leaving?" McCracken asked. "I'm sure other studios would come begging if they knew you were unhappy at Century."

"I'm under contract until 1929. Plus I'm in the middle of shooting a picture."

"Look, with your reputation, any studio you went to would stand behind you. Between the two of us, Standard would leap for joy if you ever came to work there."

Paul stared at McCracken. "They would, huh?"

"Sure. The only reason they haven't made you an offer is because they think they can't afford you. And, hell, I guess they assumed you were happy at Century."

"I don't care about money," Paul said. "All I ask is freedom to do the sort of projects I've always wanted to, not just properties that will sell."

"How about if I set something up for you with Mike Jacoby? He's creative head of Standard."

"Could you do that, Sean?" Paul asked.

"Sure, I'll talk to him tomorrow, then call you back."

"Thanks, Sean," Paul said, beaming. "I really appreciate it!"

The next morning Sean reached Paul at his office.

"Hi, Sean," Paul said over the phone. "What's the good word?"

"Jacoby wants to meet with you as soon as possible," Sean said, excitedly. "His eyes lit up when I told him you were interested in working for Standard."

"Thanks a million, Sean," Paul said.

"For what?" Sean answered. "I think Jacoby's going to give me a raise for nabbing you!"

After hanging up, Paul called Jacoby and arranged an appointment for two o'clock that day.

Paul went through the motions of shooting his picture that morning, but his interest was nil. It wasn't only because of recent developments with Standard. As far as he was concerned, he was no longer connected with Century and hadn't been for some time.

251

That afternoon he drove over to Standard Studios, a small group of neat, white buildings that reminded him of a hospital.

A harried receptionist at the front office directed him to Mike Jacoby. It was obvious that the company was still in the process of setting up. Stacks of papers, documents, and manuscripts covered the tables and spilled over onto the floors in Jacoby's office. The room was being painted, and movers and various studio staff kept filing in and out. All the noise and motion was an exciting contrast to Shore and Oakley's cryptlike dens.

There was no secretary, but Paul figured Jacoby was the man yelling into the telephone in the center of the room. He was tall and husky, like a boxer, in his early thirties, with a round, good-natured face.

"I mean it!" he yelled. "I ordered those bookcases a month ago, and they still haven't arrived! The situation here is desperate! You get a move on or we'll never do business with you people again. And I'll spread it around what a lousy company you really are!"

He hung up and sighed.

Paul approached him hesitantly. "Excuse me, are you Mike Jacoby?"

Jacoby looked at Paul and a smile dawned on his face. "Paul Hanson?"

Paul nodded and they shook hands. They were immediately comfortable with each other. Jacoby removed a stack of papers from the chair next to his desk and asked Paul to sit down.

"I'm awfully sorry," he said. "We're still in the process of settling in, and when the phone company doesn't make things tough, the movers do."

"I know the feeling," Paul sympathized.

"Plus my secretary got married over the weekend, and I haven't had time to replace her yet." Jacoby shook his head. "I wish she'd given me some warning, but you know how these things are. She just decided to elope. I think that girl's seen too many movies."

Both men laughed.

"Can I offer you a drink?" Jacoby asked. He held up a thermos bottle filled with gin.

"No thanks," Paul said.

Jacoby poured himself a shot. "Sean told me you might consider working for us."

"Yes, I'd like to," Paul said.

"And we'd be honored. I'm afraid we couldn't pay you what you're making now."

"That's not important," Paul said. "But there's something you should know—I'm under contract to Century for another two years."

"No problem," Jacoby said. "Standard could buy it up."

"You'd do that for me?" Paul said, astonished.

"If we have to, sure," Jacoby told him. "You're a very valuable man, Mr. Hanson."

"When could I start working here?" Paul asked.

"Whenever you like," Mike told him. "I'm going to call our lawyers and have them prepare a contract for you, also a letter negotiating with Century about your contract. I hope *their* secretaries are still around."

They laughed again and shook hands. Paul bade Mike goodbye and drove back to his office. There was a lot of business he had to attend to yet.

"Charlene?" he told his secretary as soon as he got back. "Would you take a letter, please?"

"Certainly, Mr. Hanson," the girl said. She followed him into his office, holding a notebook and pen.

Paul leaned back in his chair and started dictating, "This is a memo to Mr. David Oakley, dated October 30,

1927 . . . Dear Mr. Oakley, the following is a letter of resignation—"

Charlene looked up, startled. "Mr. Hanson!" she cried.

He gently silenced her and continued, "Conditions at Century have become intolerable for me. I have no artistic freedom and my ideas are not taken seriously. The tension between myself and members of your staff is another source of frustration. To sum up, the whole atmosphere at Century is stifling my creativity. I think it best for all parties concerned that the studio and I part company. I wish you the best in all future endeavors. Sincerely, Paul Hanson."

The girl looked at him, questioningly.

"Charlene, please hand deliver this, immediately."

"Yes, Mr. Hanson," she said.

After she left, Paul could not help smiling. He would have enjoyed seeing the look on Oakley's face when he read the letter.

Chapter 34

*D*AVID Oakley exploded when he read Paul's letter of resignation the first thing the next morning. He tried to get in touch with Paul, but Paul was unavailable.

That afternoon a letter arrived from Widland and Kean, Attorneys-at-Law. They represented Standard Productions and offered to meet with Century's lawyers about the possibility of buying Paul's contract. Oakley immediately called Arthur Shore and Lewis Shelby in to discuss the matter.

"He's not going to get away with this," Shore said with relish.

"I'm sorry," Shelby said, "but I can see Paul's side of the story, too. He is hot to try talking pictures and we won't let him. In fact, he reacted just the way I'd figured he would."

"Yes, he has," Shore said. "I've always known Paul Hanson was an irresponsible hothead, with no sense of duty or loyalty."

Shelby grimaced, and shook his head.

Oakley shrugged. "I don't know what to say. Paul's a talented man with no respect for anyone else's opinion. I guess the only way I could have kept him was by letting him run the studio." Oakley sighed. "Well, I suppose we should call Standard and start negotiating a price for his contract."

"Frankly David, I don't think we should let them buy it up," said Shore. "We'll be sacrificing a principle if we give in so easily to their requests."

"What principle?" Shelby demanded, irritated with both Oakley and Shore.

"Honor!" Shore barked. "I don't want people to think that I will sell out at the drop of a hat! I don't want them to feel that Century has a price, just like everyone else! We'll be losing face if we give Hanson his way. After all, there are a number of things to consider. What's to stop Joe Lamm or Ken Bruner from going to another studio without a second thought?"

"You have a point," Oakley conceded.

"What are you proposing, Arthur?" Lewis Shelby asked suspiciously.

"I think we ought to sue Paul Hanson for breaking his contract," Shore said.

Shelby threw up his hands. "I don't believe this!"

"Why not?" Shore demurred. "It's done all the time."

"That is a bit strong, Arthur," Oakley said hesitantly.

"Legally, we're in the right," Shore said. "The cards are all stacked against Hanson. And don't forget—Hanson is leaving Century high and dry in the middle of a picture. He's not even going to complete it; that's rubbing salt in the wound."

"Leaving Century!" Shelby cried, unable to endure any more. "If you ask me he's been driven away! You two have been resentful of Paul ever since...."

"Go ahead, Lewis," Shore said calmly.

"Oh, what's the use? I'm sorry Dave, but if you carry this suit through I don't care what you call it—as far as I'm concerned, it's a personal vendetta against Paul Hanson!"

"That's quite enough!" Oakley said, outraged. Shelby had never spoken to him that bluntly before. It was proof that Paul's rebellious attitude was contagious. Perhaps Shore was right; he had to exercise some power before his whole studio started rebelling.

"Lewis, I appreciate your opinion," Oakley said in a tone of dismissal. "Thank you."

"You're welcome," Shelby said tersely. He left the room.

"How much do you think we should ask for damages?" Oakley asked Shore.

"A quarter of a million," Shore told him.

Oakley whistled. "That's awfully steep."

"I think we should ask that much. It's doubtful we'll get all of it, but such an action will certainly warn others against taking their contracts lightly. Objectively, David, Hanson has it coming. Skipping out on Century this way is a slap in the face, a betrayal of the highest order. I don't know how you could let him get away with it and keep your self-respect."

Oakley quietly clenched and unclenched his fists. "You're right, Arthur. You're absolutely right."

"I'm going to phone our lawyers immediately," Shore said. "I'm going to show Hanson he doesn't have the market cornered where surprises are concerned."

Both men laughed.

Shore returned to his office, called Century's lawyers and instructed them to inform Paul Hanson that David Oakley was suing him for breach of contract.

Then he left the studio, feeling keen and light. Let Hanson try to squirm out of this lawsuit; Century had him cornered.

Shore smiled to himself on the drive home; nothing gave him greater pleasure than having an enemy at his mercy. Hanson's only alternative would be to declare bankruptcy and subject himself to public humiliation.

Visions of courtroom scenes and newspaper headlines proclaiming Hanson's ruin flooded Shore's mind.

At home, the air was rich with the aroma of boeuf bourguignon.

"Smells delicious," Shore complimented Leona.

"Why thank you, Sir," she said timidly.

"Is my wife around?"

"Outside," Leona told him. "Working in her garden."

"Fine," Shore said. "I have something very interesting to tell her."

Shore strode outside and spotted Abbie pruning her rose bushes.

"Well, aren't you a sight out of *Vanity Fair?*" he sneered. "The pretty young matron puttering around her garden."

Abbie froze at the sound of his voice.

"Heard anything from Lochinvar lately?" Shore asked.

Abbie didn't answer. When she'd returned home from lunch that afternoon, Leona told her that Paul had phoned, but she hadn't been able to reach him.

"He's going to have quite a bit to tell you when you speak to each other again," Shore teased.

"Why don't you stop talking in riddles and say what you want to!" Abbie cried.

"All right, my dear, we'll take it in steps so you understand everything. Number one, Paul Hanson is no longer working for Century. Number two, Century is suing him for breach of contract."

Abbie's jaw dropped. "What the devil do you mean?"

Shore shook his head. "I really tried to make it as simple as possible for you, but we'll do it one more time. Now listen carefully, it isn't hard to understand...."

"Oh, stop it!" Abbie cried. "When did all of this happen?"

"Within the last twenty-four hours. Hanson announced he was leaving for Standard Productions and today Dave Oakley and I decided to sue him for a quarter of a million dollars."

"A quarter of a million dollars! Are you mad?"

"On the contrary, it's one of the sanest decisions the studio has ever made. Allowing Hanson to get away with such nonsense would have been insanity."

"You slimy, low-down bastard!" Abbie screamed. "It has nothing to do with the studio! You want to destroy Paul, and you'll use any means you can find!"

She started to cry. "You're vicious and wretched! I hate you!"

"That is quite enough!" Shore bellowed. "You shut your mouth, you filthy bitch, before you get yourself into serious trouble. I shouldn't have to tell you that your well-being depends entirely on my kindness."

Abbie sobbed and said nothing.

"Now, go in and prepare for dinner."

"I'm not hungry," she said.

He shrugged. "Suit yourself."

Abbie ran in ahead of him and went directly to her room. She felt ill with misery and helpless to do anything. Her love for Paul was ruining his life. If she gave Paul up completely, she wondered, would Shore leave him alone? Would she be able to be that brave, that unselfish? Paul was the source of everything good and beautiful in her life.

She walked downstairs somberly, prepared to bargain with Shore. He was sitting in the dining room, eating supper.

"This is delicious, Monica," he commented when he saw her. "You don't know what you're missing."

"If I stop seeing Paul Hanson, if I keep him out of my life completely, will you drop the lawsuit?" she asked quietly.

"You really love him, don't you? His welfare is at the top of your list of priorities. Aren't you noble, Monica," he said. "I guess I should be moved, but I'm not."

"I mean it, Arthur," Abbie said. "If I cut off all contact with Paul, will you withdraw the lawsuit and leave him alone?"

"It's a thought," he said, smiling.

"I want something more definite than that," Abbie said.

"I'll have to think this over," Shore told her playfully.

Abbie returned to her room, weary and dispirited. She fell asleep trying to think how she and Paul could escape the traps Arthur Shore had set for them.

Chapter 35

$\mathcal{A}$BBIE was too depressed to join her group for lunch the next day. She told Claire that she was coming down with a cold, and went back to bed after breakfast, too miserable to face the world. She slept until one that afternoon then drifted downstairs for coffee.

"Mr. Hanson called before, Madame," Blanche said. "I didn't want to wake you. He said he'd be over at three."

"Thank you, Blanche," said Abbie. She was anxious to see Paul, but dreaded his news—he must have heard from Century's lawyers by now.

Abbie showered and dressed, then waited in the living room, trying to imagine his state of mind.

The doorbell rang.

"I'll answer it, Blanche," Abbie called to the maid.

As soon as she opened the door, Paul smiled and embraced her. He looked cheerful, but strained.

"Come in, Paul." She led him into a small parlor adjacent to the dining room. They sat down and she searched his face anxiously.

"What is it, darling?" Paul said.

"Oh, Paul, Arthur told me everything!"

"I'm not worried, Monica. I'm really not."

"How can that be possible? Paul, you're in serious

261

trouble—why did you put yourself in this position? Why didn't you tell me you were leaving Century?"

"It all happened so fast—I didn't plan on quitting. The opportunity just arose. And besides," he admitted. "I was afraid you might try to talk me out of it. I know Arthur still bullies you."

"Paul, a quarter of a million dollars!" Abbie said, staggered.

Paul shook his head. "It's outrageous. That's what my lawyer, Steve Widland, said. I haven't got that kind of money."

"What are you going to do?"

"I'm lucky. I've got friends, and I've got great lawyers. We've been discussing the suit all morning; that's why I look so disheveled. They've been looking through my contract for clauses and planning strategy. They're confident that I've got a good defense."

"And what's that?" Abbie asked dubiously.

"The studio didn't fulfill its obligation with regard to my creative potential. They didn't keep their end of the bargain. Also, we think that as the silents lose more and more ground, my case will be stronger."

"What do you mean?" Abbie asked.

"I'm getting out of Century to save myself, to salvage my career. It's self-protection," he said. "Also by any count, the amount of money Century is asking for is excessive. It hurts their case. They look too greedy. The only real point they have is that I skipped out in the middle of shooting a picture for them. But I already told Widland I'd be willing to spend another two or three weeks finishing it. Anyway, Monica, these suits can drag on for years, and who knows what can happen until then? I can't let the suit rule my life. How have you been, darling? I've missed you so much."

"For God's sake, Paul, you just can't move onto

another subject like we were discussing a parking ticket! How can you dismiss it so easily?"

"Because I know I'm right," Paul said. "If I wasn't sure of that, of course I'd worry. If I was drumming up a petty lawsuit out of sheer malevolence the way Century is, I'd be plenty worried. Besides, I'm not afraid of courtrooms the way some people are."

Abbie lowered her head, ashamed.

"I'm sorry, dear," Paul said. "I didn't mean that."

"It's all right," she whispered.

She turned her head and looked out the window. Like many fine directors, Paul was a skilled actor. She couldn't believe he wasn't upset over the lawsuit. Century had a tangible document, a legal contract to hang their case on. Paul was pretending to be calm for her sake. She loved him for it, but she hated the position their love affair had put him in. They were both under Arthur Shore's heel and might remain there forever.

She inhaled sharply. "Paul," she said. "I don't think we should see each other anymore."

He groaned. "Monica, for God's sake! Has this upset you so much that—"

"Yes it has!" she shrieked, pretending hysteria. "Everything about our affair upsets me! The way we meet, the awful publicity, this new mess! My nerves just can't take anymore—it's not worth it!"

Paul looked at her. "Just tell me you don't love me, and you'll never see me again."

She hesitated. "I can't, darling," she said. "I can't do that!" She burst into tears and put her arms around him.

"Monica, why?"

"Because it's ruining your life. All I bring you is misery."

"Monica, nothing could be farther from the truth and you know it. You thought that if we stopped seeing each other, Shore would be persuaded to withdraw that ridiculous lawsuit, didn't you?"

Abbie nodded, shamefaced.

"Monica, I think the business at the studio has nothing to do with our relationship. Shore is waging two wars against me. He wants to keep them separate, and he won't give either of them up."

"Everything just seems so useless," Abbie said, wearily.

"That's what he wants you to feel, Monica. When you succumb to despair, you're giving in to him. And, darling, I refuse to let that bastard beat us!"

"But what hope do we have?"

"I have you, Monica. That's enough reason for me to keep believing."

He held her close. "Now I want you to cheer up. Promise me."

"I do," she said, suddenly happy.

Chapter 36

*B*Y summer of that year, Paul had already completed his first film for Standard Productions, George Bernard Shaw's *Saint Joan*. Most new talkies, since the equipment was still rudimentary and the set was restricting, had the look and feel of photographed stage plays. Still, Paul had concentrated on creating new camera techniques to lend interest to the photography and work against these limitations. It had been extremely difficult. The actors, especially, had problems. They were silent film stars still adjusting to acting in talkies and no longer able to use space freely. Still, Paul's efforts were rewarded. *Saint Joan* was a critical and financial success and established him as a celebrated director in the new medium. He was busy looking for other properties, books and plays, that could be transferred to the screen.

He didn't trouble himself about the Century lawsuit. The case was still pending and by July 1928, Century was preoccupied with other things. Their procrastination had caught up with them. The public was completely captured by talking pictures, and almost any film with sound made money. Silents, no matter how good, were neglected. Warners and Standard had left Century far behind.

Abbie knew trouble was brewing from Shore's silent brooding. He no longer spoke to her at all. He came

265

home from the studio every night and immediately opened a bottle of scotch or bourbon. Sometimes, he wouldn't even touch his dinner. He would simply pour himself one drink after another, then put the bottle under his arm and take it up to his room. There, he would spend the night in solitude, dwelling on Century Studios and drinking.

The luncheons with Lorraine and Claire became somber affairs. The ladies continued to act lighthearted, but they reminded Abbie of royalty bravely facing exile. Finally, one day Lorraine levelled with the other ladies. That week she had purchased a jade necklace and earrings and Lewis had become upset for the first time in their married life.

"I'm not a money machine," he had told Lorraine. "Things are tough at the studio. You've got to understand that!"

Lorraine was shocked. He had never discussed the studio with her before. His work there was far too complicated for her to understand, or so he'd always claimed.

"Well, how am I supposed to know that, Lewis?" Lorraine cried. She couldn't bear it when he yelled at her. "You never tell me anything!"

"For the past five months, Century has lost business on its silent movies."

"Well, why didn't you change to talkies?" Lorraine asked.

"Arthur Shore prevented it," he answered. "Now the price of sound equipment is sky high because everyone's clamoring for it. And we've got to catch up with companies that are way ahead of us. It's going to be like resuscitating a dead man!"

When Lorraine related the incident to the group at

lunch, she tactfully didn't mention Shore's name, but kept giving Abbie peculiar looks.

More horror stories were anxiously whispered. Claire's husband's bankers had told him that they felt Century's stocks were insecure. He, too, had asked her to curb her spending habits at least temporarily. Indeed, that summer for the first time in the history of the movie colony, Lorraine and Claire gave no parties.

As the year progressed, movie studios tried to catch up with Warners and Standard by inserting snatches of hastily recorded dialogue into films that had already been shot as silents.

Movie companies waged war against each other. Paramount was so determined to get their talking pictures to theaters before MGM did, that they shot sound pictures at night on the sets reserved for silent movies during the day.

Silent stars who couldn't make the transition to sound were ruined. The most stunning failure was John Gilbert, the Great Lover of the Silent Screen, whose high-pitched voice didn't match his dark, masculine looks. Rumors spread that Louis B. Mayer had toyed with the microphone so Gilbert would record badly. He and Gilbert had had frequent run-ins and rather than pay Gilbert the phenomenal salary he was asking for, Mayer decided to short-circuit his career.

The microphone terrified all the silent stars. A person could have a perfectly nice voice, but the mike could convert it into a rasp or make it unbearably shrill. Beautiful Dolores Costello was "better seen than heard." Terra Lane's squeaky Minnie Mouse voice made a mockery of her soft, tender looks. Maura Wilder had to fade out for a while, since her heavy Brooklyn accent belied her sultry, sex-goddess image. Unfortunately, Century had waited too long to train stars like Maura to speak correctly. There was nothing for Maura to do but retire temporarily and pray there'd be a place for her in talking pictures when she was ready to return to the screen.

In the meantime, new stars had to be found whose voices were as beautiful as their faces and bodies, or at least moderately pleasant.

By the new year, Oakley had asked Lewis Shelby to work closely with Shore in trying to bring Century to its feet again. Shore and Shelby detested each other.

Shore's drinking grew steadily worse. As long as he kept it to himself, Abbie could handle the situation, but one evening his behavior became downright frightening. Abbie was in her room taking a nap, when she woke up to the sound of shattering glass.

Startled, she got up quickly and ran downstairs. On the floor was a pile of broken dishes and standing over them was Arthur Shore, raving drunk.

"I detest *chicken véronique!*" he raged at the cook. Poor Leona cowered on the other side of the room. Abbie was shocked. She had never seen him lose control of himself like this.

"And how have you been all day?" he turned to Abbie, reeling. "What did you and those other sows discuss at lunch today? I'm sure that she-devil, Lorraine, must have told you all the details."

"I don't know what you're talking about," Abbie said.

"I've been demoted!" Shore cried. "Voted out by the Board of Trustees—Shelby is now Production head! That worm, Oakley, called me in to tell me the news today. I think he and Shelby were plotting it all along. They said the stockholders blamed *me* for the state Century's in, and they wanted someone more competent to take over. Competent, ha! Lewis Shelby's as competent as a painter with no thumbs! I hope they all go to hell!"

Abbie kept silent.

"Oakley put me in charge of distribution. Distribution, God!" Shore sneered. "And to cap it off, they're dropping the lawsuit against Hanson—your lover! That shyster lawyer, Grossman, told them they've got other things to worry about, so they're letting Standard buy his contract. That ought to make your evening!"

Impassive, Abbie inwardly felt pleased and relieved.

Shore poured himself another drink. The gin dribbled over the sides of the glass as he drank. Abbie turned away in revulsion.

"And now I want to see how you spent your day," Shore said.

He grabbed Abbie by the arm and dragged her upstairs. Leona watched, her eyes huge.

"Show me what you bought. Let's see what finery you're going to drape yourself in now!" he shrieked.

He flung Abbie's clothes closets open and started flinging dresses and gowns out on the floor.

"Stop it, Arthur! What are you doing?" Abbie cried.

"I'll show you what I'm doing!"

He picked up one of her dresses and tore it down the middle. Then he grabbed others and ripped them with his hands and teeth.

"Stop it!" Abbie shrieked. "No, Arthur!"

He pushed her away, violently. She ran downstairs. Leona was in the living room, poised over the telephone with the receiver in her hand.

"Leona, what are you doing?" Abbie cried. "Who are you calling?"

"The police, Madame," Leona said, trembling slightly. "I thought he was hurting you."

Abbie was grateful that she'd caught Leona in time. In the state Arthur was in, he would yell everything he knew about her and Paul if provoked. Abbie gently took the receiver from the maid's hand and put it back in its cradle. She put her arm around Leona.

"Thank you for worrying about me, Leona, but he's just having a temper tantrum. He's been demoted. We'll just let him scream himself out." Abbie masked her own terror by soothing the maid. "Why don't you and I go for a drive?"

The maid nodded. They left the house and decided to go to the movies.

When they returned, the house was silent. Abbie tiptoed up to her room. Shore was on the floor, asleep, surrounded by the rags he'd made of Abbie's dresses.

Abbie retired to one of the guest rooms for the night.

The next day, Shore managed to rouse himself, shave, wash, get dressed, and leave for work. No one would ever have suspected that he had been a raging animal the night before.

Abbie herself felt unsettled. He had been completely irrational, uncontrollable, even dangerous. She no longer felt safe in the house. The situation kept growing worse instead of better.

The phone call from Claire did not come that day, and Abbie interpreted it to mean that the studio was blackballing her along with Arthur. She didn't really care. She had almost begun to like Lorraine and even Claire, but it was probably just because she had seen them so often. They had really been only fair-weather friends after all.

She knew that the demotion at Century was a personal defeat for Shore, but it did not really affect his financial position that much. Most of his money was tied up in stocks and corporations outside of the film industry. If he tried to get another job with a motion picture studio, he would probably have trouble, though. His fall at Cenfury had pretty much negated his talents as a movie executive.

The telephone rang. It was Paul.

"Hello angel," he said. His warm voice erased much of the ugliness of the night before. "I've got something very exciting to tell you."

"Yes I know, darling," Abbie said. "Arthur mentioned it. Century's dropped the lawsuit against you."

"No, Monica, not that," Paul said. "It's a present for you."

"Oh Paul, what?" Abbie felt drained, but feigned eagerness.

"I'm going to come over and tell you in person. Will you be home?"

"Yes, dear," she said. "Come quickly."

She went up to her room to see if there were any clothes to be salvaged from the debris. She looked through her torn, shredded satins, silks, and velvets. What a sad waste!

She went to her closet and found a pretty cotton print he had managed to pass over. By the time she was finished showering and dressing, Paul was downstairs waiting for her. They embraced.

"Now what is it you had to tell me?" Abbie asked, sitting next to him on the sofa.

"You have to guess what I bought for you. Or rather for us." He looked genuinely pleased.

"Paul, I haven't the faintest idea."

"The talking picture rights to *Madame Bovary!*"

"Oh, Paul, you know Arthur would never let me do it!"

"God, Monica, the way you let him bully you! And anyway, dear, what's to stop him? I mean, if he didn't know who was directing. His allegiance to Century? From what I hear, it would be a perfect way of getting back at them. Having his wife star in a picture for another studio and making that studio a fortune!"

Abbie had to smile in spite of herself. It was true. Arthur relished revenge more than anything, and if he didn't know Paul was connected with the project, he would probably jump at the chance. Abbie also found herself quite excited over the prospect of acting again.

"I'll have to think about it, Paul," Abbie told him. "You're a love for doing this."

"The picture will be waiting for you whenever you're ready."

"Tell me, Paul," Abbie said. "How did you know about what happened to Arthur at Century?"

"News travels fast," Paul said. "The whole town knows. How has it been for you, dear?"

"He got drunk and threw a fit last night," Abbie said. "It was to be expected."

"Did he touch you, hurt you, Monica? I swear, I would—"

"No, Paul," Abbie silenced him. "He just made a lot of noise, but actually he was quite harmless. I think he fears a scandal too much to do anything really serious."

"As much as I loathe him, I can't help pitying him in a way," Paul said. "Yesterday, he lost what was most important to him in the world—the power that justified his worth as a human being."

Abbie nodded. "He's the most loveless person I've ever known."

Paul kissed her. "And you're the loveliest person I've ever known."

"Paul, I'm the luckiest woman in the world to have you," she said. She smoothed his hair, admiring how handsome he was.

"Darling, why don't you come in and test for the

Bovary part?" he told her. "Just to find out how your voice sounds on tape."

Abbie was thoughtful. "Paul, he'd never let me have the part if he knew you were directing."

"What can I tell you, Monica? No other actress will do that part except you, so I'll just have to wait until you're ready. But why don't we go over to the studio now and make a recording of your voice just to see how it sounds. Aren't you even a little curious?"

Abbie grinned. Paul made it sound like a new adventure.

"All right," she said. "You know I can't do *Madame Bovary*. It will be just to hear how the microphone picks me up."

They drove over to Standard and Paul and Abbie went directly to the sound studio. Abbie confronted the microphone, the scourge of the studios, the instrument that determined if one could have a career in talking pictures. Paul sat outside waiting for her. A studio technician handed Abbie a page of dialogue from *Madame Bovary* and told her to start talking. After an hour or so, the technician came out and told Paul, "It's fine. She's got a voice!"

Abbie left the sound booth, and she and Paul laughed and hugged each other.

"You were swell," Paul told Abbie. "I wish we could get started on it right away!"

"Paul, I can't." Abbie looked at Paul seriously. "This test was just for fun; you know that."

He kissed her. "Someday you will do it," he said. "I know that, too."

Now Bernard

"But I want a name no one's ever used before," Lorraine said, like an author thinking up a title for a book.

Chapter 37

IN the ensuing weeks, Shore's behavior became more and more erratic. Some evenings he would retreat to his room and stay there all night. Other times, he was highly visible, abusing Abbie verbally, smashing lamps or plates, and cursing Century studios at the top of his lungs. Everyone there was out to get him. Abbie and Paul were out for his blood, too. Abbie had no recourse but to leave the house until he finally passed out from exhaustion and drink. If not for Paul, she was sure she would be losing her sanity.

A rather sensational incident reported in the papers had also aggravated Shore's paranoia. Selena Winfield had escaped from Oregon State Mental Hospital. The only reason the news merited national attention was on account of Selena's former glory as a movie actress. No posse or trackdowns were organized because a doctor had observed that Selena was not considered dangerous. However, Arthur Shore disagreed. As far as he was concerned, Selena had left the institution with only one purpose: to find him and kill him.

"She just sat there all these years, plotting to do this," Shore babbled drunkenly. "Plotting my murder! That's why she escaped."

"What did you do to her that makes you think she wants to kill you?" Abbie could not help asking.

"You keep your mouth shut, you trollop!" Shore yelled.

Abbie retreated to her room hastily.

Whenever the phone rang, Shore jumped, thinking it was Selena. He tried to calculate how far she might have gotten on foot or by hitchhiking. If she was clever enough to escape, she was probably clever enough to find some means of transportation. He wondered how long it would take her to reach California.

After about a week, however, Shore's obsession with Selena was pushed aside by another revelation.

Going to his office one morning, a young man called to him as he was passing.

"Hey, Mr. Shore!" the fellow said, cheerfully.

Shore recognized him as one of the new sound technicians Century had recently employed. Shore smiled at him stiffly.

"Heard your wife's one of the lucky ones," the young man said.

"Excuse me?"

"I've got a buddy who works at Standard and he says she came in for a sound test. He set things up for her. He told me she's got a beautiful little voice. You know, lots of stars aren't that fortunate."

"Tell me," Shore said, smiling. "Did she get the part?"

"Seems she and Paul Hanson have decided to postpone *Madame Bovary* for a while. I don't know the reasons."

"Oh, I see," Shore said cordially.

"Well, so long." The young man waved and left.

"Goodbye," Shore called after him.

Shore's face twisted into a cruel grin. The impudence, the deceit of those two, carrying on such projects behind his back! His face burned with fury at the insult. He would show them once and for all that he meant business. He would finish their affair off for good.

Instead of going to his office, he stopped in to see David Oakley.

"Hello, Mr. Shore," Oakley's secretary said.

"Hello, Bea," Shore said pleasantly. "May I please speak to David? It's rather important."

"Certainly," the woman said. She got up, knocked at Oakley's door and announced Arthur Shore. Oakley told her to send him in.

"Hello, Arthur," Oakley said, a shadow of anxiety in his voice. Shore's presence always made him tense now. They had worked together so closely in the past, until circumstances had forced him to replace Shore with Lewis Shelby. Shore's demotion had not really been his decision, but he was sure Shore held him responsible.

"Please sit down, Arthur." Oakley motioned to the chair next to his desk.

"David, I've come to ask for a favor," Shore said. He knew Oakley would do anything possible to prove his loyalty and vindicate himself in Shore's eyes.

"And what's that?" Oakley asked.

"I'd like a transfer to New York," Shore said. "I want to work with the company's branch out there."

"Any particular reason?" Oakley asked. He suspected that Shore wanted to leave the scene of his disgrace, Hollywood.

"Not really. Just a change. I'm gravitating toward the East Coast right now," Shore told him.

"Well, we already have a distribution head out there, but you know for you, I could juggle things around a little. Maybe I'll have him relocate or put him in another department," Oakley said.

"Thank you, Dave. I'd really appreciate that."

Oakley smiled. The more he thought about it, the

better an idea it was for all concerned. Shore's icy manner and blatant contempt for Lewis Shelby poisoned the air in the studio.

"When would you want to move out there?" Oakley asked.

"As soon as it might be possible," Shore told him.

"I think everything could probably be settled by the end of the year. November or December. I doubt that I could make it any earlier than that. And anyway, it would give you plenty of time to take care of whatever you have to. Like finding a place in New York and renting or selling your house here."

"Four or five months from now would be perfect," Shore said. "Thanks a lot, Dave."

Shore left the office feeling rejuvenated. The idea of avenging himself against Abbie and Paul had brought him back to life.

He completed his day's work, then drove home. Today, he did not even consider having a drink before dinner. He was too keyed-up. Abbie was outside near the pool, sun-bathing. Shore went out to greet her.

"Better be careful," he said. "You don't want to burn that baby-soft skin."

"I'm fine," Abbie said curtly.

"But then I guess you should take advantage of all this sunshine. It won't be that plentiful in the future."

Abbie turned around. What new surprise did he have in store?

"All right, Arthur," she said wearily. "Out with it."

"We're moving to New York," he announced, grinning.

Abbie looked at him, dazed. "Since when?"

"Well, I certainly expected you to be more excited than you are," he said. "After all, you once told me you liked New York better than Beverly Hills. Remember?"

He sighed. "It seems I just can't do anything to please you."

"Arthur, when did this happen?"

"Today. Oakley asked me if I was interested in taking over the office out there, since the distribution head has been asked to resign. Seems like a real shake-up is going on. Knowing how much you love the city and how much I've come to hate Hollywood, why I naturally grabbed the chance."

"Arthur, shouldn't you have asked me first?"

"Whatever for?" Shore said, his eyes glinting metallically. "Arthur Shore answers to no one, least of all you. And anyway, I thought the change would do us both good."

"Arthur, I—"

"Yes, Monica?"

"Arthur, this isn't the only reason you're leaving. Is it because of Selena? Are you so afraid that—"

"Don't mention her name!" Shore yelled. "It has nothing to do with her! If you must know, you're responsible for this move."

"Me?"

"Stop playing the innocent! It makes you more despicable than you already are. I'm going to teach you, once and for all, that you suffer when you try to deceive me. I'm taking you away from your partner in intrigue!"

Abbie looked at Shore silently. He must have found out about her sound test.

"I know all about your little scheme to make *Madame Bovary* for Hanson. Did you really think you'd get away with that?"

"I wasn't planning to make the film," Abbie said wearily, knowing he probably wouldn't believe her. "I just wanted to see what my voice sounded like."

"My, my, what a novel way to spend an afternoon!

Don't insult my intelligence, Monica! I have nothing more to say to you. We leave for New York in four months."

He walked away.

Abbie sat in the chaise lounge, desolated. She and Paul had finally overstepped their bounds and would be separated as punishment. Shore would have the final word. She couldn't even summon up the energy to move. Leona finally had to come out with a robe and gently suggest that her mistress come inside and go to bed.

Chapter 38

ABBIE told Paul the news the next day.

"Monica, that does it! We've lived in fear long enough. Let him do his worst! I think I'm established enough now to endure it."

"No, Paul," Abbie said sadly. "Anyone can be expendable. I can't let you be persecuted for my sake."

"Monica, don't you understand that if we show him we're not afraid of his blackmail, we're taking his worst weapon away from him?"

"Paul, I'm not as strong as you are," Abbie said. "The truth is I am afraid of his blackmail. If he ever ruined you, I couldn't live with myself."

Paul sighed. "All right. Look. I've got a lot of money in the bank. We'll run away together, maybe even change our names, our identities."

"Oh, Paul, stop! You're talking like a boy. You know that's impossible."

"Nothing's impossible. With my experience in movies, I could probably work in theater too, directing plays for little stage companies, or—"

"Paul, please!" Abbie cried. "Don't you think I know how important your career is to you? If you lost it, how long would it be before you started blaming me?"

"Never, Monica, I—"

"You say that now, dear, and I'm sure you think you

mean it. You'd probably even try to hide the truth from me and yourself, but it wouldn't last for long. We'd destroy whatever we had. Paul, I've learned how important, how precious real love is. If we ever poisoned our love I don't know what I'd do! It would destroy my faith in everything. Can you understand that?"

Paul nodded, quietly. "But, Monica, I couldn't live with only the memory of our love, could you? Would that be enough to satisfy you?"

Abbie started to weep. "I guess some people don't even have that. Maybe we should be grateful for the happiness we gave to each other and cherish the time we spent together."

"No," Paul said. "It's not enough for me. Knowing you were real, I could still find you in New York, touch you, I couldn't be content with memories. I'd have to be near you and by God, I'd think of a way!"

Abbie brushed back his hair and kissed his face. "Let's give ourselves time, darling. We still have each other for now."

"Yes, Monica. Give me time. I'll think of something."

Abbie nodded to pacify him. But she knew Shore had them licked.

There was nothing for her to do but treasure each moment with Paul, savor his presence, speak her love to him more than she'd ever done before. There would still be letters and phone calls after she left for New York, so a line of communication would be open. Despite the hard, realistic attitude she had forced herself to accept, she still believed in miracles. Someday, she and Paul would be together, and that possibility kept her functioning.

Abbie also clung to the hope that perhaps Shore was bluffing, that he was only using New York as a scare tactic. But when he made arrangements to rent his house out to a wealthy young married couple, the move to New York became a grim reality.

The time of departure was drawing terribly near when, in September, something happened to complicate matters still further.

Abbie started feeling sick to her stomach as soon as she woke up in the mornings. Her period was three weeks late, but she had not really paid attention until her sudden bouts with nausea.

She did not mention anything about it to Paul or Arthur and tried to talk herself out of her constant fears. What if her worst suspicion was confirmed? If one had the money, such things could be taken care of easily under sanitary conditions by skilled doctors, but Abbie knew she would want Paul's baby.

Finally, she forced herself to see a doctor and asked him to call her at home the next day to give her the results of the test. She didn't sleep at all that night and spent the morning counting the minutes until she heard the telephone ring. At last, his call came. The test had been positive; Abbie was pregnant.

Abbie could not really believe it. It took an hour or so before she accepted the news. She was carrying Paul's child.

She dared not tell him. He would demand that she divorce Shore, and the ensuing scandal would be more hideous than anything that would have occurred before. It made her sick to think that an innocent baby could be the cause of such ugliness.

If she told Shore she was pregnant, he would probably force her to terminate the pregnancy.

She was only seven weeks pregnant, according to her doctor's calculations, and there was always the possibility that she might miscarry. Her mother had had two miscarriages before bearing Abbie. There was nothing for her to do now, but wait silently and try to maintain her sanity. Abbie knew she would have to reach a decision soon.

It was torture for Abbie not to be able to divulge her secret to anyone, but somehow she managed to keep her panic and fear to herself. Whenever Paul commented on her nervousness, she blamed it on their imminent separation. Her peace of mind was completely broken.

By late October, Abbie was in a state of desperation. She was twelve weeks pregnant, and she and Shore were due to leave for New York within two months.

Strangely enough, her life with Shore had become calmer than it had been in months. His drinking had decreased, and he didn't pick on her as much. As long as people carried on as he decreed, he was content.

A friend of his in New York had already found a townhouse in the city for them to settle into temporarily. The owners were spending the winter in the South of France.

Once in New York, Shore had no intention of staying with Century, although he hadn't mentioned these plans to anyone. He was leaving the studio as soon as the right opportunity presented itself, not only because of the disgrace connected with his demotion, but because it was a dying company. Despite Lewis Shelby's Herculean efforts, David Oakley's empire was collapsing. Century was miles behind the other studios in profits. Since he had so many contacts, he would have no problems finding another job. He felt no remorse about deserting Century, just as he had never felt guilty that the studio had come apart because of his feud with Paul Hanson.

On the twenty-eighth day of October, Shore rose as he usually did and left for work. He was in high spirits. He and Abbie were leaving for New York in November, a month earlier than he'd expected. Oakley had gone out of his way to make the arrangements. The man that Shore was replacing had reluctantly shuffled his family back to California under Oakley's orders.

That morning, Abbie awoke, got out of bed and walked into the bathroom. Her stomach was fluttering as it always did until she ate something. Her appetite had become enormous lately. She looked at herself in the full-length mirror on the door. She wasn't showing her pregnancy yet, but she had put on weight. Her face and figure were fuller. Even Paul and Shore had commented on her sudden roundness.

"As soon as you girls quit pictures, you all start filling out," Shore had teased her. "You'd better be careful, Monica. You don't want to get fat."

He hadn't suspected the truth at all, but Abbie knew it would only be a matter of time before he or Paul guessed.

Abbie was frequently depressed now. She had always imagined that having a baby would be the happiest part of her life and felt cheated of the joy that should be an expectant mother's right.

She spent most of the day in bed, reading magazines or listening to the radio. She was nauseous a good deal of the time, and she wasn't sure whether the reasons were physical or psychological. She was also perpetually tired. Sleeping was her way of dealing with too many pressures. She was beyond feeling anxious anymore. She was simply waiting until she was confronted about her condition by either Paul or Arthur Shore. God only knew what would happen then. She fell asleep mulling over her plight.

At six o'clock, Abbie woke up feeling hungry again. She rose and went downstairs, wondering what Leona had made for dinner.

Arthur Shore was sitting in the living room, staring into space like a zombie.

"What's the matter with you, Arthur?" she asked.

He didn't answer. He seemed totally unaware of her presence.

"Arthur, what is it?" Abbie asked again.

"The stock market fell," he told her dully. "The losses exceeded ten billion dollars."

"It happened last week, didn't it?" Abbie said. "And it made a comeback?"

"It was a false comeback. The bankers' pool had made Richard Whitney buy up millions of dollars worth of stocks last week to instill confidence in the market and stop panic selling. All that did was slow things down. It was no real comeback."

"I don't understand," Abbie said. "In September didn't the market hit an all-time high?"

Shore didn't answer. He left the room.

Abbie didn't understand what was happening. Just two months before, she had read an article by John J. Raskob, the vice-president of General Motors and a director of the Bankers Trust Company, American Surety and the County Trust. In *The Ladies' Home Journal*, Raskob had stated that "Everybody ought to be rich. . . . Prosperity is in the nature of an endless chain, and we can break it only by refusing to see what it is." Indeed, since 1924, wealth seemed as ready and available as any of the country's natural resources. The stock market, once restricted to the upper class, had invited the average man to invest in a prosperous future. Making money was his birthright as an American, and buying stocks was proof of his faith in the destiny of the country.

Only a few voices warned that the wild, unchecked spending could hurt the well-being of the nation. People borrowed money to buy stocks, then used the stocks as insurance to cover their loans. In 1929 there were six billion dollars outstanding in brokers' loans. And the stocks just kept rising higher and higher.

The next day, October 29, Abbie listened to the news over the radio as the works caved in completely. It was Black Tuesday, the day of the crash. A guard caught in the eye of the hurricane at the New York Stock Exchange described the chaos: "They roared like lions and tigers. They hollered and screamed. They clawed at each other. Every once in a while when Radio or Steel or Auburn would take another tumble, you'd see some poor devil collapse and fall to the floor."

All the corporations were swallowed up in the crash, Dupont, Whitney, Westinghouse—the titans had fallen along with the clerks and shopkeepers who had invested every dime in Wall Street, the Mecca of Capitalism, the miracle shrine. The over-priced stocks, their value blown up by inflation, had masked the symptoms of a failing economy. The merry-go-round had stopped.

The motion picture industry would not be affected by the stock-market crash for years to come, but there were exceptions like Arthur Shore. Most of his wealth had been tied up in business corporations that were now in ruins. Indeed, Shore had shrewdly encouraged the frenzied investments of average men in over-blown stocks, since their spending had made him richer. Now, Shore suffered losses totalling six million dollars. There was nothing to be salvaged.

At six, Shore still wasn't home for dinner. He had staggered into work that morning like one of the walking wounded, but the situation then had not been as devastating as it was now. Abbie and Leona were both rather grateful that he hadn't come home yet. At least they'd be granted some peace for a while. He was probably drinking himself into oblivion somewhere.

Abbie didn't feel sad or frightened, only numb. She had

been paid back for her greed in full. As Arthur Shore's wife, she was now as destitute as he was. How many other dreams had sunk beneath the ocean that day, along with the magical decade that had promised wealth and success beyond anyone's wildest hopes? It was the end of an era, a dazzling time spun out of dreams and nonsense.

Paul called Abbie at about eight. "I had to speak to you, dear. I don't care whether he's there or not," he said somberly.

"He's not home, Paul," Abbie said. "He must be hitting every bar in town. He's lost everything."

"It serves him right," Paul said. "It serves them all right! They were too greedy to stop the circus and ward off catastrophe! It's the little man I feel sorry for. He followed the big wheels' advice and doesn't have a chance in hell now! At least Shore still has his job at Century."

"It's a dying company," Abbie said, softly. "Paul, what's going to happen? I don't mean just to us or Arthur. What's going to happen to everyone now?"

Paul sighed. "The joyride's over, darling. The great crash is going to usher in a great depression."

"Thank God, you're not affected, Paul," Abbie said.

"We're all affected, Monica. There's going to be unemployment, poverty, hunger—"

Abbie looked around at the lavish interior of her home. The carpets, the furniture, the chandeliers.

"What about you, darling?" Paul asked. "You're going to have to come back to work, and I have a feeling Shore won't stop you this time."

It was true. Arthur Shore was bankrupt. Abbie could not imagine him poor, stripped of authority. "I suppose he won't, Paul," she said.

"Why don't you go to sleep soon?" Paul told her. "You haven't really seemed well, lately. You haven't been yourself. Go to sleep, darling. I'm afraid the world's going to be a very different place when you wake up."

"Yes, I know," Abbie said.

"One positive thing at least," Paul said, softly.

"Yes?" Abbie asked.

"You won't be going to New York now, I'm sure," Paul said. "I'll bet Oakley will close down the office there."

"I guess he will," Abbie said. "Goodnight dear. I love you."

Abbie sat up a bit longer, listening to the radio. She went to bed about nine.

...through room ...ing and newspaper headlines proclaiming Hanson's ring flooded Snore's mind.

Chapter 39

LEONA shook Abbie awake the next morning.

"What is it, Leona?" Abbie asked, groggy.

"It's the police, Madame."

Abbie shuddered. Police always meant trouble. "What do they want? Did they say anything?"

"No. Just that they had to speak to you." The maid looked at her fearfully.

Abbie was terrified. What she had feared most had finally come to pass. Shore, wanting to drag her down with him, had finally told the police about the evidence she'd withheld in the Hayes case. She put on her robe and slippers, opened her bedroom door and looked downstairs. Two grim, serious men were waiting for her in the living room.

She took a deep breath, tried to compose herself, then slowly walked down.

"Hello, gentlemen," she said. "What can I do for you?"

"Mrs. Shore, I'm Lieutenant Cornell," one of them told her. "This isn't very easy for me—"

It's not easy for me, either, Abbie thought.

"It's about your husband."

Abbie's eyes widened. "What?" she asked. "What is it?"

"I'm afraid he's dead," the lieutenant said. "He hanged himself in his office, sometime last night."

The stress Abbie had endured finally overcame her. She collapsed on the floor. Leona and the detective carried her to the couch, where Leona anxiously dabbed Abbie's eyes with some cold water.

Abbie revived.

"Are you all right, Mrs. Shore?" Lieutenant Cornell asked.

"Yes," she said, dazed.

"I'm sorry," Cornell said. "I know what a tremendous shock this must be for you."

"His money," Abbie rambled. "He lost everything."

"Yes," the lieutenant said kindly. "I know. Believe me, he's not an isolated case. Reports of tragedies like his have been pouring in since yesterday." He pressed her hand in sympathy, "I know how difficult a time this must be for you. I only have a few questions to ask and I'll leave."

Abbie nodded.

"Mrs. Shore, where were you at about eight this morning?"

Abbie was startled by the question. "Why, I was—"

"She was asleep," Leona answered for her. "She was upstairs in bed until now, when I had to wake her up to tell her you gentlemen wanted to see her."

"Why do you ask?" Abbie said curiously.

"It's just that a woman was seen leaving your husband's office. The studio guard let her pass by without stopping her. It was only after Shore's body was found that he even thought to mention it."

"A woman?" Abbie asked.

"Yes. It wasn't your husband's secretary; the guard knows her. This other woman had nothing to do with your husband's death. She was seen entering and leaving between the hours of seven and eight A.M. and the coroner's report said your husband took his life at about midnight. But you see, there were some charred remnants of a letter found in an ashtray. We think the letter might have been written to you by your husband. Anyway, all our detectives could make out was the name, Monica Dane. We examined the ashtray the letter was found in and your husband's fingerprints didn't match the ones found on the ashtray. We suspect this woman might have burnt that letter for some reason."

Abbie was completely perplexed. Why would Arthur write a letter to her? Was it possible that he had asked her forgiveness for the way he had used and abused her? No. Not Arthur. It would be far more plausible that he write an accusation, shaming her in the eyes of the world. He would want to seal the lid of her coffin as well as his. And who was this mystery woman who had burned the letter?

The telephone rang. Leona ran to answer it.

"It's police headquarters," she said.

"Excuse me," Cornell told Abbie. "I'll take this in the other room."

He was gone for perhaps only a moment and then returned.

"Well, this is curious," he said. "They picked up the woman who'd been spotted at the studio and arrested her. She's been identified as Selena Winfield, your husband's first wife."

Abbie gasped.

"I'm going to head over there now," Lieutenant Cornell said. "They're questioning her."

He extended his hand. "Goodbye, Mrs. Shore," he said. "You have my sincerest condolences and my best wishes."

"Thank you," Abbie said. "Thank you so much, Lieutenant Cornell. You've been very kind."

He and the other officer left.

Abbie sat down on the couch. She was completely bewildered. Why had Selena burned the letter? Perhaps it was just an irrational act of a mentally ill woman.

"I'm going to make you some hot tea, Madame," Leona said.

"Thank you, thank you, Leona."

After Abbie finished the tea, she showered and dressed, still thinking about Selena. So much had happened, she had to focus on one incident at a time to keep her equilibrium.

At noon, Paul arrived, and the sight of him made Abbie realize how good life could be, after all. She ran to him and started to cry. He embraced her as if he never planned to let go.

"Darling, our suffering is over now," he said, softly. "Have you been outside yet?"

She shook her head, too overcome by emotion to speak.

"It's a beautiful day," he told her, his own voice husky. She nodded.

"Monica, I'm taking you to Jonas Klein's place now so you won't be bothered by reporters. I reserved a room at the Wellington for you tonight."

They both went up to Abbie's room and she hastily packed a suitcase.

"You'd better get ready, too," Abbie told Leona after she was finished.

"I'll pack later," the maid said. "Right now, I'm just going to stand guard here, answer phone calls and keep the vultures away."

Abbie kissed her, fondly. "I'll see you tonight at the hotel. Thank you for everything."

Leona hugged her.

Abbie and Paul got into his car.

"Where's Jonas now?" Abbie asked.

"He's at police headquarters with Selena. I spoke to him."

"Oh, Paul, I hope the police are being gentle with her. It must be such a frightening experience for Selena."

"I'm sure nothing much fazes her, now. Not after having been in an asylum all these years."

"It was good of Jonas to go be with her," Abbie said.

"Yes, it was."

"What do you think she was doing there?" Abbie asked.

"I guess she wanted to confront Shore about something. I'm sure she didn't expect to find him dead. I think she probably went to his office, to wait until he came in that morning."

"The police told me she burned a letter there. Supposedly, it had my name on it. Why do you think she did it, Paul?"

"I really don't know. Jonas told me about that, too. He said every time the police would question her about it, she'd just keep saying, 'Arthur Shore was a hateful man.' She didn't tell them why she burned it. But then, she's not all there."

Abbie nodded.

Paul continued. "She won't even tell them what the letter said—"

Suddenly, Abbie and Paul looked at each other. They were both thinking the same thing.

"Oh, Paul!" Abbie cried. "That dear, beautiful woman is trying to protect us!"

"My God, Monica, you're right! Of course, you're right!"

"She doesn't even know us!" Abbie cried.

"No, but she knew Shore," Paul told her. "And maybe that was enough for her. She knew how much you'd suffered with him."

"Paul, we've got to help her," Abbie said. "We've got to do everything we can to help her!"

As soon as Paul and Abbie reached Jonas' house, Abbie raced to Klein's phone, called police headquarters and asked to speak to Lieutenant Cornell. She pleaded that he cease questioning Selena Winfield. Since the letter had supposedly been written to her, she felt she had the right to have this request granted.

"This is pretty unorthodox," Cornell said. "But I respect your wishes, Mrs. Shore."

Later, Jonas Klein came over to see Abbie and Paul.

'How is Selena?" Abbie asked, anxiously.

"I don't give a damn what they say!" said Klein. "Selena isn't crazy! Sure, she's a little peculiar, but who wouldn't be after nine years in a madhouse! I'll show you how clear she is! They gave her one phone call to make and she called me. She remembered after all these years. As soon as I walked in, she knew who I was. She said, 'Jonas, I'd know you anywhere,' and I said, 'Selena, you're still as pretty as a picture.'"

Klein was close to tears. He turned away for a moment.

"And by God, she is as pretty as a picture, and I'll be damned if I'll let them take her back and stick her in that looney bin! I'll fight them with my last breath!"

"We'll fight them, too, Jonas," Paul said. "We'll get the best lawyers and doctors money can buy. We'll get Selena the best care and attention possible." Paul put his hand on Klein's shoulder. "We'll help her get well again."

"You're damned right we will," Klein told him. He looked at the floor, shyly.

"Well, I promised her I'd be back as soon as I could. I'm going to tell her what you said, Paul." Klein smiled. "Thank you. God love you both."

He went out the door.

Abbie rested her head against Paul's chest.

"I have to take you to the hotel later, dear," Paul said. "I wish I could bring you home with me, but you'll only be at the Wellington for a short time."

"I'd better be," Abbie told him.

"Do you think too many tongues would wag if I married you next week?" Paul asked her.

Abbie wasn't sure whether he was joking or not. "Do you care?" she asked, testing him.

"Not me," he said. "You're the one who gets upset over these things. You're too concerned over what other people think."

"I guess I'm just going to have to learn to get over that," Abbie sighed.

"What are you doing tomorrow?" Paul asked her.

"I don't know," Abbie said. "Probably meeting with lawyers over the estate."

"That doesn't sound like much fun."

"What else did you have in mind?" Abbie asked him.

"Would you like to get married tomorrow, after we finish shooting for the day?"

"Shooting?"

"Yes, I think we should get started on *Madame Bovary*."

"Paul, I can't," Abbie told him.

"Of course, you can. What's stopping you?"

"Paul, it's sort of—"

"Monica, I think work is the best medicine for you now, dear. Look, I know how much you've been through, but getting back on your feet and into the world again is the best way to cope with things. Monica, I'm not going to let you sit idle for long. I love you too much to let this happen."

"I know that, dear, but—"

"I'm going to hire Gloria Stone to do the gowns. She can start work on them tomorrow."

"Paul, I'm afraid I'm not going to fit into them."

Paul looked at her, curiously. "What is that supposed to mean? Are you planning to put on a lot of weight or something."

"Yes, Paul, I am."

Paul looked bewildered.

Abbie gently took his hand. "Paul, it's not that I don't want to do the part but I don't think it's a suitable role for a woman . . . in my condition."

"A woman in your condition? Monica, what are you—" Paul's eyes widened suddenly. He looked into Abbie's eyes, and she nodded.

"I'm going to have your baby," she told him.

Paul scooped her up and swung her around in his arms. "You little fool!" he cried joyfully. "Why didn't you tell me? Don't you believe in sharing happiness with people who love you? Don't you want me to be happy, too?"

"I wasn't really happy about it until this very moment," Abbie said, her voice soft with tears.

"Oh, Monica, darling! I love you so much!" He wrapped his arms around her.

"Paul," she said, quietly.

"Yes, love?"

"My real name is Abbie," she whispered to him. "My real name is Abbie Dare."